WHISPERS FROM THE DEAD

B. L. BRUNNEMER

ALSO BY B. L. BRUNNEMER

Trying To Live With The Dead
When The Dead Come A Knockin'
When To Fear The Living

DEDICATION

Thank you to everyone who helps get my stories out of my head and
into print!
Robert; thank you for cooking so much while I write.
Melissa: you saved my butt again!
To my poor Alpha/Beta readers; thank you for reading the extremely
short first version of this book and encouraging me not to throw
it out.

And thank you to Adytum Library for all your wonderful editing
ladies!
Thank you Grondin Designs for not only the beautiful cover, but the
title as well!
Thank you Susan for proofreading your butt off!

CHAPTER 1

APRIL, FRIDAY

"*L*exie."

"Hmm?"

"Can you stop looking out the window and focus?" Dr. Smith asked. I let the sheer curtain drop and turned around on the plush couch in her office. Dr. Smith was a nice woman with kind gray eyes and endless amounts of patience. At least it seemed that way to me. She'd been my shrink since January. After the abduction and assault, everyone thought I should have someone who could help me through it. Miles had found Dr. Smith, an expert in dealing with the after effects of trauma. Trauma, I had suffered trauma. I huffed to myself and focused as she asked, "How are the nightmares?"

"They are happening less, around four times a week now." My voice turned raspy. I took a sip out of my now ever-present water bottle so it would go away.

"And did you shower after them?" she asked gently. I sighed. My nightmare was always the same. Clay Ordin was forcing me to walk through the snow back to the cabin. Then he would call me 'his' and grope my chest, then between my legs. It wasn't as bad as it could have been, but that didn't stop me from feeling like I needed a shower after every dream.

"I showered after only two of them this week." The raspy note from my voice was gone.

Dr. Smith's eyes ran over my face.

"How did you stop yourself from showering the other two times?" she asked.

I reached down and ran my fingers through Hades' fur. The dog had gone through a big growth spurt over the last few months, he was getting rather intimidating. I took him everywhere with me now. "I reminded myself that it happened in January, this is April. I pet Hades while doing those counting exercises," I said. Dr. Smith smiled gently.

"That's good to hear, Lexie." Her voice was encouraging. I gave her a small smile. "Any panic attacks?"

I shook my head. "Not since that last one at Vegabond." The bar had been packed, everyone kept touching me. Not on purpose, the place had just been that crowded. I didn't like it. The next thing I knew I was having trouble breathing. Miles had realized what was happening. The boys worked together to get me out the side door and into the fresh air. I made a point not to go into crowded places now.

"Have you had any flashbacks?" Dr. Smith asked.

"Nope, not since I told the guys not to touch me from behind unless I know it's them," I replied. "But I still have flashes occasionally."

Dr. Smith's eyes narrowed at me. "Are they still walking you to class?"

"Every single one," I admitted.

She smiled and shook her head at the same time. "Have you gone anywhere alone this week?"

I smirked. "Miles is in the waiting room." Dr. Smith sighed deeply as she shook her head again. She had met the guys at our first appointment. Zeke had insisted that one of them be there, they had just forgotten to choose who and everyone had shown up.

"Lexie, you need to learn you can be without them. That you're safe even if they aren't there," she said gently. I nodded.

"I know. And I think I'm ready to," I told her. "With Hades, though."

Dr. Smith smiled. "That's a good start."

"I'm also thinking of going to see about a job at the tattoo shop in town. See if I can learn anything," I said. Dr. Smith smiled encouragingly.

"That is a great step, Lexie," she said. Then her smile faded. "How are things with the boys?"

I looked over her shoulder at the wall of bookcases. "They're supportive, loving, you know, the usual," I hedged.

"Lexie," she said in her 'come clean' voice. I sighed and met her eyes.

"Zeke and I are still having problems. I still haven't been able to hug him since the hospital," I admitted. "I tried and... had a flashback."

Understanding lit Dr. Smith's eyes. "Is this affecting your relationship?"

I shrugged. "He's distant but always around."

"He's also probably struggling, Lexie," Dr. Smith explained. "From what you've told me he's a protective person, and you were attacked. That's going to take some time for him to deal with."

"I know." I checked the clock on the wall. "Time's up."

She chuckled. "That's my line," she chided. I snorted. "Your homework this week is to go out without the boys, go to the tattoo shop and try to hug Zeke again. Remember your exercises." I nodded and got up off the couch with Hades' leash in hand.

"Thanks, Doc," I called over my shoulder as I opened the door.

Miles looked up from the magazine in his hands. His high cheek bones and angled jaw made him cute, but it was his smile that showed you how handsome he really was. That and the intelligence in his emerald eyes whenever he got excited about something. His wavy, brown hair was back to curling a little again, he needed a trim. He pushed the bridge of his black-rimmed glasses back up his nose before getting to his feet. His eyes ran over me, his mouth a tight line.

"Is everything alright?" he asked in his quiet timbre. I nodded.

"I just have some homework," I explained as we headed for the door.

Miles opened the door for me then followed me out into the hallway. "What kind?"

"The kind that Zeke isn't going to like," I admitted. Miles hit the button for the elevator then gave me a gentle smile.

"If it's what's best for you, he'll do it," Miles reassured me. I raised an eyebrow as the elevator doors opened.

I waited for them to close before I told him, "She wants me to go out alone." Miles' silence was enough to make my shoulders tense.

"If it's what the doctor suggested and what you want, we'll do as you ask," Miles said in a careful voice. He was right. I just didn't want to be the one to tell Zeke. It seemed like I have done nothing but hurt him since I came back from the hospital. After my last attempt to hug him, he's walked on eggshells around me and kept at least three feet distance between us at all times. And that conversation about our kiss? Forget about it. 'When you're ready' he'd say. I hated this. We reached the ground floor.

"I know," I muttered as we walked out into the lobby. "Our communication hasn't exactly been the best lately." Several people spotted Hades and backed away quickly. I had gotten used to that reaction lately and I honestly didn't mind.

Miles walked me to his car in silence. I opened the back door so Hades could jump in.

When I turned around Miles' eyes were full of understanding.

"He'll listen to you, Lexie," he reminded me, holding the passenger door open. I nodded. He was right. I was the only one who could *get* Zeke to listen.

I got into Miles' car, and he closed the door behind me. When Miles climbed in on the driver's side, he had a small smile on his face. "But right now, the guys are surrounded by the twins' cousins. They've been sending me an SOS every five minutes for the last hour."

I chuckled, "Let's get over there and watch the chaos."

THAT WAS EXACTLY what we found at the twins' house. Pure chaos. Well, the backyard was. The twins' four cousins were in town. They visited every spring vacation for a few days when their school had two weeks off. Lucky. This just happened to be the day that Maria, the twins' mom, and Ana, her sister, went out to the spa for some pampering while leaving the boys in charge of the kids for the afternoon. Miles and I had been more than happy to go to my appointment earlier.

We stepped out onto the back porch and gaped. Toys littered the lawn as Isaac was chasing Amelia, a four-year-old little girl in pigtails, while her twin sister, Isabel, was playing quietly with her dolls in the shade on the lawn. Their six-year-old brother, Marcos, chased Isaac trying to soak him with the hose. The oldest boy, Mateo, had water balloons and he wasn't afraid to use them on Asher. I let Hades off the leash. He ran off to join the fun chasing Marcos.

Ethan noticed us from his spot on a lawn chair in the shade near Isabel. He got up and crossed the lawn, getting hit in the process. By the time he reached the safety of the porch, his shirt had several big wet patches. Ethan's square jaw, wide full lips, and straight nose made him the heartbreaker of our school. Even with his jaw length black hair back in a tie, showing off the five silver rings running up his ear lobe, he was still yummy. His chocolate eyes had dark rings under them as they ran over me.

"Hey, how'd it go?" he asked in his smoky, smooth voice. I shrugged.

"Not bad. I've got homework though." I ran my eyes over his face. "Are you sleeping alright?"

"Yeah, fine," he assured me. "What's your homework this time?"

I looked around the backyard. "I'll tell you later. Were you hiding out?"

Ethan grinned. "Nah, it was my turn for a break. But Zeke's hiding. He's changing the oil in our car in return for not having to watch the kids." He leaned on the rail next to me and watched the chaos. Mateo nailed Asher in the back with several balloons, soaking him. Everyone started laughing as he turned to chase the eight-year-old.

Isaac stopped chasing Amelia and climbed the steps to shoot a look at Ethan. "Your turn. Who gave the twins sugar?" he asked, out of breath.

I smirked.

"That was Asher and you," Ethan said as he headed down the stairs. Isaac took his spot next to me. Isaac and Ethan were identical twins, but that only meant they looked the same. While Ethan wore all black, Isaac wore bright colors. His black hair had been dyed a vibrant blue with darker blue streaks through it. The sides were still shaved and the top shorter than it was a few months ago. Isaac nudged my shoulder and gave me a smile. I bumped back with my own and grinned.

"You up for tonight, Red?" Isaac asked. I thought about it. There was a party tonight on the shore across the lake. It'd be my first party since January.

I chewed the corner of my lower lip and nodded. "Yeah, I think so."

Isaac nudged my shoulder, getting my attention again. "We can leave anytime. Just say the word." His reminder warmed my heart.

"I know." I tucked a flyaway hair behind my ear.

Asher came up the stairs huffing and puffing. Asher was your typical boy next door. If you lived next to a model that is. His high cheekbones and sharp chin belonged in commercials. His short, sandy blond hair was freshly trimmed. His white undershirt was soaked, clinging to the muscles of his chest, arms and stomach. I had to remind myself not to stare.

Asher glared at Isaac. "Get back out there, I need a break," he huffed as he went to sit down on the wooden bench at the end of the porch. His ocean eyes met mine. And I mean ocean. With blue, light blue and white flecks, his eyes reminded me of an ocean wave crashing. I turned to watch him drip water onto the porch.

"Aren't you supposed to be this hot-shot Quarterback?" I teased. He shot me a half grin.

"Yeah, I am. But nothing can outlast a four-year-old on a sugar high," he countered.

"You gave them cookies, didn't you?" I asked. He leaned back and closed his eyes.

"Only one each," he admitted. "But then Isaac went and snuck them the whole bag."

I laughed at the anguish in his voice, then turned back and watched Marcos chasing Ethan with the hose as Ethan tried to get Amelia out of the way. I contemplated going inside when a girl's cry went up instantly getting everyone's attention. Isabel was soaked. Marcos had missed Ethan and hit his little sister. Marcos kinked the hose as he went to her already apologizing.

"No!" Isabel shouted. "I want Uncle Zeke." Isabel turned and ran toward the old garage at the back of the yard. "Uncle Zeke!" she cried, wiping her face. Zeke came out of the open garage door, frowning as he wiped the grease off his hands with an old towel.

Zeke was a mountain of muscle. Two heads taller than me and a frame that was several times wider. He was a hard guy to miss. Not that he wasn't handsome. His black hair, wide cheekbones, and a wide, strong jaw gave his face a very rough, frightening look. And when he scowled most people ran for it. His all black clothes, motorcycle boots and wallet chain didn't help. The secret to getting along with Zeke was simple. Leave him alone and he'll leave you alone. Unless you hurt me or pushed me... or insulted me... Okay, just leave me the fuck alone and you'll be fine with Zeke. Isabel ran right up to him and pointed back at her brother.

"Marcos soaked me!" she cried, tears falling down her face. Zeke sighed. When he reached her, he knelt down. Isabel threw herself into his arms, crying about how she didn't want to ruin her new dress. Zeke picked her up and whispered to her, calming her down as he strode back toward the now subdued boys. He came up to Marcos, took the hose and handed it to Isabel. The little girl squealed happily as she soaked her brother.

"Now, you're even," Zeke told her in his deep, gravelly voice. Zeke put her down and she happily chased after a screaming Marcos. Zeke's sky-blue eyes spotted me. His gaze ran over me before he headed up the steps. "How'd your session go?"

I sighed. I was starting to feel like a broken record. "Good. I have homework."

His brow drew down. "What kind?"

"I'll tell you guys about it after dinner," I promised. With the kids running around crazy it was too loud to tell them. Especially with what Zeke's reaction was likely to be.

Since I came home from the hospital, someone had been with me every time I left the house. Zeke demanded it, and I needed it to be honest. I wasn't looking forward to that conversation.

That chill ran down my neck, but it was like a finger-tip. A soul was nearby and I knew who. As the guys talked, I stepped back and headed inside.

"Red?" Isaac called.

"Just gotta use the bathroom. Damn," I shot over my shoulder. There were small chuckles as I went into the kitchen.

There, standing at the window looking out into the backyard was Sophie. The twins' little sister's soul. The eight-year-old girl was standing in front of the sink, watching her cousins and brothers out the kitchen window. She had Maria's long black hair, big brown eyes, and a sweet, pretty face. Her eyes watered.

"Sophie?" I kept my voice soothing. She didn't take her gaze off the others outside. "You can't go outside, can you? Not without using the extra energy running around?" She shook her head.

"I'm ready, Lexie," she all but whispered. She turned to me, tears running down her face.

"I want to cross soon." My pulse skipped as her energy hit my barriers. They trembled once but held firm.

"Are you sure?" I asked gently.

She nodded and wiped her face. "I don't want to watch them anymore. Mom's mostly okay but Ethan keeps pulling me back. And Isaac..." She swallowed hard as her tears fell faster. "I need to go soon." I moved to stand next to her and look out the window.

"We'll need to talk to your brothers first. You know that," I told her gently. She nodded.

"I can't keep doing this," she sniffed. My eyes burned as I blinked back my own tears.

"Can you wait till your cousins are gone at least?" I asked quietly. Sophie nodded, then gave me a sad smile.

"It was good to see them one more time," she admitted. She wiped her face.

"I can wait a few more days. When I'm ready, I'll break one of Ethan's guitars."

"Okay. Then I'll tell the twins and we'll figure out how Ethan keeps pulling you back," I assured her. How the hell were the twins going to take this? She nodded quietly then turned away from the window and walked further into the house.

I took a deep breath and let it out. Sophie was ready to go. Shit. At least I had until Monday to figure out how to tell them. I took another deep breath and let it out slowly before heading back outside.

I joined Miles and Asher at the railing.

I was in my own head when Asher nudged me with his elbow. "Hey, are you okay?"

I gave him a tense smile and nodded. His brow furrowed as he kept eye contact, silently asking. Hell, he probably heard me talking in the kitchen anyway. I mouthed Sophie's name.

Understanding filled his eyes. He reached over and gave my hand a squeeze. I gave him a squeeze back.

I turned to the yard just in time to spot Isaac turning towards us with the hose. I instantly dropped as water sprayed over the others on the porch. Shouts and curses filled the air as I stayed dry. The porch shook as the guys ran down the steps after Isaac.

Laughing, I stood up and watched Asher get the hose from Isaac. Zeke pinned his arms as Asher soaked him head to toe, getting Zeke in the process. The kids and I were in hysterics. I was just getting control of myself when the back door opened. Maria came outside followed closely by her younger sister Ana. Ana was the same height as her sister, with the same beautiful thick black hair, though her amber eyes were lighter than Maria's. She had a square face and a beautiful smile.

"What are you doing?" Maria asked, a smile on her face. All the boys immediately let go of Isaac and dropped the hose.

"Ma! They attacked me!" Isaac shouted.

"Isaac soaked us on the porch, so we were getting even," Asher explained. Maria and Ana chuckled.

"Boys, go get in dry clothes," Ana ordered. "Pizza will be here in half an hour." Isaac and Ethan ran for the house. Zeke, Miles and Asher headed for the gate between the yards. They must have had some clothes at Asher's.

Maria wrapped an arm around me. I leaned into her hug.

"How did you manage to get away dry?" Maria asked. I smiled.

"I saw Isaac with the hose and ducked," I admitted. They chuckled.

Ana was the first to sober. She looked out to the yard. "Kids. Inside and in dry clothes. Now!" The younger ones ran for the house while Mateo turned off the water before following. I couldn't help but admire the way she handled her kids.

Maria gave me a squeeze. "How are you doing, honey?"

"Better," I said.

She smiled down at me. "Good, I missed my sassy girl." She squeezed my shoulder. "Come on, let's set the table." I nodded and followed her inside, more than ready for dinner.

DINNER WAS LIVELY with so many in the kitchen. Zeke, Miles and I ended up eating at the counter. I didn't mind. I was sitting on the counter anyway.

"Miles, you really need a trim, honey," Maria said as she helped dish up Isabel's plate.

Miles reached up and felt his hair. I bit back a grin as his cheeks tinged pink. I loved watching her mother the boys.

"I'll go this week," Miles agreed sheepishly.

Maria finished helping Isabel as she asked over the noise from the kids, "Asher? How did your essay for English go?"

Asher swallowed his food. "I got an A-, I'm not really happy about it but-"

"It's still an A," Maria pointed out with a look. I couldn't seem to stop smiling. At least until she turned to me.

"Lexie, what are your plans for tonight?" she asked. "We're having a board game night with the kids."

"Um, well, we're going to a party on the lake," I said carefully. I didn't know if the twins told their mom about going to the party or not. Maria nodded then looked at all the boys.

"You boys keep an eye out for her. I'm not asking," she warned.

"I'd like to see someone try and stop us," Isaac offered. The guys chuckled. I just shook my head at them and kept eating. Maria went back to questioning each of us, making her way through the room.

"You know, we could skip the party," Zeke reminded us.

"Zeke, I'm going," I told him. "Jake and Derrick are coming down. I haven't seen them in weeks."

"It should be manageable," Miles reminded him. "There's another party out on the Simmons' property. The crowd should be smaller than usual."

I looked up at Zeke with a grin. "See," Zeke grumbled wordlessly, sounding resigned. I lost my grin. "If you don't want to go then you don't have to, Zeke." He shot me a look. I looked up at him with understanding. A few months ago, Zeke had kissed me. Then I was kidnapped by my stalker. We still hadn't talked about the kiss yet.

"Not happening," he grumbled before biting into a slice of pizza. I went back to my own dinner, dropping the subject.

After dinner the little ones had to clean up. I took the opportunity to signal to the guys to meet me on the porch. We all slipped out as Maria and Ana started talking in the living room.

The porch was large and had enough seating for most of us. Putting Sophie out of my mind for now, I sat on the railing in front of the boys since I was going to be talking. I took a deep breath and let it out slowly, hoping it would help with the knots in my stomach. Zeke leaned against the railing on the far-left side of the porch while the others took the wicker couch and chairs. All eyes turned to me.

I took a deep breath and began. "Today, the doc gave me several things to do this week. The first was to try and get a job at the tattoo parlor in town." I looked around the group trying to judge their reactions. Asher nodded; everyone else was calm. Now the big one. "Another was to go out alone. Without anyone but Hades."

Everyone went still. The only sound was my heartbeat in my ears. It was forever before one of them spoke up.

"Are you ready for that, Ally?" Asher asked gently. I bit the corner of my bottom lip as I thought about it again. Then nodded.

"I think it's time," I said. "You guys have been so patient with me being scared and clingy-"

"You're not clingy," Isaac snapped.

"You needed us," Ethan added.

"Ally..." Asher sighed.

"Lexie, you're family," Miles pointed out, "we'd do anything to help you." He leaned forward, his elbows braced on his legs. His emerald eyes on mine. "Don't factor us in when you think about this. Are *you ready* to go out on your own?"

I took a deep breath and thought about it. It was scary, and made my stomach twist but...

I nodded. "Yeah, I'm tired of hiding behind you guys. I'm tired of being afraid all the time." My voice turned scratchy. I took a drink from my water bottle before continuing. "I want my life back." The guys gave me understanding smiles.

"No," Zeke growled. And there was the hiccup. Zeke shook his head, his arms crossed over his barrel chest. "No way are you going out without one of us with you."

I looked at the others. "Can you guys give us a minute?" The others got to their feet and headed inside. I waited until the door was closed before I got off the railing and moved to stand a few feet in front of Zeke. "Zeke-"

"Lexie, no," he growled, his voice hard. His posture was rigid.

"Zeke. I need to do this," I said gently. "I can't hide behind you guys all the time and I don't want to. That's not who I am." Zeke clenched his jaw. I kept going. "I haven't had a flashback or panic attack in a month. I'm ready for this." My voice was confident. I had to make this okay for him otherwise it'd just be a huge fight.

Zeke looked down at the porch and took deep breaths. It was

12

several minutes before he met my eyes. "You text me, tell me where you'll be and when you get back," he stated. I went to protest but he cut me off. "It's the only way I can, Lexie." I thought about it. He was right. Zeke had his own issues to deal with. We needed to work together on this.

"I can do that," I agreed. He nodded. I wanted to hug him. But it seems Clay took that away from me. Instead, I reached up and touched the tip of his nose. "Boop." His lips moved into a half grin, the shadows in his eyes lifting a bit. I smiled up at him.

I was going to get my life back. I was going to hug Zeke again, get a job, and go out without the boys. I could do this. I got this. Right?

AFTER DARK, as we left the twins' house, the guys were deciding who was going with who.

"Red's with us," Isaac announced. I rolled my eyes.

"I have room for everyone," Zeke pointed out.

"Yeah but you'll want to leave before everyone else," Ethan countered. Zeke shrugged. Ethan wasn't wrong.

"I'm riding with Miles," I announced. "You've had too much sugar and are bouncing around like a rabbit." Isaac blew a raspberry at me as he headed towards the car he and Ethan shared. Everyone climbed into their cars and headed for the north shore of the lake.

"We can leave if you get too uncomfortable, Lexie," Miles said.

"Miles, I'm going to be fine. I'm actually looking forward to the party," I assured him. "And if I have an issue, you guys will be there and you can haul my ass out caveman style."

He chuckled. "That may be more Zeke's style." I grinned. Zeke had done it before, I doubt he'd have a problem doing it again.

Miles pulled into a spot near the back of the lot where there were enough spaces for all of us. The others parked next to him. I got out and took a deep breath as we headed across the lot. Music was blasting, and the bonfire was already roaring. I wrapped my arm around Isaac's as we walked.

"You're not drinking tonight?" I whispered. It wasn't necessary, not with Ethan and Asher talking about some baseball game.

Isaac's other hand came up and squeezed my hand on his arm. "Nah, I don't want to be wasted if you have trouble."

I squeezed his arm. "Thanks, Cookie Monster."

He smirked down at me. "No problem, Red." I smiled up at him then turned back to the party on the shore.

I had already dealt with the dead this morning, and I was determined to have fun. Especially since Sophie's crossing was coming up. Before dread could ruin my night, I pushed it to the back of my mind and looked around.

Since the party was on the beach, I hadn't bothered changing my jeans or shirt. I just took one of my black hoodies with me, pulled my hair into a ponytail and called it good.

By the time we hit the sand, I could tell the beach wasn't packed with people and that was perfect for me.

"Let's grab some drinks," Asher suggested. We headed for the drink coolers, Miles behind me, the twins to my sides and Zeke in front of me with Asher. It had become our usual walking pattern. While I appreciated it, I was trying to get *out* of the safe zone I had put myself in the last few months. I grabbed a bottle of water and looked around the beach.

A tall, lilac-haired girl darted through the crowd. I flinched but she was on me in a heartbeat.

"Lexie! You came!" Riley practically deafened me with her shout. I relaxed, laughed and hugged her back. The guys around me relaxed. Riley pulled back. Her pretty oval face and almond eyes beaming down at me. Zeke's ex-girlfriend was one of my favorite girls around, hands down.

"I said I would," I reminded her.

Riley rolled her eyes and turned to the boys. "Hey guys! Can I take Lexie or are you guys going to tag along for girl talk? Again?"

I turned to the guys. This would be a good way to ease all of us into me going out on my own.

Every one of them was frowning, Asher was rubbing his neck,

Ethan twisting his rings, Miles tapping that staccato rhythm on his leg and Zeke was running his hand through his hair.

"If you stick to her like glue," Zeke said. Riley went still. I tensed. Being friends with Zeke's ex was complicated. So far, they hadn't had any major issues, and I was hoping that wouldn't change.

"I promise not to leave her alone," Riley offered. Zeke's jaw was clenched as he nodded stiffly. Riley wrapped her arm around mine and pulled me away from the guys.

We walked to the other side of the fire where Jake and Derrick were standing in the sand. Jake was cute, there was no way around it. He was a head taller than me, his short, styled blond hair was streaked with lighter blond highlights. His green eyes were sparkling as he looked at his boyfriend, Derrick.

"Look who I managed to pry away from the boys!" Riley announced as we reached them.

Jake turned to me, squealed and practically jumped on me in his rush to hug me. I forced myself to relax as I hugged him back.

Since January we hadn't really been able to have our coffee shop gossip sessions. We'd settled for phone calls but it wasn't the same. He let go only enough to wrap his arm around my shoulders. I turned to Derrick.

The goth boy was the same height as Jake. His dark hair was streaked with purple and spiked. His average face had a nose ring, eyebrow stud, and lip ring that, oddly, seemed to suit him.

I smiled. "Hey, Derrick." Derrick grinned, came forward, and shoved his boyfriend away so he could hug me tight. I chuckled, braced myself and hugged him back.

"I'm so glad to see you out tonight," he whispered to me as his light cologne filled my nose. "We've missed you. Jake has been impossible." I giggled as he let me go.

"Well, I'm back." I looked over at Jake's smiling face. "You can't get away with that anymore." Jake made an 'aw shucks' face as Derrick moved back to his side.

"So, how'd you get away from the guys?" Jake asked.

"Yeah, I never thought they'd let you out of their sight," Riley added.

"I'm probably not," I admitted. "I'm sure one of them has me in sight at all times." Jake, Derrick and Riley looked around me in unison, and they weren't subtle. I laughed.

"Yep," Derrick confirmed.

"It's Asher, he's trying to make it not look obvious," Jake explained.

"And failing miserably," Riley added. "He's barely talking to the other football players."

They were giggling as they turned back to me.

"We're trying something new," I hedged. I really didn't want to get into it. I looked at Jake and Derrick. "So, how's coupledom?"

Jake's cheeks turned red as Derrick answered, "It's not bad."

I smiled mischievously. "Oh, really?"

Jake smacked my arm, his face beet red. "Stop it, woman." I chuckled as he fanned himself. Derrick laughed quietly, making Jake turn vermillion.

"That good, huh?" I asked, dying to know now.

Derrick turned to me. "I got my tongue pierced." Everyone burst out laughing except Jake.

"Oh my God." Jake closed his eyes, a pained look on his face. "TMI, babe!" I kept laughing.

Jake opened his eyes then eyed me. "Don't make me ask about your love life."

"I don't need a love life, I'm surrounded by hot guys all the time," I pointed out. Everyone chuckled.

"Well, you can't argue with her there," Derrick admitted with a smile.

"Now if only she'd do something about it," Jake added. I rolled my eyes and changed the subject.

"Derrick, tell me more about this tongue piercing...?" I asked innocently. Jake's face turned crimson again.

"Well, so far-"

"Don't you dare," Jake warned Derrick as he held back a smile. Riley and I cracked up. I let the subject drop.

"So, what's the latest gossip?" I asked.

"Well, the latest is that Jason is cheating on Jessica with Michelle Hart," Riley offered. My mouth dropped.

"How did I miss this?" I demanded. "Ethan is slacking on his gossip skills."

"Word is they were seen going at it at a party last weekend," Jake supplied. I cringed.

"Ew," I stated. An upbeat song came on. It made me want to dance instantly. I reached out and took Jake's hand. "Sorry, Derrick, but I need to borrow your guy for a dance."

"Go for it," Derrick said, his hand shooing me as I dragged Jake out near the bonfire where everyone was dancing.

I moved to the music and danced with Jake to the upbeat tempo. After a couple songs, the music changed to slow song. Jake pulled me in.

"So, how's the crush situation?" he whispered. I was so grateful for Jake. He was the only one who knew I was crushing on Zeke, Miles, and Asher. And he didn't judge me for it.

I sighed. "Not great. I'm still crushing on them but at the same time I haven't really felt it for a few months."

"What do you mean felt?" He raised an eyebrow and gave me his mischievous grin.

I shot him a look. "Butterflies, heart pounding. You know. That rush you get when you're around your crush."

Jake's gaze met mine, the sympathy filling his eyes made me want to squirm. "That might have something to do with January, Lexie," he pointed out gently.

"That's what the shrink said," I muttered. "She says it'll come back when I'm ready."

Jake's eyes unfocused. "Or you've moved past the 'oh my God he's so cute' phase."

"Nope, no, no way. I like that phase," I stated emphatically. "I don't even know what's past that phase." Jake was laughing when a hand came down on his shoulder.

"Care if I cut in?" Asher asked. Jake grinned wickedly.

"Asher, you already had your chance. I'm with Derrick now," Jake chided. I snickered as Jake let go of me and turned to Asher. "But I guess I can make an exception. Just this once."

Jake went to grab Asher to dance with him.

Asher batted his hands away playfully. "Don't make me tell Derrick!"

I started laughing as Asher called for Jake's boyfriend. Jake stopped messing with Asher.

"Tattle-tale," Jake chided before turning to a smiling Derrick. "Hi, babe."

"Are you causing trouble?" he asked, pulling him in to dance. Jake draped his arms over his shoulders.

"Never," Jake teased. They moved off, dancing in the crowd. Asher moved closer, took my hand and held it as he placed the other on my waist.

"How are you doing, Ally girl?" he asked softly.

I smiled up at him. "I'm having fun. How about you?"

He smiled as we turned in the sand. "Not bad."

"How's Zeke handling the change in our routine?" I asked, curious.

"He's handling it in typical Zeke fashion," he hedged. I sighed.

"He's being a grumpy ass?" I guessed. He chuckled.

"Yeah, pretty much." His eyes ran over my face then back to my eyes. "But I get it. I got used to you being around more."

"I'm not disappearing. I'm just... getting back to normal," I reminded him. "Normal is good."

"I know and I'm glad you feel up to it," he said. "I'm just going to miss you a bit more."

I smiled up at him then enjoyed my dance with Asher. The song ended and a fast one with a hard beat came on. He took his hand from my waist and he held my hand a little longer before letting go.

"Shout if you need me," he reminded me.

"Will do," I promised. He headed back to his other friends while I went back to Riley, Jake, and Derrick.

Over the next three hours the beach got more crowded. Jake and Derrick had gone off for a 'walk' and Riley dragged me over to talk to her other friends. Looking around I realized the guys weren't within sight. They must have relaxed. I smiled to myself as I tried to listen to the story Riley was telling.

Someone bumped into me. I jumped, my heart slamming into overdrive as I turned. The girl was drunk and staggering. Her friends helped her move off towards the cars. The crowd seemed to press in on me. I took a deep breath and let it out slowly. Everyone was jumping, dancing and having a good time. But all I saw were people I didn't know around me. The crowd was getting to me. I needed a breather.

I excused myself and slipped away from Riley's group into the crowd. I kept taking slow deep breaths until I could get out of the crush and closer to the shore. I walked away from the party towards the lake, people bumped into me making me jump and shaking my insides. I focused on breathing.

When the music wasn't so overwhelming, I sat down in the sand and watched the waves lap onto the shore. The knots in my stomach eased. I focused on what was around me. The full moon shined down on the water, making the small waves shine. It was cool out but not too cold.

Clouds were moving in over the lake, it looked like a storm might be on the way in. Other than that, it was a nice night.

I started to regroup. I had come out with confidence in my ability to deal, but with the crowded party that confidence was fading. I was going to have to stay on the edges. That's okay, as long as I don't leave because of it. You can do this, Lexie. Clay is in jail. No one here is going to hurt you. The guys are within ear shot. You got this.

I had just calmed myself down when someone stepped next to me. Ryan, the drummer in Ethan's band, was standing there with his hands in his pockets.

Ryan wasn't a bad looking guy. He was just big and burly. His brown hair was still buzzed down to his scalp. He had a horseshoe shaped ring through the septum of his nose and a new gunmetal stud in his eyebrow. His gray eyes were warm as he grinned down at me.

"Hey, what's going on?" he asked, crouching down in the sand.

"I just needed a breather from the party," I admitted. He nodded before he sat down. His rich, musky cologne came over the breeze. My stomach rolled as I was instantly thrown back to that night in January. Clay's face flashed in my mind. His grip on my neck. He had worn the same cologne the night he kidnapped me, the night he.... I shook my head and forced myself to stay in the present. I could do this. Just because it's the same doesn't mean Ryan will.... It's Ryan and he isn't going to hurt me. The guys are only a shout away.

My shoulders grew tense anyway. I hadn't been alone with anyone except one of the guys or family for months. Breathe, Lexie. You're okay. You've got this. Ryan's gray eyes were on me, his face curious.

"You okay?" he asked as he settled in the sand next to me.

I nodded and forced a smile. "Yeah, it's... just your cologne." I changed the subject. "How's the new singer working out?"

"She's not as good as you," he stated, "but she's working."

"She'll get better," I offered. "Ethan says you guys just need to find your niche with her." He shrugged.

"Yeah, it just stinks." He looked over from the waves. "How are you really doing?"

I resisted the urge to growl. I was getting tired of that question. "I'm doing alright."

"Where are your guards tonight?"

I grinned. "They're here. We're trying something new." Slowly, the tension started to ease in my shoulders. This was Ryan. The guy was a big sweetheart.

"Oh yeah? Going stir-crazy?" He chuckled. I smiled at him.

"Something like that," I admitted. "I'm just ready to get back to normal."

"That's good to hear," he muttered. "So, how big is Hades now?"

"Mid-thigh and still growing."

He shook his head. "You should bring him by practice sometime. He could be our mascot."

I shrugged. I really didn't want to see Ethan and their new band member singing together. Something inside me told me I wouldn't like it. "I'll see what I can do." I looked back out on the water as an awkward silence fell. Ryan was probably just being nice and trying to keep me company. The least I could do was keep the conversation going. "So, what are your plans for the weekend?"

He sighed. "I don't have much planned," he admitted. "I was hoping to maybe get a date."

"That shouldn't be too hard," I said. "You're in a band after all." He chuckled.

"Yeah, I don't know. This one doesn't seem to be impressed by that," he countered.

I glanced back at him before looking out at the water again. He had a thoughtful look on his face. "You're a nice guy, Ryan. She'll probably say yes," I said absently. I should probably head back to the party before one of the guys started looking for me.

"You think so?"

I nodded. "Sure, why not?" I started to turn back to him. "We should head-" His lips met mine.

Surprised, I gasped. Rich musky cologne filled my lungs. I wasn't on the shore anymore. I was in the woods being dragged back to the cabin. I shoved him away from me and scrambled out of reach. Horror filled me as Clay squeezed my neck then ran his hand over me. I pulled my knees to my chest and wrapped my shaking arms over my head. Oh, God... no, no, no.

"Lexie?" a voice asked. That cologne. Terror tore through me.

"Don't touch me. Please, don't touch me," I bit out, trying not to scream. Clay grabbed me between the legs, hard. Tears fell and my stomach churned as he kept forcing me toward the cabin.

"Lexie?" The voice was uncertain. "I'm getting one of the guys, okay?" I knew Clay was in jail. I knew I wasn't at the cabin. But logic was out of reach. The cabin was all I could see. All I could feel as he tackled me to the floor. Heart slamming in my chest, Clay pinned me to the floor then drove his knee into my groin. I felt it. Every blow, every hit. The fear, the pain, the nausea. All over again.

"Lexie." A smoky, smooth voice got my attention. The musky cologne changed to spicy. That wasn't Clay, that was Snoopy.

"You're outside, at the lake," Ethan said gently. I stopped rocking. I was still seeing the cabin. I reached out to him desperately, as if he was the light switch in a dark room that I was desperately looking for because something was breathing in the dark.

Ethan gathered me in his arms, holding me to his chest. I buried my face into his shirt, my hands clinging to the fabric, rubbing the cotton material between my fingers. The anvil in my chest was making it hard to breathe.

"What's going on?" Ryan asked, his voice worried. Ethan ignored him as he held me in his arms, rocking me side to side.

"You're not in the cabin, Beautiful. You're safe with me, we're sitting in the sand on the north shore of the lake." His voice helped ground me as Clay's weight pressed me into the floorboards. I nodded, so he knew I heard. "Lexie, what month is it?"

I focused on his voice, his question. "April."

"Good, what day?" he asked patiently.

I fought to turn away from the memories and think. "F-Friday."

"That's right," he said. "What did you do after school?"

"I came over to your house, and your cousins were there," I answered, his questions helping ground me.

"Then Zeke got totally suckered by a four-year-old. Remember?" he asked. I nodded again, still clinging and trying to breathe as Clay's hands tightened around my neck.

"How did you get to the party?" Ethan's voice brought my attention back to him.

I swallowed hard as I struggled to come back. "Miles drove."

"That's right. Now, where's Hades?" he asked gently.

"At home," I mumbled as tears poured down my face. Footsteps ran towards us.

"Who am I?" he asked.

"Snoopy. Ethan," I whispered, my heartbeat filling my ears.

"That's right. I've got you, Lexie."

"Flashback?" Asher's rich baritone brought me back a bit more. Asher hadn't been at the cabin. I'm not at the cabin, I'm sitting on the shore of the lake... Tears kept falling as I felt it all fresh again.

"Yeah," Ethan said, his hand moving to hold my cheek. It helped ground me even more. "Who came with us tonight?"

I focused on answering and not the memories, "Everyone."

"Name them, Beautiful," he whispered.

"You, Isaac, Asher, Zeke and Miles," I recited through the knot in my throat. The flashback was fading. I knew where I was but the aftermath... that wouldn't let up.

"It's okay, Beautiful, cry all you want. I've got you." I nodded against his shirt as his arms tightened around me. He kept rocking me and telling me about his day, how nice the moon looked over the lake. Eventually, limes mixed with spice in my nose.

"Red, breathe for us," Isaac's rich honey-like voice said before a hand rested on my shoulder.

It helped. I was safe, Isaac and Miles got me out of the cabin. Clay Ordin was in jail. It was spring. I'm not in the cabin. I kept thinking it over and over. The jingle of keys started somewhere far off.

"What happened?" Asher asked, his voice hard.

"Nothing, she was fine one second and the next she wasn't," Ryan said, his voice concerned. The key jingle grew louder, then stopped.

"Not buying it," Isaac said. "She's been doing better for the last month."

"What the fuck did you do?" Zeke's snarl helped pull me back more. There was a scuffle.

I focused on the fact that I was on the shore. That Clay Ordin hadn't touched me in months. He couldn't get to me. I didn't need a shower. Isaac and Ethan started humming that tune I loved.

"Let him go, Zeke!" Asher snapped. "Ally's having a flashback. It's not a good time for you to lose it around her." Leather and engine grease filled my nose.

"Give her to me," Zeke growled. My flashback may have been over but I wasn't ready to face anything yet. I was still struggling to breathe.

"You know I can't, man." Ethan reminded him quietly. Zeke cursed.

"What happened?" Miles' silky-smooth timbre reached my ears. The pressure in my chest began to ease.

"Flashback." Asher, Ethan, Isaac, and Zeke answered in unison.

"What triggered her?" Zeke demanded. There was silence.

"Ryan, tell us what happened?" Miles asked calmly, in a firm voice.

"She said something about my cologne when I sat down," Ryan told them, baffled.

Isaac's hand left my shoulder. Wintergreen tickled my nose. I stopped burying my face in Ethan's chest. I laid my cheek against his shoulder, my forehead against the warmth of his neck. I was back but I was still in pieces in the sand. I kept my eyes closed and tried to pull it together.

"What the hell are you doing?" Ryan snapped.

"He's wearing the same fucking cologne Ordin was." Isaac bit out. All the guys, except Miles, cursed.

"How do you know that?" Ryan asked.

"I got a real good sniff when I was beating the shit out of him," Isaac said, his voice boiling.

"Is that it? You sat down and this happened?" Asher's voice demanded an answer. I listened to Ethan's heartbeat, that soothing tune slipping through my ears. It helped ease the tightness in my chest even more.

"I..." Ryan began awkwardly. "I might... have kissed her." Ethan stopped rocking me. His body grew tense around me.

Isaac cursed "You son of a-"

"What the fuck, Ryan?" Ethan snapped. "I told you not to make a move! I told you she wasn't there yet!"

"I know! I should have fucking listened." Ryan shouted back. "She just... seemed fine."

"Of course, she did," Miles explained. "Because she was. Until you did that." Miles' calm voice helped; I realized the guys were pissed at Ryan, but it wasn't his fault.

"It was the cologne." I managed in a small shaking voice. Everyone stopped yelling.

Fingers brushed my hair back from my face. I opened my eyes. Miles was kneeling in front of me. His emerald eyes warm on mine.

"Was it only his cologne?" Miles asked gently. I hesitated. He noticed. "Lexie?"

"He... he just surprised me," I mumbled. Zeke let out a deep growl.

Isaac and Asher blocked Zeke before he could reach Ryan. Ryan backed up even more, his hands up and away from his body.

"Get out of here, Ryan!" Isaac grunted as he fought to keep Zeke away. "Or Zeke's going to kill you!" Ryan sent me an apologetic look before heading back towards the bonfire.

Zeke stopped fighting the others only to pace up and down the shoreline. I closed my eyes and tried to stop crying. I focused on taking deep breaths and knowing that the guys were around me.

When I finally stopped, I opened my eyes.

Miles wiped my cheeks with Zeke's handkerchief. "Are you ready to go home?" I nodded. It was humiliating. I had been fine, confident even. Then one smell, one surprise and bam! I was a crying mess. I hated it.

"I'll carry her." Isaac's voice said not to argue.

"I can walk to the car," I said quietly.

Isaac crouched down in front of me. "You're sure?"

"I need to," I muttered.

Ethan kissed my forehead before letting me go. Isaac reached out, took my hands and helped me to my feet. He wrapped his arm around me as we started moving through the crowd. I leaned against him a little, feeling exhausted. It was as if I had just run a marathon, and in a way, I had. The others made a path as we walked through the party and out to the parking lot.

I had let them down. I had promised that I was okay to be left alone and I let them down. I pushed that thought away as my eyes burned again.

When we reached the twins' car, Isaac opened the passenger door. Ethan made sure I was buckled in. I hid my face in my hands.

"I'm sorry, guys," I told them, my voice tired.

"It's okay, Ally."

"This is all part of the healing process." Miles reminded me.

"Don't be stupid Red, this party sucked."

"Yeah, we were talking about leaving anyway. You're just giving us a reason, Beautiful."

Zeke was quiet. I dropped my hands and looked up at them. Not one of them seemed angry or frustrated as they closed my door. I kept my gaze on the floor of the car as Ethan pulled out of the lot and headed back to town. Through the drive my mind became clearer.

By the time they pulled up to my house I was doing better. I took off my seat belt.

"Thanks," I said.

"No problem, Beautiful" Ethan said instantly.

My door opened. Isaac reached in to help me to my feet. I took his hand and climbed out of the car. I shut the door then turned to the house. I had a flash of being grabbed on the front step. The lawn had been covered in snow, the porch light was only bright enough to see my keys. I hadn't even realized he was behind the tall bushes next to the door. I hated the front of Rory's house now. The sage green craftsman was a great house, pretty even. I just didn't like the bushes next to the door or the shadows all over the yard. I shuddered. Isaac's hand tightened on mine as he gave me a small tug to get me going.

I unlocked the door, then Isaac went in first. I followed and disarmed the new security system Rory had installed. After punching in the combo I turned back to Isaac. He wordlessly pulled me into a hug.

"It'll get better, Lexie." he reminded me.

"Promise?"

"Promise." He gave me a squeeze then kissed my cheek before heading out the door. I turned the deadbolt and turned the system on again.

I went to my bedroom and shoved a snoring Hades to the other side. I laid down, not bothering to change out of my clothes. My phone vibrated in my pocket. It was Ryan.

Ryan: I'm sorry. Please tell me you're alright?

Poor guy, he probably thought it was all his fault.

Alexis: I'm okay.

Ryan: I'm so sorry. I didn't know about the cologne.

Alexis: It wasn't your fault. Don't worry about it.

Ryan: You're tired, go to sleep. Night.

Alexis: Night.

I held my phone half expecting Zeke to text me. Sure enough, ten minutes later someone did.

Ethan: Are you okay?

I smiled to myself.

Alexis: I'm okay. Just tired.

Ethan: Do you want some company?

Alexis: Nah, I'll be fine.

Ethan: Are you sure? I'm more than willing to sneak out.

Alexis: Yeah, I'm good.

Ethan: Alright. Get some sleep.

Alexis: You too.

CHAPTER 2

SATURDAY MORNING

I ran through the tree line, following it, staying under the trees where the snow wasn't so thick.

"Alexis!" His shout echoed through the woods. I fought for breath as adrenaline surged through me, pushing me. Footsteps were behind me. I swerved through the trees. I was hit from behind. My face hit the snow. Something wet touched my face...

I jerked awake, gasping. Already sitting up, my eyes darted around the room looking for him. It took me a few seconds to realize I was in my bedroom, safe at home. Heart racing, sweat running down my skin, I sat back against the wall. Hades whined next to me. I reached out and let him climb in my lap. Trying to ignore the memories running through my mind, I focused on petting Hades; the texture of his fur, the way his ears felt under my fingertips. It was April. Clay Ordin was in jail without possibility of bail. He can't hurt me anymore. I ran through my exercises until the tension in my chest eased. I hugged Hades. He must have woken me up before the worst this time. He was *so* getting treats today.

When I could, I got to my feet and headed to the bathroom. I started the shower, not because I felt I needed one, but because it was morning. I braced my hands on the counter and took stock.

I was never going to get back to 'normal.' It was time to face it. The doc was right. I wasn't going to be the same person I was before the cabin. I was going to have triggers, more nightmares, and have trouble in crowds. I looked into the mirror. My green eyes with gold flecks stared back at me out of my heart shaped face. I wasn't the same person. But that didn't mean I couldn't take my life back. My eyes ran over my long, copper hair. I wasn't the same person and I wasn't going to be. Maybe it was time to show that. A fire began burning in my belly as I pushed away from the counter and climbed into the shower.

I quickly ran through my morning routine, determined to make this day a good one. After my shower, I pulled on clean jeans and a simple gray t-shirt before grabbing my keys and phone.

I headed downstairs to find Rory and Tara in the living room. Living room didn't quite cover it. It was one great room with the kitchen in its own nook.

"Rory, do you care if I head out to the park or maybe get my hair cut?" I asked as I reached the first floor.

Rory didn't even look up from the paper. "No, go ahead. Which of the guys are going with you?"

"None," I stated simply.

His head snapped up, his gaze ran over me. Rory was a good-looking man. Even I could see that. His Delaney copper hair was rumpled, his brown eyes searching.

"You're going out alone?" he asked carefully, his worried eyes meeting mine.

"Yeah. The shrink said it's time to try. So, I'm trying," I bit out. His eyes narrowed at me.

"Bad dream?" he asked. I grumbled wordlessly. His lips moved to a half smile. "Okay, Kid. If you're ready, you're ready."

"Thanks," I said as I let Hades out back and closed the door behind me. Tara had been oddly quiet this morning. I half expected her to make fun of me or something.

Putting it out of my mind, I looked around. It was a nice, crisp spring morning. The perfect morning to start over. I pulled out my phone and texted Zeke.

Alexis: I'm heading out to the cemetery alone. Then I might be going to a salon.

It didn't take long for a response.

Zeke: Which one?

Alexis: Don't know yet, I'll let you know when I do.

There was a long pause before he responded.

Zeke: Fine. Don't forget or I'll start looking for you.

Alexis: I know.

I tucked my phone away and let Hades back into the house.

I ate a quick breakfast and was at the door with Hades in less than ten minutes.

My stomach shook as I looked outside. For the first time in months, there wasn't someone waiting for me. That was good. I had this. I'm taking my life back. My hands shook as I stepped outside and closed the door behind me. My body grew tense as I walked to the Blazer. A bird chirped. I jumped. My heart started racing. Come on. It's broad daylight and you're just walking to your damn truck. Had the Blazer always been this far away? I growled at myself.

A neighbor started their lawn mower, I didn't jump this time but I did tighten my grip on Hades' leash. My hands began to sweat and my skin was too tight. Being this jittery was starting to piss me off. Okay. I can use pissed off. Pissed off was better than scared. This was my life and I wasn't going to let some fucker take it from me.

When I reached the Blazer, I was steadier. My pulse was still racing but I was steadier. I had this.

As per my normal routine, I drove out to the cemetery. It was your average cemetery. Grass, headstones, some trees and a large group of souls waiting around the flagpole in the Veteran's section. Okay, that part wasn't normal but lately it had been my normal. Hades immediately started barking.

"Shush," I told him as I looked over the massive crowd. It seemed as if the group never got any smaller. More dead had been showing up every day demanding to be crossed over.

Luckily, I had figured out a trick in March.

We had been standing in a big storm with Isaac holding an umbrella over our heads. I had been making trip after trip with souls, the multiple trips were wearing on me.

"This is taking too long," I grumbled as I rubbed my temples. Isaac rubbed my lower back gently.

"Yeah, it is." he agreed. "Too bad you can't take more than one." I went still as I thought it over. Why couldn't I take more than one? It'd be tricky…

"Let's give it a shot," I suggested. "The after effects can't be too bad."

He eyed me. "If you die, take me with you. Or Zeke will kill me, painfully."

I chuckled before turning to the next two souls. Their names were Patty Sinclair and Noah Moore. The two had been high school sweet-hearts who died in a car crash before graduation. I focused on their need to move on. That golden ribbon of will reached out, split and wrapped around their wrists. I threw up my arms in victory. "Yes!"

Since that rainy day, I've been increasing the number of souls I took in one trip to the Veil, little by little. But lately I've been stuck at twenty. And the dead were still getting impatient.

I zipped up my black hoodie, left Hades in the car and approached the group.

"About time you showed up," one of them snapped. I eyed him. Mr. Davis had died in the 70's, judging from the mustache and polyester suit. There were several murmurs of agreement through the crowd. I ignored him.

"Okay, we did twenty yesterday," I announced. "We're doing twenty today. Whoever is crossing step forward." A group of souls lined up. Normally I'd care who they were. Today, I didn't. I just wanted to get this over with. "Alright, we're forming a chain. Hold hands with the person next to you. There's going to be a long dark fall, then we'll land in the Veil. DO NOT let go of the person next to you or they won't make it to the Veil." I didn't know if that was true or not but I didn't want to take the chance. As the group did as

I said, I went to one end of the line. "What's your name?" The guy was about my age. He was wearing a Kiss shirt and had 80's band hair.

"George," he said. I slipped off my beads. My stomach immediately rolled hard. Ugh, he must have died from a drug overdose.

I focused on everyone's need to move on. That gold thread wrapped around his wrist. It serpentined through the group catching everyone's wrists down the line. I closed my eyes and dropped down, dragging the line of souls with me. It wasn't comfortable, but it was faster than doing one at a time. Midway down I visualized where I wanted to come out in the Veil. Soon we hit grass. I looked behind me to see all twenty had made it. I let go of the souls and took a look around.

The Veil had changed over the last few months. Instead of cracked dirt, lush green grass grew, the burnt stumps of trees poking through the waves. Wild flowers grew here and there in groups. It reminded me of a forest growing after a fire. Life was returning to the Veil, slowly but surely.

I turned back to the group to see if anyone needed any help crossing today. Several doors of gold light were already closing, others just opening. Everyone rushed to the other side happily. I smiled. That was a first, there were usually one or two who needed a little encouragement. Today was going to be a good day. The doors closed one after another, turning to balls of gold light that shot up into the sky like rockets. They disappeared through the Way.

I looked around and spotted several new flowers and vines that hadn't been there before. I eyed the walls of the Veil. They were still gray and smoky. How many souls was it going to take before they even began to thin? I wished I had the answer. I closed my eyes and pulled myself out.

I blinked at the sunlight before looking to the rest of the large group.

"They're across. I'll see you guys tomorrow." I told them as I slipped on my beads.

"What about the rest of us?" Davis barked.

I reminded myself to be patient. "I'm not going to burn myself out for you."

"You need to cross more of us. This wait is getting ridiculous." he shot back. I blinked at him, stunned. I had been letting their attitude go. But this...

"I will cross however many is safe for me to do," I snapped. "and not one extra." I turned back to my Blazer as the grumbling crowd began to disperse.

I climbed in and used my phone to find a salon. Then I got an idea. I called Riley.

"Hey, girl. I heard you left early last night, are you okay?" Riley asked instantly.

"Yeah, I had a flashback. I'll explain later." I said, hoping she'd forget by then. "I was thinking about getting my hair cut and was wondering if you wanted to go have girl time?"

"Oh, hell yeah!" Riley exclaimed. "My aunt runs a beauty shop here in town so let me see if I can get us in. I'll call you right back." Riley hung up on me. I snorted and took Hades' leash.

We walked around the cemetery. It was quiet, as you'd expect with no living people around. Hades lifted his leg to a headstone near the road.

"No! Bad Hades! You don't do that there," I told him as I pulled him away from the headstone. He looked at me, confused. I brought him over to a tree. He sniffed around then lifted his leg. When he was done, I gave him praise and love. He licked my face. I'm assuming that was dog for 'I get it now and forgive you.' My phone rang.

"Hey."

"I got us in!" Riley announced. "Except it's not until tomorrow at one."

"That works," I said, "I have voice therapy today anyway."

"That sounds like fun," she said sarcastically. There was shattering glass in the background. "Shit! Gotta go, the cousins are loose." Riley hung up on me.

Smiling, Hades and I climbed into the Blazer and started driving.

I ended up at Chester Park on the east side of the lake. It had several bike paths and walking trails that I had heard of. Before getting out, I texted Zeke.

Alexis: Salon was a no go. I'm at Chester Park, taking a walk on the main path.

Zeke: Hades with you?

Alexis: Yep.

Zeke: Good. Pay attention around you anyway.

I tucked my phone into my pocket before climbing out. Hades jumped down, his tail wagging. His tongue lolled out of his mouth as we walked. He looked happy as can be.

Following Hades' lead, I headed down the empty main path. The trees towered over us, and the brush was thick here and there. Occasionally, a small patch of wild flowers peeked out of the long grass. The breeze brought pine to my nose, easing the tension in my body. It was a beautiful morning. Birds chirped, the lake was calm, and the sky was clear.

Several times I had to pull Hades from the huckleberry bushes. He kept trying to eat them. See Lexie? You can do this. You're going to be okay.

After some time, I found a bench near the water and sat down. Hades sat, then leaned against my legs. The silence surrounded us. I was outside, alone, for the first time in months. I smiled to myself. I actually managed it.

A stick snapped somewhere in the woods. I turned and scanned the area with my heart in my throat. I took a deep breath and let it out slowly as I listened for anything to tell me if someone was there. The woods were quiet again except for birds and the waves on the shore. Swallowing hard, my stomach was in knots as I pulled out my phone. Just in case. Memories brushed my mind. I pushed them away as fear filled me. This wasn't the same thing. I'm in daylight and Hades is next to me. But my body wasn't listening. I looked down at my phone to find my hands trembling. My lungs grew tight. All I could hear was the blood pounding in my ears. Shit! It was getting hard to breathe. I tapped my phone to call someone.

Heavy footsteps came up the walkway.

My gaze darted that way, my mind already planning on how to get away. I blinked. Zeke strode down the path towards me with a scowl on his face. Instantly, I could take a full breath. His eyes ran over me, his frown deepened as he moved around the bench to sit near me. Leather and engine grease reached me. I breathed deeply, taking it into my lungs as my heart slowed.

"I didn't make it," he muttered. I let out a long breath as Hades moved to get scratches from Zeke.

"Me neither. I was starting to have a panic attack," I admitted sheepishly as I held up my phone. "I was about to call someone."

His eyes ran over me, assessing. "How about now?"

"Better," I admitted. Whenever one of the guys was around, I was always better, calmer.

He looked out on the water. "Well, aren't we a pair?" he grumbled.

I huffed. "I have trouble leaving the house alone…"

"And I have to fight tooth and nail to let you," he admitted quietly.

I reached over and took his big calloused hand in mine. His fingers were warm as he gave me a squeeze.

"My shrink says it's like a muscle," I told him, as his thumb made small circles over my knuckles. "The more I do it, the sooner I'll be able to with less trouble."

"Sounds like a good doc," he said. I nodded.

"We can try again tomorrow." I offered quietly. He took a deep breath and let it out slowly.

"Sounds like a plan." he agreed, still looking out at the water.

I gave his hand a shake so he'd look down at me. Those sky-blue eyes met mine. "Let's get out of here." he nodded, let go of my hand, then got to his feet. I had to remind myself that Zeke wasn't into PDA. Not to mention he'd been walking on eggshells around me since he found out he couldn't hug me. We had been close, we always seemed to understand each other. But now… things were different. I didn't like it.

We walked back to the cars in silence.

When we reached the cars I let Hades jump inside before turning to Zeke. "Maybe we can start with you not following me to Miles' house?" I offered. He struggled with the idea for a moment. I just waited patiently.

"Text me when you get there?" he asked, his face hard.

"You got it." I gave him a small smile. He waited until I climbed into the Blazer, closed and locked the door before he headed for his '97 Jeep Cherokee.

I missed the old Zeke. The Zeke that wasn't afraid to touch me or even stand near me. Heart aching, I pulled out of my parking spot and headed to Miles' house as my new routine dictated.

My official Voice Therapy sessions had ended weeks ago. Ethan, on the other hand, had other ideas.

I drove through the gate and up the driveway. Ethan thought the more therapy I had, the better the chance of me getting my singing voice back. I had told him what the therapist said but he didn't care.

I pulled up to Miles' house. House was a relative term; it was really a mansion. The gray stone three story house sat on top of the hill with new ivy trying to climb the walls. The old, dead ivy had been cut away. Huh, he must have had gardeners come out.

I parked in the circular gravel driveway and texted Zeke that I made it before I headed in. I didn't bother knocking.

"I'm here!" I shouted, wincing as my voice came out scratchy.

"Kitchen!" Miles called back. I headed through the foyer and down the long hall to the kitchen.

Miles was putting away groceries. Grabbing a bag, I started putting away the cans in the pantry.

"You were busy this morning," I said as I turned around.

Miles closed the fridge then turned to me. "I usually go shopping Saturday mornings." His gaze ran over me. "How did leaving the house go?"

I closed the pantry. "Zeke and I got a big fat F for today. I was starting to have a panic attack when he showed up."

Miles gave me a small understanding smile. "How long were you out alone before you had an issue?"

I thought it over. "A couple of hours."

His smile grew. "That's progress, Lexie. It might not be the big step you wanted but it's still progress." I grinned at him. He was right. I might have had a problem, but I still went out alone.

"Thanks, Miles."

"You're welcome, Lexie."

I tossed the grocery bag into the recycling bin. Then went to sit down at the counter before I met his gaze again. "I need to talk to you." His brow drew down as he moved to stand across the breakfast counter from me.

"Sure. What's on your mind?" he asked, his voice that silky smooth timbre that I loved.

I took a deep breath and told him. "Sophie wants to cross soon." His face turned somber. He placed his hands on the counter as I continued. "And I need to tell the twins so we can find out what pulled her back here." Miles made his thinking face, the one that left a little wrinkle between his eyes.

"When does she want to cross?" he asked, his voice quiet.

"After the cousins leave at the earliest, she said she'd break a guitar when she was ready," I replied.

He started tapping out that staccato rhythm on the countertop.

"I have no idea how to even begin to tell them," I said softly as I rested my arms on the counter. He let out a deep breath.

"We," he said, his eyes meeting mine. "We are going to tell them. We all knew Sophie was in the house and we decided not to tell them."

"I don't want you guys to take the fallout," I admitted. "They can blame me, it'll be better-"

"No," Miles stated clearly. "We're going to do this as a family. The way we always do things."

I sighed deeply, tension melting from my shoulders. To be honest, I didn't want to have to tell them by myself. "How do you think they'll take it? That we didn't tell them?"

"It's not going to be pleasant," he admitted, his gaze on the counter top. "Ethan will probably be angry. But Isaac... I don't know what to expect from Isaac."

I cursed.

Miles reached out and took my hand. I met his gaze. "But we'll all be there for them and we'll help them get through it." I looked down at our hands. I held on tight, wanting to believe it'd be that easy.

"Lexie." I met his eyes again. "It's going to be alright." I nodded. Miles' thumb ran over the back of my hand. "Now, they leave Monday morning?" I nodded again. "I'll do some research and see if I can get a better idea of how to help them through the initial shock."

"Thanks, Miles." I squeezed his hand again. He squeezed back.

"Of course." The front door opened.

"I'm here!" Ethan shouted.

"Kitchen!" Miles' hand slipped from mine before he moved to the coffee maker.

It wasn't long before Ethan walked in smiling. "Ready for therapy?" he asked.

I sighed wearily as I picked up my water bottle. "Sure."

"Come on, Beautiful." He gave my arm a tug. I got up, a heavy weight settling on my shoulders.

I followed Ethan down the long hallway that ran the length of the house and into the music room. The room was beautiful. The walls covered in bookshelves. The only things in the room were a guitar, a cello, and a grand piano.

Ethan sat down at the piano and opened the folder he brought. I sat next to him and waited with a heavy heart.

"Ethan…" I tried again to get him to understand.

"No. Screw what that therapist said," Ethan stated cheerfully. "We can get your voice back to where it was." He handed me the sheet music to Green Day's 'Still Breathing.' It didn't require a huge range, but first I needed to do my warm up exercises. His chocolate eyes were determined when they met mine. "Okay?"

I didn't have the heart to tell him it was hopeless. I nodded. "Okay."

CHAPTER 3

SATURDAY AFTERNOON

*I*t was over an hour later and I was still sitting next to Ethan at the piano. He played the guitar as we sang a duet. I was trying to sing my verse of Seether's 'Broken.' On my second line my voice cracked. We ignored it. On the fourth line my voice strained to reach the higher note, it came out scratchy and sounded awful.

Enough! I stopped, threw my sheet music, put my elbows on the closed piano and hid my face in my hands. My chest was tight as tears fell. I sounded horrible. I couldn't hit the notes I used to, my range was small enough that it was laughable.

I took a deep breath. My throat burned with the need to scream. It wasn't enough for Clay Ordin to take Zeke, no, he had to take this too. That fucker! I took shaking breaths as tears fell. I didn't even realize how much I loved singing with Ethan until I couldn't anymore. And now... I wished Clay was in front of me so I could stomp his nuts into the ground.

Ethan's hand went to my shoulder as I tried to get myself under control.

"It's not... going to... happen," I managed while taking deep breaths.

"Lexie…" his voice was smoky and gentle. I dropped my hands and looked at him. When he saw my tears, his face grew pained.

"Don't 'Lexie' me," I croaked. I cursed and took another drink from my water bottle. "My range is gone and it's not coming back."

His eyes softened on mine. "Then we'll pick songs in your range-"

"There aren't that many-"

"Then I'll fucking write 'em!" he snapped. He reached out, wiped my cheeks and held my face in his hands. "Don't give up on me, Beautiful."

I took one deep breath, then another. He pulled me against him. I laid my head on his shoulder. His touch starting to calm me down. He rested his cheek against my forehead and held me tight.

"You might not sing with the band again, but you'll always be able to sing with me," he whispered.

I nodded and held him tighter. "Love you," I whispered.

"Love you, too." He held me until I had stopped crying and could breathe again.

When I moved out of his arms he chuckled. He reached up, using his thumb to wipe under my left eye.

"Your makeup is destroyed." He smiled. I snorted and then wiped my face under my eyes.

"I'm not surprised," I said, my voice hoarse. "I think that's a day."

"Yeah, breaking down into tears usually means the end of my practices," he offered. I grinned a little. He gave me a small smile as I drank from my water bottle again. "It might take a long time, but we'll keep trying."

I nodded. "I'm going to go wash my face." My voice was hoarse as I got up and headed down the hall to the bathroom.

When I saw my reflection, I shook my head. My mascara was destroyed. I thought about what Ethan said as I warmed up the water. Did he really think we could get my range back? He kept being so certain. When the water was ready, I washed my face until my makeup was gone. I dried my face and looked in the mirror. My eyes were still red from crying. Oh well. There was nothing I could do about that.

I headed back to the kitchen to get my usual 'after voice therapy tea'. Miles was there already, pouring hot water out of a kettle into a mug. By the time I reached him he had put in a tea bag and passed it to me.

"Thanks, Miles," I croaked. He gave me a gentle smile as I sat on the counter next to the stove. I blew on my tea as he leaned against the kitchen side of the breakfast bar. I took a drink, the warmth soothing my throat.

"Ethan headed out, he said he'd see you tonight." Miles' gaze ran over me. "Are you alright?"

"Just had a breakdown," I admitted, meeting his eyes. "My voice hasn't improved in the last month."

"If you want to stop these lessons, I'll talk to Ethan about it," he offered.

I shook my head. "I think they're more for him than me." I took a sip.

"It's possible," he said quietly. "Are you guys really going out to that old hospital tonight?" Miles grinned.

I chuckled. "Yeah, it was Isaac's idea." There was an old hospital that closed down in the forties. It remained empty and was pretty much abandoned at this point. Everyone at school swore it was haunted.

Miles narrowed his eyes on me. "Why?"

"Because of the rumors," I explained. "The twins want to see if it's really haunted or if it's just stories. And since I'm the world's best ghost detector…"

He shook his head. "I'll be here in case you guys get caught and need bail."

"Why don't you come with us?" I asked. "I think Asher and Zeke are going too."

"Walk through a large, abandoned building?" He looked out the window over the sink. "I live in one. It's not necessary to go looking for one." I looked him over. There were shadows under his eyes.

"Are you having trouble sleeping again?" I asked softly. His gaze met mine.

"As usual," he admitted. "I've tried music, I've tried television, I even tried Melatonin. The only thing that works is working until I'm exhausted." I hated that Miles couldn't fall asleep normally. He was brilliant and that was when he was exhausted. I wanted to see what he could do with a full night's sleep.

"Well, if you're up one night, give me a call." I offered with a grin. "I'll probably be awake too."

He smiled the smile that made him handsome and wreaked havoc with my heart. "Deal."

Miles waited until I was done with my tea. "If you don't want your dance lesson today, I'll understand," he offered.

I smiled. "Nope."

He held back a grin. "Alright, then let's go."

BY THE TIME I finally got the moves Miles was teaching me right, we were both sweaty and breathing hard.

When the song ended, Miles lifted me from the dip then went to turn off the stereo. He looked good when he was sweating, the wave of his hair curled more, making me want to run my fingers through it. I pulled my mind back from where that train of thought was taking me.

He shut off the music then turned back to me. "You're making a lot of progress."

"I'm trying to," I admitted before taking a drink of water.

Miles wiped the sweat off his face. "You're a fast learner. By this summer I'll be able to take you to one of the salsa clubs in Missoula."

My eyebrows went up. "We're underage."

He finished his drink from his water bottle. "Some of the clubs let in minors." Did I want to go salsa dancing with Miles this summer? Yeah, I *really* did.

"Sounds good to me," I said as we started putting the furniture back in place. "Why do you like salsa dancing anyway?" I began shoving one of the couches back to its spot. Miles was instantly there, practically moving the couch on his own.

"It's all about the woman," he said quietly as he slid the coffee table back into place.

"How's that?" I asked as I started pushing the other couch. Miles went to the other side and helped move it into place.

"If you watch the dancing in a salsa club, you'll see it," he said as he met my eyes. "Salsa dancing isn't really about the men. It's about the women. The man's job is to make her look great. Which isn't really difficult." He turned away from me to the stereo. "Your hair spins around you, your body moves with the music, and you start to glow. You let go." He reached up and pulled out the CD and put it in its case. "It's my job to make you look even better." My face warmed. What the hell did you say to that?

"Well, this woman is going to go take advantage of that bathtub," I announced. I picked up my bag of clothes. Miles' back was still to me. "Thanks, Miles. I really enjoy these lessons."

"You're welcome," he said, not bothering to turn around. "I enjoy teaching you."

I walked into the long hallway and headed to my room in the house. It was the classically elegant master bedroom. It had been Miles' mom's but she decided to bail and not come back. I still wanted to yell at her for it, but I settled for donating all her clothes to charity. Miles thought it had been a great idea.

I shut the door behind me and made a beeline for the bathroom. It looked like a spa. Teal walls, and white tile. Especially, with the giant Jacuzzi tub. Hello heaven.

As soon as the water was high enough, I dropped a rosemary bath bomb in before I stripped down and climbed in. Oh, God. The hot water went to my chin. This was bliss.

I reached up, grabbed one of the rolled-up towels and put it behind my head. Then I hit the jets. Jets of water massaged down my back and the bottoms of my feet. I groaned and closed my eyes.

Rosemary scented steam filled the bathroom.

I looked up at the row of bath products that had been appearing over the last few months. Brands I didn't even recognize. All of them had either rosemary oil or extract. The shampoo and conditioner were even for curly hair. Not to mention they were hydrating, exactly the kind I used. Only these were better. Whenever I used the tub here I left with my curls defined and smooth without any help from me. Miles never said anything. Bath stuff just kept showing up. I smiled to myself and closed my eyes.

Somedays I wondered if Miles cared about me the way I did about him. Others... I had no clue. I took a deep breath, sank into the heat of the tub and let the world drift away.

CHAPTER 4

SATURDAY EVENING

*I*t was four in the afternoon when I trudged up to my room for my 'nap.' At least that was what I called Veil work when Tara was around. Hades followed as usual, the dog had been my shadow for months now. I laid down on my bed and groaned when Hades instantly took up more of my bed. I scooted, bitching the whole time. He just laid his head on my pillow and looked adorable. The brat knew how to play me.

I closed my eyes, focused, then dropped down to the Veil. Over the last few months, bypassing my center had become a habit. I dropped to the grass then straightened. The Veil was the same as this morning. Nothing ever changed here unless I brought the dead. I was at the center of the Veil, exactly where I needed to be.

I sat down in the grass, making sure I didn't crush any flowers, took a deep breath and brought up a memory of the guys that made me feel safe.

It was the night after I came home from the hospital. Hades was with me, hogging the bed. The guys were spread out over my floor. Well, most of them. Zeke had been sleeping sitting up against the wall between the door and the closet. The twins were on the floor beside my bed. Miles was down near the foot and Asher's long legs were in the hallway. They refused to leave that night. So, Rory agreed to let them crash in my room as long as the door was open.

My barriers dropped.

The energy of the Veil washed through me gently, making my skin tingle. I opened my eyes. My energy was still close around me in a golden dome. That was fine for what I was doing.

I closed my eyes and focused on an image of an apple. That hard feeling in my chest grew, my will reached for the energy of the Veil. A small weight grew in my right hand. I opened my eyes and smirked. A shiny red apple sat in my hand. It felt solid and real. Mostly because it was. Following the book from Serena, I learned how to use the energy in the Veil, much like a Witch in the real world, only in here. I left my eyes open as I focused on dissipating that energy. I pictured it gone, its energy absorbed back into the Veil. The apple burst into gold light, then there was nothing.

"Okay, one down, thirty to go." I thought out loud.

I ran through the exercises that were in the book, twice. I worked on doing it faster and faster. Once I was warmed up, I could create almost anything instantly.

I was playing with fire as it ran along my arm when I had an idea. I smirked at the flames as they smothered out.

"Zahur!" I shouted. Over the last few months, Zahur had become more of a teacher than the creepy Imposter Me. Whatever she was, she was always willing to help if I got stuck on an exercise.

It was only a couple minutes wait before she popped into the Veil, looking like me again. I instantly dropped water on her, soaking her to the bone. I burst out laughing. She pushed her hair out of her face and glared at me.

"If you wanted a fight, you just had to ask." She smirked. Oh shit. A ball of water shot towards my face. I dropped onto my back barely in time for it to pass over me. I somersaulted backwards to my knees and shot Zahur a challenging look. She wasn't wet anymore but she was smiling.

I conjured a ball of fire and threw it at her. She ducked, her smile grew.

"Good," she stated in an odd voice. It wasn't mine... it sounded deeper. "Now, let's see what you have learned." I grinned wickedly.

We went at it like that for some time. She scored some hits, which hurt like hell, and I scored a few myself. Eventually, she called it.

"Good," she said as the shield of energy she created disappeared from around her. "But you need to be faster. If the other one comes back you need to be able to take them down quickly before they can do more damage." She walked towards me. I met her in the middle. When she was close enough she reached out, her hand glowing with green light. Before I could ask she ran that hand around me. The spots she hit didn't hurt anymore.

"What did you do?" I asked when I got my breath back.

"Simple healing. I can only do it here," she said before meeting my eyes. "Now, you need to start on making an alarm."

"Yeah, I'll start tomorrow," I agreed. I needed that alarm soon. If whoever shut off the Veil came back, I'd need to know immediately.

"See that you do," she said a second before she disappeared. I hated that she could do that.

I looked at the flowers blooming around the Veil. There were even some vines now, climbing over the charcoal stumps of trees. The Veil was finally healing but if it took a hit like before, it might just kill it off for good.

Worried, I pulled myself out of the Veil and back to reality.

I HAD JUST PULLED on my black hoodie when a car honked outside. I looked through the blinds and spotted Zeke's Jeep. I hurried downstairs, Hades on my heels.

"I'm heading out with the boys," I told Rory. He eyed what I was wearing. Black jeans, black shirt, black boots and hoodie.

"What are you guys up to tonight?" he asked suspiciously.

"The twins want to check out the old abandoned hospital to find out if it's really haunted," I admitted. Rory chuckled.

"Be careful and don't get caught," he told me as he looked to Hades. "Hades, want to stay, eat pizza and watch sports?" Hades gave a small bark and left my side to join Rory on the couch. I smiled as I opened the door and almost ran into Asher.

"I wasn't taking that long," I pointed out as I slipped outside and closed the door behind me.

"I know, but Zeke was starting to growl." Asher shrugged. We headed across the lawn toward the running Jeep.

"Ash, I need to talk to you guys without the twins before Monday," I whispered as we slowly walked out to the car.

He nodded. "I'll send a text to Zeke to show up early to brunch tomorrow." he offered. I gave him a smile.

"Thanks," I mumbled before opening the back door and climbing into the middle of the seat next to Isaac.

Zeke's car still slightly smelled of smoke, but the interior was brand new and black. Big surprise there.

I buckled my seatbelt as Asher climbed in next to me. Isaac shifted and laid his arm along the back of the seat as I was squeezed between the two of them.

Zeke pulled onto the road and out of my neighborhood.

"So, tell me about this place and why everyone thinks it's haunted?" I asked the guys.

"It was a hospital that closed in the 1940's," Asher began. "It was the only one around for miles."

"Why'd it close?" I asked as Zeke pulled out onto the highway.

"That's where the rumors come in," Isaac explained. "Some rumors say bad treatment of the mental patients and others say that with the new smaller hospitals in towns they ran out of funding."

"Wait, there was a mental ward?" I asked.

"A small one." Ethan pulled out a notebook and turned on a small penlight. "In the... east wing."

"Is that a map?" I asked, incredulous.

"Yeah, I sketched it from what I could find online." Ethan held a copy up to show me. "I figured it'd be easier to get around." Good idea.

"So, what have people seen that made them think it's haunted?" I asked as I shifted to get more comfortable. Vanilla and limes mixed in the space of the back seat. It wasn't unpleasant but it was distracting.

"Loud noises, doors slamming, cold spots, weird shadows," Isaac began. "There's a couple of sightings of a woman in a white hospital gown."

"You guys really did your homework," I said, impressed.

"Me and my brother have been wanting to do this since we found out you could see the dead," Ethan admitted. I shook my head at that.

"Did everyone bring their charms?" I asked. Everyone but Zeke held up their charms against the dead for me to see. "Zeke?"

"Hmm?" Zeke seemed to have not been listening.

"Did you bring your charms?" I asked. Zeke nodded.

Why was he so quiet? Maybe I'll get him alone later and ask. The rest of the drive the guys continued to fill me in on the information they found on the hospital. It wasn't very exciting, which I was fine with. That meant there probably weren't any ghosts there, we could just look around and leave.

Half an hour later Zeke pulled off the highway onto an overgrown gravel road. Isaac started bouncing in his seat. I put my hand on his leg to try to get him to calm down. It didn't work.

It wasn't long until we pulled in front of a large, desolate building. Zeke parked the car.

"Everyone grab a flashlight out of the back and a copy of the layout," Zeke ordered.

Isaac and I jumped out of the Jeep and looked up at the building. Three stories of brick, set in a U. The building was enormous. Ivy was crawling up the walls and over the roof. Chimneys were crumbling. Some of the large windows were busted out, letting the ivy inside. It was awesome.

I was suddenly just as excited as Isaac. I walked to the back of the Jeep and took a heavy Maglite from the pile and a map from Ethan.

"Looks like a couple found the place too," Asher announced. I turned to where he was looking. There was a gray sedan parked closer to the building.

"We could scare the hell out of them," I suggested wickedly. Isaac started nodding.

Zeke looked down at me with that glare. "No," he said in his 'don't even think about it' voice.

"It was just a suggestion," I said innocently. The others chuckled.

Once everyone had what they needed, I peeked up at Isaac. His gaze met mine, his mischievous grin appeared. We were both thinking the same thing. I turned back to the guys and tried to hide my excitement.

"So, why don't we split up?" I suggested. "We can cover more ground." The others looked at me with confusion.

"You're the only one who can see the dead," Asher reminded me.

"Yeah, but there are other signs you look for. You know, weird noises, those doors slamming, all that stuff." I inched my way toward the building with Isaac just a step behind me.

Asher was eyeing me. He knew I was up to something. When our backs were to the building entrance I added, "So, let's split into teams. I'm with Isaac." Before they could say a word we both turned and bolted for the entrance.

"Lexie!" Zeke bellowed. I giggled as we climbed the crumbling front steps and carefully slipped through the sideways door. We were both laughing as we turned on our lights and kept going.

The foyer was decaying. The plaster on the walls gone in most places. The floor littered with dust and debris. There was a dusty, dank, stale smell to the air. But I didn't care. I knew Zeke, he'd try to find us as fast as possible. I grabbed Isaac's hand.

"Quick, second floor!" I hissed. We could barely stop snickering as we raced up the stairs and down the left hall. We slowed down.

The walls here were covered in peeling paint, making them looked cracked. We walked down the long corridor. Doors ran down each side of the wide hallway. It looked straight out of a horror movie.

Isaac's light shined on a doorway whose door was on the floor.

"Hey, Red, let's check this out," he whispered. I went with him and shined my light inside.

It was a small room. The green paint cracked and peeling off the walls, the floor covered in dirt and grime. It was empty.

"Just a hospital room," I thought out loud. I let go of Isaac's hand and moved further down the corridor and around the corner. Isaac with me every step of the way.

"This is one of the reasons I love you, Red," Isaac said as we kept moving. "You're willing to do the same crazy stuff I want to."

"Like driving Zeke nuts?" I offered, smiling. He nodded.

"That is high on the list," he admitted. He was quiet for a bit. "This shit doesn't bother you?" he asked as we reached large double doors on one side of the hall.

"Not really." I pushed one of the doors open and stepped inside. Isaac followed. "Does it spook you out?" The light from our flashlights bounced off the green tile. There were bathtubs lined up against the wall across from us.

"Not really," he said as he went to one of the tubs and looked in. "Too many video games maybe." We went back into the hallway and started walking.

"Maybe." I shrugged. As we looked around, I thought back to what he had said. "I don't like all the stunts you do. The really crazy ones actually scare me." I told him. His gaze ran over me then met mine.

"My stunts scare you?" he repeated, sounding doubtful. "The woman who sees the dead all the time? The girl who laughs at horror movies?"

"Yeah, they scare me," I said simply. "Like that surf tubing in January, that scared the hell out of me." I turned my flashlight to the walls and kept walking. "Climbing without gear in October," I reminded him.

"That's just fun," he explained.

I turned back to him. "When you do that shit, it scares the hell out of me," I said sincerely. He wouldn't meet my gaze. I stepped up, grabbed his chin and made him look at me.

"I care about you. Hell, I love you, Cookie Monster." His jaw clenched as I continued. "I just don't want to see you get hurt."

He sighed deeply, shadows filled his eyes. "So, you, what? Want me to stop being me?"

I shook my head. "I just don't want you to take stupid risks anymore." His fingers brushed along my jaw. He leaned down and kissed the corner of my lips. My heart gave a hard throb. Whoa. Where did that come from? I'd never felt that before, not from Isaac. Hell, not from anyone lately. He pulled back and gave me a small, sad grin.

"Alright, Red," he said softly. "For you, I'll try to pull back on the stunts." I gave him a big smile and practically tackled him as I hugged him tight.

"Thank you, Isaac," I whispered. He squeezed me back.

"Only for you, Lexie," he said softly.

Cursing came from down the hall. We went still. The voice was gravelly and deep. We let go of each other.

While talking we forgot what we were doing. Zeke must have finished searching the first floor. Smiling, I hurried to the nearest door. It was a closet. I gestured to Isaac, we squeezed in and shut the door behind us.

I shut off my light and he covered his with his shirt so it wasn't completely dark. The closet was musty and small, forcing us to be pressed against each other. Zeke's heavy footsteps came closer. He was mumbling about how he was going to kill us both. Isaac snorted. I looked up. He was trying to stop himself from laughing, his face was red from it. I couldn't stop smiling as I put a finger to my lips to remind him. His shoulders started shaking. I felt my own control slipping. I let out a giggle. I covered my mouth with my hand as the footsteps came closer.

The door jerked open, light blinding me. I couldn't help it. I started giggling.

"Not funny," Zeke growled as he lowered his flashlight. We broke out laughing. He reached in, grabbed my arm and pulled me out of the closet to his side.

Isaac and I kept laughing as Zeke marched us back downstairs to where the others were waiting. By the time we reached them I had my breath back.

"How'd you find us?" I asked, wiping a tear from my eye.

"Your footprints in the dirt," Zeke bit out.

"Oh, clever." I smiled up at him. He glowered down at me which set me off on another round of giggles. Asher shined his light at the ceiling so we could see everyone.

"Are you two finished running off on your own?" Asher asked in a very Miles-like tone.

I tried not to smile too much as I said, "Yes." Asher shook his head.

"Back to what we came here for," Zeke growled. "If you two are done, let's get to it." I peeked up at him. Was the hospital getting to him? Maybe.

"Fine," I agreed. "Where were the most sightings of the woman?"

"Third floor common room," Ethan announced. "In the east wing." Great, the mental ward wing.

"Third floor it is!" I declared and turned toward the stairs. Zeke stepped in front of everyone as Asher stepped up next to me.

"What did you think you were doing?" Ethan hissed at Isaac behind us.

"Exploring," Isaac countered.

"The group sticks together, that was the deal," Ethan snapped.

"Fine, God, relax will you," Isaac grumbled. "It was just a joke."

As we reached the second story landing, something moved. I only spotted it out of the corner of my eye. I looked to the left and shined my light. There was nothing there to move. Huh. Must have been a bug or something.

We turned and headed up the staircase to the third story.

"Are you guys sure you don't want to look around some more?" I asked, almost begging.

"Maybe, if you don't run off again," Zeke called over his shoulder. I rolled my eyes.

Zeke tested each step before he let us on the staircase. After all, if it could hold him, it'd hold all of us. It took a while to reach the third floor. The air was colder up here; every window was broken letting the spring wind in.

"Which way to the common room?" Zeke asked.

I pulled out my map and looked at it. "To the left, I think."

We started walking down another wide corridor that was exactly the same as the second floor. Everything was normal until I noticed I could see my breath. "Um, guys. I think there's a soul somewhere. And a pissed off one at that." I announced. The guys started looking up and down the corridors. I saw nothing. That chill ran down my neck, only it felt like a punch. I grunted and closed my eyes with the pain. It was only a few seconds, but when I opened them I was surrounded by the guys.

"Ally?" Asher asked.

"There's a soul alright, and close." My voice turned raspy. I reached for my water bottle and realized I had left it in the Jeep. Shit.

I was looking down the hall at a pair of double doors when the soul walked right through it. She was in a hospital gown and muttering under her breath. Her stride was long as she cursed stupid teenagers. She looked up and stopped. Her brown hair was wild, her eyes furious.

"Great, more stupid teenagers looking for ghosts," she groaned. "I don't want you here! Stop bothering me!"

I bit back a smirk as I stepped out from behind Zeke. "I see you." She froze, then frowned at me.

"You can see me? Now?" she asked, her voice full of disbelief.

"Yeah." I nodded.

She sighed with relief. "Great, can you tell those morons to stop coming around here and trying to talk to me?"

The two doors down the hall opened. Two boys around our age came out. One with a video camera and another with a gadget in his hand.

"The temperature is dropping out here!" the shorter one said. "The cold spot is moving!"

I went still. Were they... no. They finally noticed us and jumped about three feet in the air.

"Shit!"

"What the..." The taller one swallowed hard. "What the hell are you guys doing here?"

"Checking out an old building. What about you?" Asher asked moving to my side.

"I'm Travis," the shorter one said. He had an average face with dark hair and gray eyes.

He gestured to his taller, leaner friend. "That's Keith. We're looking for proof there's a ghost here."

Isaac tried and failed to cover his laugh with a cough. I elbowed him in the side.

"So, you're what? Ghost hunters?" Ethan tried to cover for his brother.

"Yeah." Keith had a nice face, black hair and silver-rimmed glasses.

The woman waved her arms around. "See what I mean? They're here every other day now and I'm sick of it." I made eye contact with the soul and tilted my head toward the back of the group.

"Asher, stall please," I barely whispered.

"So, how do you do that?" Asher asked walking over to them. The guys began explaining as I slipped back behind the twins. The ghost joined me.

"I can't deal with them but I can help you cross," I whispered. Her brown eyes lit up.

"Oh, yes, please. Get me out of here," she said adamantly. "I'm so ready."

"What's your name?" I asked my voice still low.

"Esther," she said. I gave her a smile. I pulled off my bracelets and tucked them into my pockets. Esther's energy hit my barriers. Thankfully, they had gotten stronger. I vaguely felt pressure in my chest, a heart attack? I wasn't sure.

I focused on Esther's need to move on. That gold thread wrapped around her wrist. I dropped down immediately.

The Veil was quiet as we hit the grass. Esther let out a deep sigh of relief as I let go of her.

"Thank you so much. You have no idea how long I've been there." Esther said emphatically.

"It's what I do." I shrugged. "Should I expect any other souls in the building?"

Esther shook her head. "There were others once. But over time they disappeared." Her eyes focused as she met my gaze. "You need to get those boys out of there. There are these... things there."

"What things?" I demanded instantly, my pulse picked up.

"I don't know. I've been hiding from them for years," she admitted. A golden door shimmered into sight.

"I'll get them out of there," I promised. She smiled.

"Thank you."

"You're welcome." I didn't bother to wait for her to cross. Something was in the building with the guys. I pulled myself out immediately.

I opened my eyes and blinked hard trying to get my bearings.

"The temperature is rising," Travis snapped. "Damn it!"

"Sorry, I was just curious about how you did what you do," Asher offered. I was about to turn around and let the guys know we needed to go when the hair on the back of my neck stood up. The sudden feeling of being watched washed over me. My heart pounded as I looked down the other side of the hall toward the West Wing and lifted my light. There, near the walls, was a pitch-black shadow figure. My skin crawled.

"Ethan," I whispered.

He turned to me. "Yeah?"

I swallowed hard. "Can you see that?" I asked quietly. Ethan looked to where my light was.

"No," he whispered back. "You see something?" I nodded. My stomach knotted as I looked at it. It wasn't just a shadow where you could see through to the other side. No, the black of its body was so thick I couldn't see past it. Dread filled me. This was definitely not a ghost.

"Asher, we need to leave," I whispered, knowing he'd hear me. "All of us. Now."

"Well since you're done here, why don't we all hit the diner for some late-night food," Asher offered. "Our treat for ruining your night." I kept my eyes on that shadow figure. And it kept watching me. It felt...

"I can see it now," Ethan said. Shit.

"We're not done, we still have a couple hours to work," Travis said. Another shadow figure emerged from another door. I threw subtlety out the window.

"We need to go," I ordered. The figures started moving down the hall towards us.

"Now!" Zeke and Asher grabbed Keith and Travis. They dragged them down the hall. We turned and ran back the way we came. Travis and Keith were shouting, asking what was going on.

When we reached the staircase, I skidded to a stop and let the others go first. I watched as the two shadow figures came towards us. Sweat ran down my back as I turned and ran, following the boys down the stairs. When we hit the second floor there were two more on the far side of the corridor.

"Anyone else see that?" Keith asked.

"Faster!" I shouted. Everyone picked up the pace. When we hit the first floor it was clear.

Everyone ran for the door. Zeke stopped and made sure the others got through first. "Run, you ass!" I shouted as I bolted through the door. Zeke followed right behind me.

We ran until we reached the gravel. I turned, out of breath, to look at the doorway. Nothing was coming. I took big, gasping breaths as I watched the entrance. What the fuck were those things? They felt...

"Everyone okay?" Zeke demanded. There were several yeses and yeahs.

"Why the hell did you guys yank us out of there?" Travis demanded. Asher started making something up. Zeke stepped between me and the building. I looked up.

"Lexie? You alright?" he asked. I nodded quickly several times as I reached up and wiped some dust off my neck with a trembling hand.

Frowning, Zeke reached out, his hands cradled my face gently, forcing me to keep meeting his eyes. His hands were warm on my skin.

"Lexie, what did you see?" he whispered.

I swallowed hard. "I don't know," I whispered back. "But it was bad. Really bad."

"If that was true, then why is she white as a sheet?" Travis demanded. The scent of limes and spice mixed with the scent of engine grease as Zeke let go of my face. His large hands moving to my shoulders, the weight comforting.

"She probably has low blood sugar right now," Asher offered. "She didn't eat much at dinner."

Keith eyed me.

"Bullshit. She saw something," Travis declared.

"Something we didn't see. Not until we were already moving..." Keith seemed to be thinking out loud.

"Ethan, get her in the car," Zeke ordered. Ethan wrapped his arm around me and started walking me back to the Jeep.

Travis came toward me. "What did you see?" Isaac moved to intercept. Zeke moved with Ethan to get me in the Jeep.

Isaac held his hands up and gave him a charming smile. "Man, she just has low blood sugar, diabetes runs in the family."

"I don't buy that," Keith announced before pointing at Ethan. "Because you said, 'I can see it now.' Then you were hauling us out of there." Travis moved around Isaac and headed straight for us. Zeke moved between us.

"Are you psychic?" Travis demanded, a light sparkled in his eye. Zeke blocked his view of me. I sat down in the Jeep. Ethan stayed in the door, he leaned over me then handed me my water bottle. I took a sip.

"She has low blood sugar and a seizure disorder," Zeke growled. "That's it. Now leave her the fuck alone."

Keith came over and grabbed his friend's arm. "Come on man, we got enough footage for tonight." They both began to walk away.

Everyone stayed put until they drove off. There was a collective sigh of relief.

"What did you see in there, Beautiful?" Ethan asked gently. The others gathered around the open door.

"When I got back from helping the ghost cross, I got this really bad feeling," I explained. "A solid black figure walked into the hall from the other wing. That's when I told Asher we needed to go the first time."

"The first time?" Isaac asked.

"She whispered it so those guys wouldn't hear," Asher explained. Isaac nodded.

"It watched me, I watched it. And it felt…" I swallowed hard. "It felt… it felt evil and hungry. It scared the shit out of me. So, when another one walked into the hall and started coming towards us I just yelled run," I admitted.

"She asked if I could see anything, and I couldn't." Ethan offered. "Until right before we ran."

"But, what were they?" Isaac asked.

"I have no fucking clue," I admitted. "I'd never seen anything like it in my life." The silence was thick as everyone absorbed that.

"Get in, we're out of here," Zeke ordered. I was happy to scoot over so Ethan and Asher could get in beside me.

We were halfway back to town when Zeke broke the silence. "Lexie, do you want to stay at Miles' tonight?"

"I can't. Hades is at home and I need to figure out what those things were." I replied.

Isaac held up his phone. "It sounds like shadow people," he announced. I raised an eyebrow. He continued to read from his phone. "Thought to be an entity from a separate dimension, demon or ghost; most, if not all, are parasitic," he looked back to me. "That sound about right?"

I gave him a small smile and nodded. "Yeah, that feels right."

When Zeke pulled up to my house, I was still a bit out of it. Asher slid out of the Jeep. When I climbed out I stumbled, Asher caught me with an arm, then made me meet his eyes.

"Ally?"

"I'm fine," I said instantly. "Just, a little off balance."

Turning to the house, I shuddered. I really hated the front of this house.

Asher took my arm and walked me to the door. I didn't really need to hold on to him, but I wanted to, so I didn't complain. I walked into the house and turned back to him. His worried eyes ran over me.

"You sure you're okay?" he asked quietly.

I nodded.

He frowned even more. "If you need to talk, call me, alright?"

I nodded again.

"Night, Ally girl."

"Night." I locked the door behind him and turned on the alarm. I was feeling numb as I turned to find Hades on the couch.

"How'd it go?" Rory asked as he walked into the living room area with a beer bottle in his hand. I met his eyes. His smile disappeared. "Lexie?"

"Where's Tara?" I asked immediately. Rory put the bottle on the end table and strode over to me.

"She's at a friend's house tonight," he answered. He lifted my chin and checked my eyes. "What happened?"

"I just saw something I've never seen before." I began. "And it was scary as hell." Rory pulled me into his arms, I held on tight.

"What did you see?" he asked gently. I explained what happened as he let go and we moved to sit down. The numbness slowly ebbed away as I spoke.

Eventually, when I was responding enough to his questions, he went into the kitchen. When he came back, he handed me a mug of hot chocolate with marshmallows. It made me smile. He sat down on the couch and leaned forward with his elbows on his legs.

"Now, Kid, didn't Serena say you were going to be seeing more things as you got stronger?"

I nodded absently. "Yeah, she said I'll see stuff then need to figure out what it is."

Rory raised an eyebrow. "You've been dealing with groups of dead people since March. You're crossing them in groups still, right?"

"Yeah?" I didn't see where he was going with this.

"Kid, you are way beyond what any of our family has known," he explained. "Before you came here, I had never heard of the Veil. Or that there was a way to cross souls. Hell, I didn't even know that you could. From family stories, the girls always had extreme trouble dealing with it. And they..."

"They all died before they turned thirty." I finished for him.

His mouth pressed into a tight line. "Yeah. But Kid, you're ahead of the curve here. You have Serena to call and ask when something like this happens. You have the guys out there who know how to help if you get jumped. You have an enormous advantage over every generation of women that came before you. And you don't go down without a fight." I sighed. It felt that way a lot lately. And I was sick of it.

"I just wish there was a manual. An Idiot's Guide to Necromancy," I admitted with a grin.

He smiled. "Maybe you'll write one. For your future kids."

I snorted and shook my head. "Oh no. No kids for me. I'm not passing this shit on," I stated adamantly. His smile turned sad.

"Wait till you're at least twenty-five before you make that decision," he advised. "See how things are then." The air took on a heavy weight with the elephant in the room. Tara, she was obviously going to live a long life.

"A manual, huh." I thought about it. It wouldn't be a bad idea. I wonder... "Rory, do you think that any of the women in our family could have written down what they knew already?"

Rory's eyes were thoughtful. "Maybe. I could find your grandfather. He still has all the family stuff." His eyes focused again on me. Grandfather? I'd never heard Rory talk about him before, not really. "I'll see what I can do. But for now, go get some rest."

I nodded before heading upstairs with Hades. I changed into my jammies, and laid down, nudging Hades toward the edge of the bed. The bugger had started taking the outside of the bed after I came home from the hospital in January. I hadn't minded then, but now he took most of my bed.

I quickly called Serena and got her voicemail. I explained what happened and asked her to call me back. I needed to know what those things were...

I was still laying there looking up at the ceiling, dreading going to sleep, when my phone vibrated on my desk. I reached over a sleeping Hades and checked my texts.

Miles: I heard about tonight. Are you alright?

I smiled to myself. Of course the guys told Miles.

Alexis: Yeah, just spooked.

Miles: Are you sure?

I looked up at the shadows moving over the ceiling. Was I okay? I was getting tired of that question. Tired of asking myself over and over.

Alexis: I'll survive. Can't sleep?

Miles: As usual. Sweet dreams.

Alexis: Night.

CHAPTER 5

SUNDAY MORNING

The hand on my shirt dragged me through the snow. I didn't want to go. I fought his hold until he pulled me in front of him, his hand on my throat, squeezing.

"In time, you'll see. Our marriage will be perfect. Our children will be beautiful," he said confidently. Rich musky cologne was thick on my tongue.

"Planning to rape me?" I snapped through my teeth. His free hand moved...

I jerked awake, biting back a scream. I was still gasping when I recognized my room.

Feeling Clay's hands, smelling his cologne, I got out of bed and started pacing. My heart slammed in my chest as I ran my hands through my hair. It's April. I'm at home. Clay Ordin is in jail. Isaac beat the shit out of him. I'm safe. I don't need a shower. I kept pacing in front of an anxious Hades until I realized what was happening. I was having a panic attack. I needed to do something.

Hands shaking, I changed out of my jammies then hurried down stairs. I needed to do something, anything. I could cook breakfast... I walked into the kitchen and began pulling out pots and pans. I needed... I needed.... Shit! What did I need? Asher would know... Asher... yeah...

I left the kitchen, grabbed my keys from my hoodie and hurried outside. Hades trotted beside me as we went to the Blazer. It's April. It's morning... I ran over it again and again until I pulled up in front of Asher's house. Sunlight barely peeked over the mountains, warming the ground causing fog to rise. My pulse was pounding in my ears as I turned off the truck and climbed out. Hades pressed against my thigh as I went up the front steps and tried the door. It didn't budge. Why wasn't it unlocked? Asher usually left it that way when he was home...

Still dazed, I unlocked the door. Asher would probably be in the kitchen... it was morning so that's where he'd be... I headed for the kitchen with Hades still pressed against my thigh the whole time. I didn't mind, it was comforting. The kitchen was empty... Where was he? My mind raced around in frantic circles as I looked out the window and watched the fog rise off the grass. I was so lost in my mind that I didn't hear anyone come down stairs.

"Ally?" I jumped. My heart skipped as I turned around. Asher came into the kitchen in a pair of Marvin the Martian PJ bottoms and a white tank undershirt. His hair was everywhere while he blinked at me. The world came back into sharp focus.

"Sorry, I... I didn't mean to wake you up," I said, feeling guilty. He stopped a foot from me. His eyes ran over me, growing worried.

"What's wrong?" he asked gently. "Did you have a nightmare?" I looked down at Hades and nodded. I bit the corner of my lower lip as my eyes burned.

"It was the cabin. I started... I woke up and had a panic attack," I admitted, looking up at him. "The doc said do stuff to stop it, to distract myself. I wanted to make breakfast and I couldn't figure out what I needed so... I ended up here."

Asher's face softened. "Come here," he said in that rich baritone that I loved. I stepped into his arms and rested my head on his chest. He held me tight, one hand cradling the back of my head. I took a deep breath and drew in vanilla and cinnamon, all the tension inside me easing a little.

"I didn't mean to wake you up," I said pitifully.

"You can wake me up anytime you need me," he said softly.

I smiled into his shirt.

He gave me a squeeze before letting go. He kept one of my hands in his and gave me a tug. "Come upstairs, you might be able to catch a couple more hours of sleep."

I nodded and followed him upstairs with Hades on my heels. Asher led me into his bedroom. His big double bed called to me with its slept-in white sheets and blue and orange striped comforter. I didn't hesitate, I toed off my sneakers and climbed in. The bed dipped and moved as Asher got comfortable.

His arm wrapped around my waist as he tucked me into the curve of his body. I was half asleep when I remembered who else was here.

"What about your sister?" I muttered. Asher's face was buried in my hair at the top of my head.

"She can go to hell," he mumbled back. I smiled as I fell asleep in his arms.

AN ANNOYING HUMMING woke me up. Groaning, I tried to move only to find I couldn't. Something was heavy across my chest. I opened my eyes and looked down. A muscular forearm was between my breasts, the hand spread against my upper chest. Fingers brushing my collarbones. Hmm? Asher? Still half asleep, I held his hand as I felt him start to wake up.

Asher's face rubbed against the back of my neck.

"I did it again, didn't I?" he mumbled, his lips brushing my skin.

"Uh-huh," I muttered as I tried to wake up. His fingers squeezed mine, I let go of his hand so he could pull his arm away from me. He rolled away.

"Sorry." He did something to make the annoying vibrating stop.

"Don't care." I snuggled further under the covers to go back to sleep. The blankets were pulled off my head.

"If you want to get to Miles' before the twins, we need to get going," he told me.

I grumbled, rolled onto my back then opened my eyes to look up at him. He was on his elbow next to me, his other hand holding my blankets.

"Do I have to if I don't want to?" I asked seriously. He snorted.

"Yeah," he countered. His eyes narrowed on me. "Why did you want to meet with us before the twins got there?"

I sighed and met his eyes. "Sophie is ready to cross."

"Shit." He laid down on his back next to me, his shoulder touching mine. There was silence for a few minutes. "When does she want to go?"

"She was willing to wait to talk to the twins until after their cousins left." I reached up and wiped gunk from my eyes. "I have to tell them when she breaks a guitar."

"And you want to talk to us about how to tell them," he surmised. He rubbed his hands against his face, hard. "Okay, coffee. We need coffee." He dropped his hands and sat up on the side of the bed. I grumbled as I got out of the warm blankets and went in search of my shoes.

Hades simply lifted his head and watched. Apparently, he didn't feel the need to abandon the comfy bed so soon. I found my shoes near the door and pulled them on. When I turned back to Asher, I froze.

He was by his dresser on the other side of the room, shirtless. My mouth grew dry as my gaze ran along the sculpted muscles of his shoulders, down his muscled back and dear Lord. He had two dimples near his butt, just above the waistline of his pajama bottoms. Damn. I swallowed hard and forced myself to turn around.

"Ash. You could have waited to change until I was out the door," I pointed out.

He chuckled. "Jessica is downstairs. Do you really want to deal with her this morning?"

I started weighing my options. Stand in the same room while a hot as hell Asher changes and *not* look... or deal with his twin sister Jessica. Yeah, not much of a choice.

"I'll take your sister," I admitted. "I've got to take Hades out anyway." I patted my leg.

Hades came to me instantly. I kept my back to Asher as I slipped into the hallway.

When the door was closed I let out a deep breath. Holy crap! That guy was... and his back... dimples! Come on Lexie, get it together. I moved downstairs slowly, hoping I could get outside before Jessica saw me. This was not the day to hope.

I was almost down the stairs when footsteps came from the kitchen.

"What the fuck are you doing here?" Jessica shouted. I sighed. I had to remind myself I made a choice. I stepped off the stairs to turn to Asher's twin sister. She towered over me, her pretty face furious. Her mouth hanging open. She was wearing pink Hello Kitty pajamas with her sandy blond hair back in a ponytail. The whole image was rather funny.

"I came by early to talk to Ash-"

"Are you fucking my brother?" she shouted. I sighed.

"No, I'm not fucking your brother. I'm friends with your brother," I reminded her patiently. She scowled at me as she looked at my hair and lack of makeup.

A door opened upstairs.

Jessica shot Asher a dirty look. "Are you bringing ho-bags into the house now?"

I shook my head and headed for the front door. There was no talking to Jessica, she hated me and there was nothing I could do to change her mind. And quite frankly there was nothing I wanted to do either.

Asher, however, had something to say. "Shut it, Jess!" Asher snapped. I turned at the door to watch him step off the last step. "I'm sick and tired of your issues with Ally," he stated clearly, his face hard, his eyes bright. "She's my friend and is welcome in this house at any time, day or night. You can ignore her, or you can treat her as a guest. But your screaming is over. I'm done with this bullshit."

Asher stepped away from a gaping Jessica and came to the door. Stunned, I opened it and headed out with Hades.

Hades was taking a leak on the mailbox before I could say something.

"Wow. Ash," I said, impressed. He rubbed the back of his neck as he looked back at the house.

"I've just... had it, Ally." he sighed. "She's been acting like a stranger for years. I'm tired of trying to find the sister I remember in that person." I reached over and took his hand. He took a calming breath and let it out. He squeezed my hand before tugging me toward his red truck. "Come on, we've got to grab groceries for brunch."

I let Hades jump into the back of the cab before climbing into the front seat. Asher was quiet all the way to the grocery store. I rolled down my window a bit so Hades would be comfortable before getting out. It didn't seem to matter, he was on his back asleep anyway.

We headed into the store and grabbed a cart. I pushed while Asher checked out the cantaloupe in the produce section. He was so thorough, making sure everything was ripe that it made me smile. He noticed.

"What?" he asked.

"Nothing," I shrugged. "I just didn't know you did brunch every week." We headed into the bakery section.

"It's cheaper than ordering it in," he hedged.

I smiled. "You like doing it." His cheeks tinged pink as he focused on picking out fresh croissants from the bakery. He pointed out which ones he'd like then turned back to me, his eyes full of shadows. "Ash? Is something wrong?" I asked gently. He sighed.

"My dad's been giving me a hard time lately," he said as he took the box from the woman. He thanked her and put them into the basket before continuing. "He's on my case about Jessica's grades. Apparently, she's been ditching a lot."

I scowled. "That's not your fault. You're her brother, not her father," I reminded him.

He started looking at some oranges. "I know. But he won't deal with it and she'll keep doing what she's doing." His ocean eyes met mine. "And my sister might end up in some trouble she can't get out of."

"Those are her decisions, Ash. She decides what she's going to do. Not you," I pointed out. "Your dad's the one who should deal with it." he nodded, his gaze unfocused.

"I know," he said softly, his eyes focused before they met mine. "Which is what I'm going to tell him next time I talk to him." I went still. Asher was going to stand up to his dad. That's...

"You surprise me, Superman," I told him, a small smile tugging at the corners of my mouth.

He grinned, then it started to fade. "That's not our biggest worry right now. I'm dreading talking to the twins," he admitted.

My smile dimmed. "I don't know how it's going to go, but they need to talk to her."

"That's what I'm worried about," he said quietly. With that thought lodged in our minds we got back to shopping.

I WAS SITTING IN MILES' kitchen at the breakfast counter. Asher was making eggs and bacon while Miles was getting the coffee ready as Zeke arrived. The front door slammed.

"Here!" Zeke barked.

"Kitchen!" Asher answered. Zeke came in with scruff covering his face and his eyes half open. Miles immediately handed him a cup of coffee. He grunted his thanks before coming to sit on the stool next to me.

"Why the hell am I up so early?" Zeke grumbled before taking a drink of his coffee.

I waited until he finished drinking before answering. "Because, on Friday Sophie told me she was going to be ready to cross soon."

Zeke grew still, then slowly set down his coffee. "When does she want to cross?" Zeke asked, his gaze on the counter.

"She was willing to wait until their cousins left, so, tomorrow maybe. She'll let me know by breaking a guitar," I explained. "But I still haven't told the twins."

Zeke let out a deep sigh, braced his elbow on the table and rubbed his eyes with that hand. "Fuck."

"One of the reasons we're here is to figure out the best way to tell them," Miles said as he brought his own coffee mug to the breakfast counter.

Zeke dropped his arm to the counter and shot Miles a look. "There is no 'best way' to tell them," he growled. He pointed toward the front door. "That's their little sister who has been stuck here because one of them pulled her back."

"And we all knew about it." Asher took the skillet off the burner and moved across from me at the breakfast counter.

"And we didn't tell them," Miles added. The silence grew thick.

"That day is going to suck," Zeke growled. The others nodded in agreement. "What we need to do is figure out who's watching who?"

Miles turned to Zeke. "Do you think that you and Asher can handle Isaac while I take Ethan? Ethan will be angry, but he is less likely to do something dangerous."

Zeke nodded, his eyes full of shadows. "Yeah, we can handle him. I'll sit on him if I have to."

"Call me if you need a hand," Miles added. Zeke nodded.

"So, that's the plan?" I asked. All eyes turned to me. "Tell them, and you guys stop them from flipping out?" They all nodded. "Okay. That's not scaring the crap out of me." I said sarcastically.

"Who is going to tell them?" Asher asked, looking over at Miles.

"I am," I said immediately. The guys all opened their mouths to protest, I cut them off. "I'm the one who can see her. It's my responsibility to tell them."

"Fine," Zeke bit out. "But make it clear we all knew about it too. Don't even think about taking all the blame yourself." I shot him a look, mostly because the guy had read my mind. His piercing ice-blue eyes stayed on mine until I had to give in.

"Fine," I grumbled.

Asher lifted his head. "They're coming up the drive."

We all waited until the front door opened.

"We're here!" Isaac shouted.

"Kitchen!" we called back in unison. The twins came in, still half

70

asleep and in their jammies. I smiled at the monster slippers on Isaac's feet.

Everything grew busy as everyone dished up their plates. Once we were in the living room and eating, we were able to talk.

"What are everyone's plans for the week?" Asher asked before taking a drink of coffee.

"Ethan and I have that trip down to Missoula Art Museum tomorrow," I reminded them. "That should be fun."

Zeke's head snapped up, his gaze went to both of us. "Take a kit."

"As if we'd forget," Ethan huffed. Months ago, Miles had created an emergency kit for if I ever got jumped around them again. It was really only salt and salted holy water but everyone had a stockpile of them everywhere. It had saved my ass in December, so I didn't mind the reminder.

"I've got one in my hoodie and two in my bag," I reassured him. Zeke nodded. Appeased, he went back to his breakfast.

"You guys are coming to the barbecue Rory is doing tonight, right?" I asked. Everyone agreed.

"Yeah, even Aunt Ana and the monsters will be there," Ethan offered.

"Other than the Championship and practice, I have nothing planned." Miles announced. I smiled.

"How's training going?" I asked before I took a bite of melon.

"It's going well. We're keeping it a bit lighter since the meet is on Friday," Miles said.

"That'll be fun," I said.

"Then we can have a victory party," Isaac pointed out.

Miles shook his head. "I haven't even won yet."

"You will," Ethan said confidently. His phone vibrated on the table. Ethan picked it up and checked it.

"We could have a Miles party," I suggested. "Game marathon and snacks." Miles sent me a grateful smile.

"Or we can hit a big party and Miles could actually meet someone." Isaac countered.

Miles picked at his plate, his ears turning pink. "I'd rather have a night with my friends."

"That decides it," Asher declared. "Video game party Friday night."

"Hey guys, Joslyn Clark just texted me that her whole neighborhood had a power surge. It blew the transformer. It's the fourth time in a month." Ethan announced. He looked up from his phone.

"Now that you mention it, there have been more electric company trucks in town lately." Miles said. "More transformers are breaking around town."

"I saw four yesterday alone," Asher added.

"Are they just old and breaking?" Isaac asked before biting into a slice of bacon.

"I don't think so, the electric company came through three years ago and updated the entire system," Miles said. I had a hunch.

"Where does she live?" I asked them.

"Over on Walnut," Ethan answered.

"And Walnut is right by the cemetery," I thought out loud. "Where an ever growing group of ghosts get together almost every day."

"You think the energy from the souls are affecting the transformers?" Miles asked.

I nodded. "With all the extra energy floating around out there... yeah, it seems likely."

My phone rang on the table. I set my coffee down, leaned forward and picked it up. It was Serena. "I need to take this, guys." I got up and moved into the long hallway before answering.

"Hey."

"Tell me again what you saw?" Serena demanded. I moved further down the hall so I could have some privacy.

"These human shaped figures. They were completely black, as in, you can't see through them black," I told her softly. "One of my friends looked them up and said he thought they were shadow men."

"How did they feel to you? Sad? Confused?" she asked.

I licked my lips before answering. "Evil. And hungry." There were several heartbeats of silence.

"What you're describing is a Shadow Man," Serena finally said. "How many did you see?"

I ran through my memories again. "Four, I think."

"Where?" she asked, her voice cold. Her attitude was starting to irk me.

"The old abandoned hospital off the freeway. Thirty minutes east from Spring Mountain," I answered, my voice growing hard.

"Well, they were Shadow Men. There's nothing you can really do about them," Serena said in a lecturing tone. "I need to go-"

"Hold on!" I snapped. "What the hell are they?"

"Lexie, haven't you been doing research?" she chided me.

"Yeah, and I still don't know what they are or what they can do," I shot back. She sighed in my ear.

"They are parasites. No one knows where they come from. They latch on to a place or sometimes even a person and slowly kill them. Just stay away from the building and you should be fine," she said in an irritated voice. "You really need to do more research."

That's it. "Oh, I'm sorry. I've just been busy getting the dead to cross over and trying to fix the Veil," I snapped.

"Lexie, that's not my area. It's yours." she reminded me.

"Except it affects the entire world and you know how to do more than you're telling me." I countered.

The silence on the line was thick.

"I answered your question, next time figure it out yourself. Good-bye." Serena hung up.

I resisted the urge to throw the phone into the wall. Ever since I learned Serena had lied to me about how much she really knew about working with the dead, our relationship had been on the downslide. I kept getting the run around and I was sick of it. I took several deep breaths before heading back into the living room.

Asher was just finishing a story as I sat down and picked up my coffee mug.

"Who was on the phone?" Asher asked.

"Serena," I said, keeping my voice light. "She was just answering some questions for me." More like dodging them but I couldn't tell them that. They had enough to worry about with the twins right now. Asher looked like he wanted to ask more but Isaac jumped in.

"So, Red," Isaac turned to me, "are you still coming to the skate park with me?"

"Yep." I thought about telling them I was getting my hair cut then quickly decided against it. They were guys, it's not like they were going to care about my hair anyway. "I just have some girl time scheduled with Riley first."

"What do you girls do anyway?" Ethan asked. "Gossip and get manicures?"

I smiled sweetly at him. "If that was the case, you'd be there right along with us." The guys chuckled.

"That's true..." Ethan admitted.

The rest of brunch went on as usual, though I was quieter than normal. Serena's attitude and rush to get off the phone was still in the back of my mind. Why was she so reluctant to give me the answers I needed? One day soon, I was going to have to have a long talk with her. And it wasn't going to be a pleasant one. Everything was starting to feel like it was on a timer and when time was up, all hell was going to break loose.

I pushed away the feeling of time slipping away and focused on enjoying my time with the guys. Tic tic tic...

CHAPTER 6

SUNDAY AFTERNOON

*R*iley, Hades and I were sitting in the waiting area of the salon looking through magazines when I remembered I needed to tell Zeke where I was. I pulled out my phone and opened our usual group chat.

Alexis: Zeke, I'm at a salon getting my hair cut. Just so you're aware.

I was about to put my phone away when it blew up.

Isaac: What salon?

Asher: You're cutting your hair? How short?

Ethan: Awesome! Get an undercut!

Zeke: Why are you cutting your hair?

Miles: You never mentioned wanting to change your hair.

Surprised, it took me a few seconds before I could reply.

Alexis: Because I want to. I'm over at Torren's Salon, Riley's aunt runs it, I'm still looking at styles. I'm doing it because if I roll over and yank my hair one more time, I'll start screaming.

My phone blew up again.

Isaac: We're on our way, we want to see what you pick!

Oh God. No. They wouldn't... "Shit."

"What?" Riley asked putting her magazine in her lap.

"The guys," I said absently as I read the incoming messages.

Asher: Me too, don't get in the chair until I get there.

Zeke: I don't think you need to cut your hair.

Miles: I suppose I'll join you guys. I'm in town already.

I raised an eyebrow. Seriously?

"What are they doing?" Riley asked.

"I made the mistake of saying I was getting my hair cut," I told her. "Now they all have an opinion." Riley started laughing.

Alexis: Don't you dare.

Ethan: Too late, we're in the car. LOL.

Oh great. I looked to the stylist. She was just finishing cleaning the hair up from her last client. I grabbed a magazine and looked through it as fast as I could.

"Quick, help me find a style before they get here," I hissed. Riley instantly started searching.

"Why do they think they get to have an opinion?" she asked, smiling.

"I don't know," I admitted as I looked up at the stylist who was fixing her station.

I mentally urged the leggy blond to hurry up. I didn't know what the guys were thinking. The stylist came towards the sitting area.

"Lexie, right?" she said. I nodded and rushed to my feet. "My name's Mira." She led me to her station. I sat down so fast Riley began snickering. "So, what are we looking to do today?"

I pulled my hair out of its ponytail and let it fall down my back. Mira gently lifted it over the chair. "Oh my, when was the last time you had a trim?"

I thought it over. "A couple years ago?" I offered. "I know I want to take some length off. I was thinking just about the middle of my shoulder blades." I watched Mira nod in the mirror as she began to pull my hair into a braid.

"With your curls, I'll have to cut longer than that or your hair will be up to your shoulders," she explained.

"Works for me." I resisted the urge to tell her to hurry up and cut.

"You know, your hair is very healthy. It'd be perfect for Locks of

Love." Mira wrapped a band around the end of my braid. "They make wigs for kids with cancer, women suffering from hair loss."

"Might want to hurry," Riley warned. Shit!

"Sounds good to me, it's not doing me any favors," I stated. Mira chuckled as she reached for her scissors. Come on, come on! The door to the salon opened. Oh no.

"Stop!" Isaac shouted dramatically. Both Mira and I spun around. Riley was in the waiting area shaking her head. Isaac was standing in the doorway still in his PJ's. "Don't cut that wench's hair!" He puffed up his chest. Ethan gave him a shove from behind so he could come inside. Ethan was also still in his pajamas. I bit back a smile as they came over.

"Uh, what's going on?" Mira asked.

"Incoming," Riley warned. Before I could explain, Asher strode through the door.

"You're not buzzing your head, are you Ally?" Asher asked, a grin on his face.

I began to answer.

"Screw that, she should buzz half her hair off," Ethan announced, smirking.

Isaac shook his head. "What about a pixie cut? I heard some girls talking about it at school, they said they were in trend or something." Riley fell into a fit of giggles, all but falling out of her seat.

"Do you know what a pixie cut is?" I asked. They shook their heads. I smiled as I looked to Ethan. "It's what your ex had."

Ethan's face cringed. "No pixie cut! No way!" he announced dramatically.

The door to the salon opened again. Zeke strode over to the group now surrounding me and Mira.

"What are you doing, Lexie?" he asked.

"Cutting my hair," I said clearly.

Zeke gave a slight cringe "How about just a trim?"

"It's heavy and it's down to my butt," I pointed out. "I need more than a trim." Riley started laughing harder. The bell over the door rang as Miles walked in. His gaze went to me.

"You haven't cut your hair yet?" Miles asked puzzled.

"I would, but everyone is being opinionated," I announced sweetly.

"Yeah, well, I love your hair the way it is." Asher offered, his cheeks tinged pink. A flutter of butterflies went off in my stomach. It had been a long time since I had felt them. They weren't huge, like they used to be, but the butterflies were there.

"Because it's heavy, catching on everything and I want to," I explained. The twins opened their mouths to argue.

"Lexie should cut her hair any way she likes," Miles declared.

"Hell no!" Ethan countered going so far as to point a finger to the ceiling. "I say we call for a vote." I snorted.

"Yeah, a vote as to how she cuts her hair," Isaac added. I smiled. I was so not going to follow the vote and they knew it.

"We are not voting on how I cut my hair," I told them, holding back laughter.

"I propose a trim," Zeke announced. The others nodded. I shook my head smiling. I knew exactly how to end this. I looked up to Mira who was looking at the guys as if they lost had their minds. She met my eyes.

"Yeah, I can settle for a trim." Isaac voted.

"Alright." My voice grew raspy as I raised it over all of theirs. I went to drink from the bottle in my lap to find it empty. Crap. "I'm cutting my hair now. Mira, for every new opinion or complaint, take another inch off."

The guys instantly went silent as Mira burst out laughing, Riley joining her. Asher took my water bottle from my cape covered lap then went over to the water cooler and filled it. When he came back he handed it to me. I smiled gratefully and took a sip. "Now, what were you guys saying?"

The boys looked at each other then looked at me.

"Cut your hair however you want," Isaac offered, smiling. I rolled my eyes. Riley was down to giggles.

"Okay, now, get out. This is our girl time. I'll see you guys later," I told them playfully.

Ethan leaned in and kissed my cheek, Isaac did the same on the other only to give me a raspberry instead. They all filed out of the salon door. When they were gone, Mira looked down at me.

"Who were those guys?" she asked.

"Those were my friends."

"They're pretty sweet," she said as she turned me in the chair towards the mirror.

"They're my guys," I said quietly, that feeling of being loved warmed me. Mira smiled and got to work.

Another stylist came in and put Riley in the chair beside me.

"So, what happened Friday night?" Riley asked. Damn, I had hoped she had forgotten.

"I had a flashback," I said simply, hoping to drop it.

"How'd that happen?" Riley asked, looking down at her lap so her stylist could work on the back.

"Um... Ryan's cologne set me off." I admitted.

She lifted her head and eyed me playfully. "How did he get close enough for you to smell his cologne?"

I cursed myself. I just shouldn't have answered. "He kissed me."

Her eyes grew wide. "Shut. Up," she all but yelled. "Ryan kissed you?"

Mira asked me to look down. I was looking at my lap as I answered. "Yeah."

"How was it?"

"I had a flashback Riley, I wasn't exactly in the right mindset to judge his kissing abilities," I reminded her sarcastically.

"Yeah, but..." She shook her head. "Ryan kissed you."

"And got chewed out and almost killed by the guys for it," I added.

Riley sobered. "Zeke almost lost it, huh?"

"Everyone but Miles almost lost it," I corrected. "I'll be surprised if he ever comes near me again."

There were several heartbeats of silence except for the cut of the scissors. "Do you want him to come around?" she asked.

I sighed. "I'm not interested in him like that." I lifted my head to look in the mirror again.

Riley eyed me before looking back at her mirror. "Is there anyone you are interested in?" she asked carefully. Mira told me to look left. I did happily.

"I'm not looking to date right now, Riley." I reminded her. Even if I wasn't crushing on three of my best friends. "What about you? I saw you talking to a few hotties Friday night."

Riley waved her hand dismissively. "Those are just my friends. You know, the three I was trying to hook you up with."

"Was trying?" I asked with a smirk. "Have you finally given up?"

"In a way," she said in an odd voice. "Never mind that, tell me how things went down with Ryan. Every detail." I sighed and told her everything up until my flashback.

"I still can't believe you didn't know he liked you," she said.

"I still can't believe he kissed me." I countered.

Riley changed the subject to what happened after we left. Apparently, drunken antics by the football team occurred. She had me laughing for over an hour.

RILEY DECIDED to get her nails done and it was tempting to stay, but I was meeting Isaac at the skate park.

I looked at my hair one more time in the mirror. The curls were frizz free and a little below my shoulders. Mira hadn't expected my hair to have that much curl to it. I liked it anyway.

As I finished paying I said, "Go ahead and send my hair to Locks of Love."

Mira smiled as she handed me my receipt. "You're going to make one little girl very happy." I smiled back then headed out the door with Hades.

I was almost to my Blazer when I noticed him. Asher was sitting in his truck playing on his phone. I walked across the parking lot and knocked on his window. He jumped, then gave me a sheepish look as he got out.

"What are you still doing here?" I asked with a smile.

His cheeks turned pink as his gaze ran over my hair. "I wanted to see how your hair came out."

I ran my hand down the back of my hair suddenly feeling self-conscious. "And?"

He grinned. "It looks good."

My cheeks warmed. "She took a little too much off," I muttered.

"It still looks good," he reassured me.

I met his ocean eyes. "Thanks."

"You're welcome." He looked away from me to the Blazer. "You're headed out to meet Isaac?"

"Yeah, he's going to try to teach me to skateboard," I said, my voice full of doubt. He chuckled.

"Don't get hurt," he warned.

"I won't," I grumbled.

"I'll see ya at the barbecue tonight, Ally." Asher got back in his truck. I waved good-bye as I headed to the Blazer with Hades in tow.

The drive to the skate park wasn't long. It was just on the south side of town. I pulled up and climbed out. Hades' tail was wagging as we walked towards the cement section of the park.

There were several others already there. A couple were riding down rails, a younger kid was practicing making his board jump. I didn't know the terms. I knew nothing about skateboarding whatsoever. I walked to the railings of the skate park and looked for any sign of Isaac. I found him standing with several others around what looked like an empty swimming pool. Isaac had his skateboard braced against the cement, the other end in his hand.

I was about to shout to get his attention when he moved onto the board and rode it into the swimming pool. I watched as he moved across the surface and up the side only to slide along the edge before dropping down into the pool again. He was moving fast as he rode up one side, flipped his board over under his feet, before hitting the wall of the pool again.

Impressed, I watched him run through several more tricks. Eventually, he was riding horizontally along a wall when he lost his balance. Instead of falling, he took several running steps to slow down.

Several of the guys hooted and whooped. Isaac picked up his board and hurried up the side of the pool. He climbed out practically in front of me.

"Hey, Red. Nice hair." He grunted as he pulled himself up onto the walkway around the swimming pool.

"Hey, Cookie Monster. Glad you like it, I guess I'll keep it." I grinned down at him. "That was impressive."

He chuckled as he got to his feet. "You have no idea what you just saw, do you?"

"Not a clue," I admitted, unembarrassed.

His grin turned mischievous. "Well, you're going to learn."

I eyed the empty swimming pool then looked back to him. "Oh, no I'm not."

"Just the basics, Red," he assured me as he took my hand and started walking.

We walked over to the other side of the skate park where there were fewer people and more open space. Hades found a spot on an empty bench, he immediately began to hog it. Isaac set his board down and stopped it from rolling with his foot.

He tugged me to him. "Okay, first, are you right handed or left handed?"

"Right."

"Then you're going to want to put your left foot in front and your right in the back. At least that's what feels right to me. Come on, step on."

I grumbled as I carefully stepped onto the board and immediately lost my balance. I grabbed his shoulders instantly. Isaac's hands went to my waist, steadying me.

"How's that feel?" he asked.

I thought about it. "Like I'm going to roll away any second," I said dryly. He chuckled.

Hades gave a short half bark with his own grumble at the end. I smiled. Even Hades agreed this was nuts.

"Relax, Hades, she's not going to fall," Isaac said. Hades grumbled again but stopped. He turned his attention back to me. "Okay, now to move, shift your front foot until it's straight. Just like when you're walking."

I shifted my foot, still holding on to his shoulders.

"Good. Now, you use your other foot to push off on the ground. Again, just like walking." He was using his 'instructor voice' now.

I lowered my leg and gave a small push.

"Good." He moved with me. "Now, bring your back foot onto the back of the board. Shifting your front foot sideways on the board at the same time, if you can."

I did as he said, wobbling a bit. He steadied me again.

"This is the ride position. After pushing you always come back to this position. This is where you do all your tricks." he said, still holding on.

I looked up at him doubtfully. "I doubt I'll be doing any tricks."

He smirked. "You never know." He looked down at my feet. "Let's just get you used to moving."

Isaac kept a hand on my lower back or hip as I slowly moved around the area. "Okay, big push and glide."

I did as he said then started listing to the left. I tried to correct only to start falling forward. Isaac became the only thing that kept me on the board.

"Yep. No tricks for me." I stated as I clung to his shoulders. He chuckled as he made sure I got off the skateboard safely. He picked up the board before we walked over to sit on the bench so we could watch the other skaters.

"Thanks for coming out, Red," Isaac said. "I feel like I don't get to see you much anymore."

"You see me every day," I pointed out.

He looked down at the ground. "You know what I mean."

I bumped his shoulder with mine. He bumped back. "Yeah, I do." I wrapped my arm around his and gave him a squeeze. "Ethan does have a habit of hogging the car."

"You're telling me," he muttered.

I shook his arm. He looked down at me. "You know you only have to call me to go somewhere."

He gave my arm a squeeze. "That's not really better."

"Is that how you started skateboarding? It was faster than walking?" I asked, curious.

He looked back out to the crowd. "Nah, Ethan actually started skateboarding when we were nine. He learned pretty fast too. Then he taught me."

Ethan knew how to skateboard? "That doesn't bother his back?"

He moved his arm so he could take my hand. "He can't anymore."

I gave him a sad smile. "That's why you let him have the car more. Because you could always skateboard."

"Or ride a bike. Yeah." He scratched his eyebrow, his face pensive.

"You miss skateboarding with him," I said softly. He just squeezed my hand.

"Red, leave it," he said quietly.

I rested my head on his shoulder. "So, what exactly *were* you doing in the empty swimming pool?"

He smiled then began explaining to me what I was seeing.

We talked for a couple hours about nothing and everything. With Isaac, every conversation was always different, we never stuck to one subject. We bounced around wherever the conversation took us.

I didn't realize how late it was getting until my phone rang. It was Rory.

"Hey, Rory."

"Hey, Kid. I forgot some things at the store. Can you stop by and pick them up?" Rory asked.

"Sure, hit me." I listened to the short list that happened to include buns and chips. When I got off the phone I turned to Isaac. "Want to go shopping with me?"

He grinned. "Sure." He picked up his skateboard and got to his feet. "Let's go."

WHEN WE PULLED up to the house we had the groceries that Rory had asked me to pick up. The street was already lined with cars I knew. I climbed out, grabbing as many bags as I could carry. Isaac got the rest as I headed for the door. Once I opened the door Ethan got up from the couch to take several bags from me.

"Thanks. Where is everyone?" I asked as I got out of Isaac's way.

Ethan headed to the kitchen. "They're outside. Miles and Asher are already here, so are Ma and Aunt Ana."

Isaac took his bags into the kitchen and set them down. He winked at me before heading upstairs, probably for the bathroom.

"Are the kids driving Rory crazy yet?" I asked as I began pulling large bags of chips from a bag.

Ethan chuckled. "Nope, he's actually out there playing with them." I shook my head as we threw the bags away. Ethan turned to me and eyed me. "Nice hair, Beautiful."

I smiled back. "Thanks, it feels about ten pounds lighter." I picked up several chip bags while Ethan picked up the buns. We headed out back to the others.

Rory had set up a couple of long tables and folding chairs on the patio. He was busy playing with the four-year-old twins. Amelia was sitting in his lap while they played a game with his fingers. Isabel was watching intently from Tara's lap. I looked around for the boys. Rory must have given Mateo and Marcos fishing poles since they were fishing off the end of the dock. Ethan was called over by his mom.

I put down the chips and looked for the other guys. I found Asher at the grill with Miles. Asher was talking while Miles listened. I grabbed a soda from the cooler and headed over to see them. Miles was the first to look up.

"Lexie, your hair suits you," Miles offered, his ears turning pink.

"Thanks," I said with a grin. He smiled as I looked at the grill. "So, how long until food is ready?"

"About five minutes," Asher said as he flipped the burgers on the grill.

"Good, I'm hungry."

"How was the skate park?" Miles asked. I turned to him.

"It was kinda fun," I said as I popped the top on my soda. "Until I almost fell on my ass." The guys chuckled.

"Things are usually fun until then," Ethan pointed out as he joined us. I shrugged. The back door opened. Zeke and Isaac came out arguing. Out of the corner of my eye, I noticed Tara's posture straightened.

"She didn't fall," Isaac snapped.

Zeke shot him a look. "Put a helmet on her next time," he growled. Isaac rolled his eyes as he headed towards us.

Zeke dropped off a large plastic closed bowl on the table before coming over.

"What's got you all pissy?" Ethan asked.

"Interacting with people. I've hit my quota for the day," Zeke countered, his voice dry. I snorted.

"Did Sylvie send that garden salad over?" Asher asked.

"Yeah. It's on the table," he bit out. His shoulders were tense, and he kept clenching and unclenching his jaw.

I met Zeke's eyes. "It's a barbecue. Stop growling." I ordered. He shot me a look that told me it wasn't likely. "Please?" The look went away as he sighed.

"Fine," he muttered.

"I'll go get the ketchup, mustard, and all from the kitchen." I turned to walk away. Miles fell into step beside me. His fingers tapping that staccato rhythm on his thigh. What was going on?

When we were inside loading our arms up I finally asked, "Did something happen while I was gone?"

"No, it's just..." He hesitated. "It's Tara. She tried to, well, interrogate me, earlier."

I narrowed my eyes at him. "About what?"

Miles shrugged. "She was jumping subjects. She didn't stick to any specific subject but she wouldn't stop asking me questions until Asher arrived."

"That's weird," I thought out loud as I closed the fridge.

"Though, she kept asking about your bloody noses and that party in October," he informed me.

"Huh," I muttered. "Why would she suddenly care?" Miles opened the back door and held it for me.

"I have no idea," he said softly as we walked to the table where everyone was grabbing chairs. I took a spot between Miles and Maria. The twins were down the table with their cousins, trying to keep the chaos at a minimum. Asher and Zeke sat across from us.

Tara immediately took the chair to Zeke's right.

"Hi, Zeke. How have you been?" Tara greeted cheerfully. Zeke's posture grew rigid. Ever since Zeke punched a guy out at a party for her, it seemed Tara had started thinking of him as some kind of knight in shining armor. Even though, before that night, she had never even acknowledged his existence. Now, she couldn't seem to stop paying attention to him.

"Fine," he muttered as he passed down the buns. I started getting my bun ready for my hotdog.

"How was your week?" Tara asked. That was just the start. As everyone ate, laughed and visited, Tara flirted with Zeke. I tried to ignore it and smile, but it wasn't easy. Especially when Tara reached over and touched Zeke's forearm. He immediately pulled his arm out from under her hand.

I glanced over and met his eyes then quickly looked away. I couldn't pretend it didn't bother me. It did. But I didn't really have the right to be jealous. Yeah, we kissed. But since then... nothing. I focused on eating and talking whenever I had something to add to the conversation.

Eventually, the table broke up. Zeke took Mateo and Marcus to the docks to show them a better way to fish. Tara followed. Asher and Miles went off to watch the four-year-olds while Ethan and Isaac were talking with their Aunt Ana.

I, on the other hand, started gathering plates and silverware to take inside. I couldn't watch Tara hitting on Zeke anymore.

Why did she need to hit on my friends anyway? She's pretty and rather popular. I'm sure she could get any guy she wanted at school. So, why did she have to go after one of mine? I paused at the back door. Mine? Zeke wasn't mine. Neither were Asher and Miles. I needed to stop thinking that way.

I started adding the dishes to the left sink as I began to fill the right with rinsing water. What the hell was wrong with me? Three guys?

Really, Lexie? I sighed wearily as I shut off the water and started washing the plates first.

I was lost in thought when the back door opened. I looked over my shoulder. A scowling Zeke was striding through the great room.

"Your cousin is annoying the fuck out of me," he growled.

"Sorry." I offered.

He glanced over his shoulder. "I'll see you tomorrow." He all but slammed the front door behind him. I bit back a smile and went back to the dishes. A part of me wanted to laugh.

Another part of me was just glad Zeke wasn't interested in Tara. Or Asher. Or Miles. I sighed. What the hell was wrong with me?

Ethan

I WAS ON STAGE, playing my heart out for the crowd. Instead of cheering they were booing.

Saying fuck it, we stopped playing and headed off stage. Cursing, I took off my guitar and resisted the urge to throw it once I got into the backstage area. The area was empty. The other guys... were somewhere else. I turned towards the back doors and froze.

Sophie was standing there in her jeans and shirt, her hair the way she always had it. Down and wild.

"Sophie?" My voice shook.

She smiled up at me with her amber eyes. "Hi, Eth."

"You're... here," I said, stunned.

She stepped closer. "Yeah, I'm here. And I need you to listen." I blinked down at her. That didn't sound like my Sophie. She sounded... older. "You need to let me go."

I began shaking my head. "You don't get it..."

"Eth. You need to let me go," she repeated. "Please, for me." I shook my head again.

How could I let her go? With Isaac the way he was... I couldn't.

Suddenly, I was shivering. The backstage was covered in a layer of ice. Sophie was crestfallen. I didn't understand...

I jerked awake, gasping as I looked up at my ceiling. My breath was fog in the air.

My room was freezing. I pulled my blankets over me and waited as I had the other nights.

For the last week, I've woken up to my room freezing cold. That's all the ghost ever did. Freeze my room and knock over my guitars. I rolled over to check on them. All four of them were still in their stands but this cold wasn't good for them. The air started warming again.

I sighed. I was getting tired of this bullshit. I needed to get Lexie to move this fucker on. I'd ask her tomorrow. I quickly fell back to sleep.

CHAPTER 7

MONDAY MORNING

I hurried to the cemetery. My stupid alarm hadn't gone off and I was running late. I pulled up to the group of souls and jumped out, pulling off my bracelets as I strode towards them. What I saw had me slowing down. A ghost was being held by one of the others. What in the fresh hell? I stopped at the grass line.

"What's going on?" I asked. The skin on his face seemed to be melting off. His flesh peeling away from his neck.

Mr. Davis struggled with the rotting soul. "It's Martin, he's taken in too much of the energy-"

"He's rotting out," I finished for him. "There's nothing I can do for him. Get him out of here."

Mr. Davis met my gaze, then let go. Fucking asshole! My heart slammed as the rotting soul ran straight for me. I pulled my will to me and waited. My skin tingled as if electricity ran over it. He was almost on me.

"No," I growled, whipping out with my will like a whip. His feet went out from under him, then he hit the grass. I threw that golden thread around one of his wrists and dropped immediately. He fought me. He cursed, clawed, and howled. But I held on. My drop slowed, it

WHISPERS FROM THE DEAD

was because of him. I cursed. I pictured myself getting heavier and heavier. We started to fall again.

Then I yanked hard. The soul slammed into me. His nails dug in, I deflected and tried to direct us to the Veil while keeping his hands off of me. Eventually, I managed to wrap the golden thread around both his wrists.

When we hit the grass, we hit hard. The air was knocked out of my lungs as I hit. I rolled onto my back and forced my lungs to work.

When I could I sat up; the ghost wasn't being held by me anymore. The Veil had grown vines that wrapped around his wrists and legs. All the plants near him reached out for him. I watched dumbfounded as the vines all but covered Martin's rotted soul.

A shudder rocked the Veil, almost throwing me back to the grass. I knelt there, stunned, as the vines shimmered, grew thicker. Martin was screaming.

All the greenery around him changed. Thicker grass sprung up, vines wrapped around a burnt stump and kept growing till they bloomed. Holy shit.

The vines were draining the energy from him. I knelt, frozen where I was. Just as I started to worry that it might drain him too much, his screaming stopped. The vines dropped away showing me a normal, healthy soul. His stunned gaze was on his shaking hands. When those gray eyes met mine, he smiled.

"Wow," he said. "What just happened?"

I got to my feet. "Apparently, the Veil drained you of all the extra energy you absorbed."

He eyed me. "Did you know it could do that?"

"No," I bit out.

"Then what were you going to do?" he snapped.

"I didn't exactly get a chance to figure it out!" I shouted back. "In case it missed your notice, they just threw you at me." They could have fucking killed me. Movement out of the corner of my eye told me that a door had come for him.

I ignored him and looked at my body. I had scratches on my arms and shoulders. Please don't let me have them in the physical world.

Otherwise, Zeke was going to be pissed. I looked up in time to watch that ball of light shoot up into the Way.

"You're welcome!" I shouted, completely irritated. What a dick. I closed my eyes and pulled myself out.

THE CEMETERY WAS JUST how I left it. I quickly looked down then cursed a blue streak. The scratches came with me. Shit. I took a deep breath then looked at Mr. Davis.

"I managed to get him across. But don't you ever fucking do that again," I growled. "That hurt like hell." I turned away to head toward the Blazer.

"What about the rest of us?" someone shouted.

"Fuck you!" I shouted over my shoulder before climbing into the Blazer.

I drove off, still furious that they had thrown a rotting soul at me. Did they ask me to try? No, they just went and did it. The dead were pushing it more and more. It was time to start pushing back.

I had just turned off the Blazer when it hit me. I had just crossed a rotting soul. I sat there for a full three minutes just absorbing that. I hadn't even known that was possible. If I can cross a rotting soul... I grabbed my bag and ran to meet the guys.

I met them at our usual table outside. They saw me coming. Everyone got to their feet as if to come to me. I reached the table first.

"I managed to cross a rotting ghost this morning," I announced. Their mouths dropped. "Rotting, like Mary Summers."

Miles was the first to recover. "That's amazing, Lexie."

The others began to say similar things when Zeke growled over them, "What happened to your arms?"

I looked down at them. Blood streaked my arms and was still dripping from other scratches. "He put up a bit of a fight, but once I got him to the Veil... the Veil just... sucked the extra energy right out of him. Then he was himself again." I kept my voice light, wanting him to focus on what I was telling him.

"Asher, do you have your first aid kit?" Miles asked.

Asher opened his bag and pulled out a small box. Everyone sat back down, including me.

"You guys know what this means, right?" I asked as Miles pulled out antiseptic wipes.

"It means you can cross the really bad cases," Asher offered.

"Which is great news but they can hurt you in the process," Zeke added.

I hissed as Miles hit a particularly deep scratch.

"Sorry, but it needs to be cleaned out," Miles told me. I didn't argue. I sat there as they watched me get patched up. When he was done I had several band aids covering my arms along with one really long scratch on my inner forearm that ran to my wrist.

"Guys, I crossed a rotting soul," I reiterated. "Let's focus on the good."

"You're right," Miles said. "It's amazing that you got him to the Veil."

The others agreed, except Zeke. Zeke was quiet.

The bell rang for first period. I picked up my bag and got up.

"I'll take her to History," Zeke announced. "Asher, do you want to take her to English..."

I tuned them out as they decided who would walk me to English. Yeah, I was going out on my own now. But here, in the overcrowded halls, I still needed a little help.

Everyone split up. Zeke walked beside me in silence to History. At the door his eyes ran over me one more time before leaving for his own class. He really didn't like the scratches.

Everything went on normally until it was near the end of English. Our teacher, Mrs. Hayes, asked to see me at her desk in the back before I left. Wondering if something was wrong with my latest essay I walked back to her desk when there were a couple minutes left of class.

Mrs. Hayes was a small woman. She'd given birth to a healthy boy in January and she still had a little roundness to her body. She eyed my arms, her face concerned.

"Lexie, what happened to your arms?" she asked quietly as if I didn't want this to be overheard.

"I petted a friend's cat's belly one too many times and it got even," I lied. Her worried eyes met mine.

"You can talk to me if you need to," she said. I was stunned for a whole five seconds.

Shit. "I didn't cut myself," I stated. "A cat got me."

She still had that worried look in her eyes as she nodded. "Alright. I just wanted to check on you." She went back to her computer.

The bell rang. Irritated, I went back to my desk and slung my backpack over my shoulder. When I stepped out into the hallway Eric was waiting.

His brown hair was still short, but not shaggy anymore, he still had enough that I could tell he used something to keep it up and back that way. He had a nice open face, a pointed chin and angled jaw. His amber colored eyes were killer, though. Too bad he was kind of a dick and had an issue with who I was friends with. At least he was pretty to look at, until he opened his mouth.

"No giant bodyguards today?" Eric asked with a smirk.

"Go fuck yourself," I snapped as I walked past him and down the hall.

Before he could say anything else I was out of ear shot. What the hell was his problem anyway? And why did he have to express his opinion every chance he got?

Putting it out of my mind I headed for the buses for the trip to Missoula. From the long line, it looked like I was running behind. Thankfully, Ethan had said he'd hold the seat for me. I got in line behind a couple of girls and waited until I reached the teacher.

Mrs. Archer was a bird of a woman, thin and always moving. This morning she seemed to be fluttering in excitement. "Ah, Alexis. Good," she said. "I think you'll learn a lot from this trip. "

"That's the hope," I said. She checked off my name as I climbed inside.

The bus was almost packed, the noise annoying. I spotted Ethan in the middle on the right side. I dropped down next to him. "Hey, Snoopy."

"Hey, Beautiful." He ran his eyes over me. "Are you okay?"

I sighed. "My English teacher thinks I'm cutting myself."

Ethan raised an eyebrow at me.

I shook my head and continued. "I know. Then on my way out the door Eric asked about my 'giant bodyguards.'"

"What did you tell him?" he asked grinning.

"I might have told him to go fuck himself," I admitted.

He chuckled. "I love the way you tell people off, Beautiful." Ethan bumped his shoulder into mine. I bumped back. "We're going to be away from the guys for several hours," he pointed out. A mischievous light in his eyes.

"Let's try not to get suspended." I suggested. His smirk probably should have had me worried. But I was actually looking forward to some time with Ethan.

THE MISSOULA ART MUSEUM was full of classic and modern art, which meant there were many paintings, photos, sculptures, engravings, even textiles.

I was practically jumping up and down in happiness. Mrs. Archer had us go through the basic tour then she let us explore on our own.

Ethan walked with me from painting to painting, listening as I talked about the ones I liked, what I saw in them or what other people might see in them. It wasn't until my voice grew raspy and I took a drink from my water bottle that I realized I had been rambling on. Ethan had a small grin on his face as he met my eyes.

"I've been talking a long time, haven't I?" I asked, cringing. He smiled gently.

"I like listening to you talk about art," he admitted. "You don't do it enough."

"Because I go on and on until someone stops me." I looked up at the next painting.

"More like, you get excited," he corrected. "And you're cute when you're excited."

I turned to look up at him to see if he was joking. He looked down at me with warm eyes. He wasn't. My heart gave a hard thump. "Is there anything you wanted to see?"

He shook his head. "Not really."

I turned back to look at the landscape in front of us. "Why did you sign up for an art museum field trip if there was nothing you wanted to see?"

He chuckled as we moved through the room. "Well, it did get me out of classes for the day."

I smiled. "Ooh, good point."

"The other reason I came was because you were looking forward to it," he said. I slowed to a stop then turned around.

Ethan stepped closer, his spicy cologne surrounding me. "You got really excited about this trip." His eyes ran over my face before meeting mine again. "And you don't get excited about a lot of things anymore. I wanted to see what you were so passionate about."

I didn't know what to say. What were you supposed to say to that? Feeling awkward I was, naturally, a smartass. "And now you're bored to tears and counting the seconds until you can go home."

He chuckled as he looked over at the painting. "Not really. But I think I get why you like art as much as you like music now."

I turned and moved on to the next piece. This one was a black and white photo of a church in France. "Why's that?" I asked quietly.

He kept pace with me, staying close. "Because it expresses something that people are afraid to say out loud."

We came to another painting, he pulled me to a stop. "And everyone sees something different. For instance," he pointed at the painting in front of us, "what do you see in this one?"

I licked my lips and looked up at the painting. It was of a young woman in a gown simply sitting in a dark room. It was... interesting.

I looked over the painting and thought about it. "I see a woman waiting for the axe to fall."

Ethan stepped closer until he was behind me, his breath slipping through my hair. The museum faded as his hands went to my shoulders.

"Why's that?" he asked in that smooth, soft, smoky voice he rarely used.

"She's sitting in the dark. It looks like she's been crying; her makeup is smudged. It looks like she's half dressed. She's in her corset and skirt, as if she doesn't want to be vulnerable to whatever happens next," I said softly.

"I can see that," he admitted quietly. "Do you want to know what I see?"

"Yeah."

"The woman I see is tired. She's had a hard time, but she's not taking off her clothes." His voice was light and soft in my ear. "It's morning, and she's stopped in the middle of getting dressed to take a minute to give herself time to think about what she'll face that day. To remind herself that she can handle whatever it is coming at her." His squeezed my shoulders gently as his voice slid through my ears. My eyes burned as he continued. "I see a woman getting ready to fight again. And I think that's why the artist painted it. To show her strength." I bit my bottom lip hard to push back the tears. It helped. "Or she's been dancing all night, drunk and she's sitting down because her feet hurt," he added lightly. I chuckled as he squeezed my shoulders again before he continued, "There's a lot of interpretations for a song, just like with a painting."

"I guess that makes sense," I said. I pulled my eyes from the painting to look up at him.

"You know, we might actually know what the artist wanted to show if we get the audio tour for the entire museum."

He grinned down at me. "But it's fun making up stories for them," he protested.

I smiled and shook my head at him.

"I'll go get them. Stay here." Ethan headed towards the front of the museum.

I turned back to the painting again. Trying to see it the way he had. The darkness around her eyes could be bags from not enough sleep. She could have just had her corset cinched and was sitting for a moment... I liked Ethan's interpretation better than mine.

I was deep in thought when someone stepped close to me. I instantly stepped to the side and moved into a better defensive position.

"Sorry, I didn't mean to scare you," he said. He was definitely a high school student. Dark blond hair and slate gray eyes smiled at me in a rather pleasant face.

"It's fine, you just kinda came out of nowhere," I said.

He winced. "I guess you're right." He met my eyes. "Sorry."

"It's fine," I muttered before turning back to the painting. My shoulders growing tense. I didn't like how close he was.

"Are you dating Ethan Turner?" he asked.

I shot him a look. "Why are you asking?" Who was this guy?

He looked sheepish. "I just wanted to warn you about him. He's a player."

I gaped at him for a full minute before I could say a word. "That is none of your business."

He looked away from me. "I know, I just wanted to warn you." He gestured over his shoulder toward where Ethan had gone. "He's dated a lot of girls, and not for very long."

I had enough. "First off. That's one of my best friends you're talking about. Second, I don't know you, so why would I give a damn what you think?"

"You okay, Beautiful?" Ethan's strained voice had me turning. Ethan moved between me and blond boy.

"Yeah, I'm fine," I assured him. Ethan met blond boy's eyes.

"Don't you have something else to do, David?" Ethan asked pointedly before turning his back on the taller boy. He handed me one of the headsets. "Let's go check out the rest of the museum." His voice was still strained when he spoke to me. David must have really bothered him.

I took his hand and tugged him with me further into the museum. David didn't follow. For the rest of the visit Ethan was quiet. I missed my usual Snoopy.

We were having lunch in one of the city parks. Everyone from the field trip was scattered in groups here and there with their brown bagged lunches. Ethan and I sat off to the side in the shade of a pine tree.

I was sitting next to Ethan, in the middle of eating my sandwich when I decided to ask him, "Ethan, who was that guy in the museum?"

Ethan finished chewing before he answered, "That was David Harris." He looked out over the lawn. "I dated his sister Olivia for a couple weeks during the summer."

"Wow, and he's still pissy about it?" I asked as I opened my carrot sticks.

Ethan put his half-eaten sandwich down. "It didn't end well."

I bumped my shoulder into his. He lifted his head to meet my eyes. "What happened?"

He sighed as he began twirling the silver rings on his fingers. "She wasn't the most stable person." He looked out at the large lawn.

"What do you mean by stable?" I asked, before taking a bite of carrot.

"Things got strange right off," he said dryly. "She started talking about conversations we'd never had. Movies we'd never seen. She even said I climbed in her bedroom window to sleep with her." He met my eyes. "I never slept with her and I still don't even know where she lives." My eyebrows went up. Wow. He continued, "She got weirder as time went on, so, I broke it off."

"Damn," I said surprised. "So, why is big brother still pissy about it?"

Ethan sighed as he looked down at his lunch. "She started hurting herself. Using lighters to burn her hair. Her parents found out and got her help. They eventually figured out what was wrong. She ended up going to a hospital for some kind of treatment. Now, they medicate her and home school her to control her schedule and keep her level."

"And he blames you?" I couldn't believe that.

He shrugged. "I don't exactly have the best record with girls."

"Yeah, but she was mentally ill. Him blaming you for that is majorly fucked up," I snapped. I began looking through the crowd to find David.

Ethan turned and grinned at me. "Thanks, Lexie."

"For what?" I asked absently, still looking.

"For wanting to find him and tell him off," he said casually. Busted, I stopped looking to turn back to him.

"I... wouldn't do that," I said innocently.

He chuckled. "You would and you know it."

"Well, no one messes with my friends," I mumbled as I went back to eating my lunch, my face warmed under his gaze. He wrapped his arm around me and gave me a squeeze.

"Everyone pack up, it's time to get on the road!" Mrs. Archer announced as she fluttered around the lawn. We both got to our feet and tossed our lunches before climbing into the bus.

I sat on the inside this time. We went back to talking about music as we headed back to Spring Mountain.

CHAPTER 8

MONDAY AFTERNOON

I woke up surrounded by spicy cologne. A heartbeat was under my ear when I realized there was a weight across my chest, holding me. Something breathing was buried in my hair.

I opened my eyes slowly to find my knees against the side of the bus. I was somehow laying across Ethan's lap and against his chest at the same time. I tried to move and found I couldn't.

"Ethan," I mumbled. Whatever was in my hair disappeared.

"Yeah?" he said, his voice sleepy.

"How'd I get here?" I asked rubbing my cheek against his shirt.

"You fell asleep and almost climbed in my lap to get a snuggle," he told me, waking up a bit more. Yeah, that sounded like me.

"Oh, sorry," I said, rubbing my eyes.

"I like snuggling you, Beautiful," he reminded me. I smiled as he let go of me so I could sit up. We were back in town and pulling into the school parking lot.

"Well, you're very easy to snuggle," I countered. He snorted. I stretched as we stopped.

Everyone grabbed their bags and started to get off the bus. Several girls shot us curious looks as they walked by. I rolled my eyes and ignored them.

We got off the bus last then began walking across the parking lot to our cars.

"I'll see you over at Miles'," Ethan said.

"I'm heading over after I pick up Hades," I told him.

Instead of going to the gym today Miles thought it would be better to workout at his house. But first, I needed to get Hades.

I climbed into the Blazer then headed home. I wasn't looking forward to today's lesson.

Isaac was going to teach me grappling today and Miles thought privacy would be better. I didn't disagree with him.

After picking up Hades, I drove over to Miles' house and walked inside.

"I'm here!" I shouted as I let Hades off his leash.

"Family room!" voices shouted back. Moving into the long hall I ran into Isaac.

"Did you bring your gym bag?" Isaac asked. My pulse picked up.

"I have some clothes here," I said quietly. "I'll go change." I walked down the hall and into my bedroom.

I took my time getting ready, braided my hair twice and triple checked my shoes. I was stalling and I knew it.

I took a deep breath and left my room then headed down to the basement with Hades at my side.

Everyone was waiting outside the weight room. Most of them had changed into their gym clothes. But not Zeke.

"Are you not coming in?" I asked. He shook his head, his face like stone. I looked to the others who took the hint and headed into the weight room. I waited until the door was closed before looking up to meet his eyes. "Why?"

He clenched and unclenched his jaw. "Do you really think it's a good idea for me to be in there when one of them is pinning you and acting like they're choking you?" he growled softly, his voice thick. I reached out and took his hand in mine.

"Good point," I said quietly. Isaac was planning on teaching me how to get out of the holds Clay Ordin had used on me. It really wasn't a good idea to have Zeke in there. He squeezed my hand, making me look up to meet his eyes again.

"You're probably going to have a flashback, or at the very least flashes of the cabin," he reminded me. "Take breaks and take your time." His eyes began to glow. "But if it gets to be too much, you stop." I nodded but that wasn't enough for him. "You hear me?"

"I hear ya," I whispered. He took a deep breath, gave my hand a final squeeze then let go.

"I'll be out here with Hades when you're done," he muttered as he walked by me. I took a deep breath and headed for the weight room door.

I looked over my shoulder. Zeke was there, sitting on the stairs. His elbows braced on his legs, petting Hades as he watched me. I had the urge to walk over and hug him. I reined it in and just gave him a small smile before going inside.

The room was filled with tension as I closed the door behind me. I moved to the corner with the mat where the others were waiting. I clapped my hands loudly.

"So, let's get to it," I said cheerfully. The guys gave nervous laughs. I walked onto the mat. "Okay, who's choking me?" I smiled at them.

"I thought we'd start with Asher, he's bigger than you. But not Ordin's size." Miles suggested. I nodded, licked my lips nervously and swung my arms.

Asher stepped onto the mat and moved around me.

"Isaac is going to give you instructions, Ally," Asher said before touching my shoulder. I nodded. "Okay, I'm going to grab you," he warned. Asher's arms moved around me and put me in a choke hold gently. Immediately my pulse picked up, my stomach lurched. Sweat rolled down my spine as I took a deep shaking breath. Asher dropped his arms from me instantly and touched my arms.

"Ally, breathe," Asher told me as he stepped around me. "I don't think I'm going to work."

Miles nodded.

I closed my eyes and sighed. "Sorry, Ash."

"Nothing to be sorry about, Ally girl," Asher reassured me. "We'll just try someone else. The technique will transfer, we just wanted you to have practice with someone a lot bigger than you."

"Isaac?" Miles suggested. "With you giving instructions from behind her it might work better."

Isaac nodded, his eyes running over me. He came onto the mat and walked around me.

"Okay, Red," he began. "I'm going to put you in a choke hold, but not really." Isaac's voice was soothing as he stepped up behind me. He put his hand on my shoulder and gave me a squeeze. I took a deep breath and let it out slowly.

When I was ready, I nodded. Isaac slowly moved his arms around me, placing his forearm against my throat. I took a deep breath, his lime scent calmed my racing heart. This was Isaac, he'd never hurt me. I focused on what he was saying.

"Now Lexie, the first thing you need to do is breathe. You're going to grab my forearm, pull it down as you bend forward and turn a little into me." I reached up and pulled on his forearm, bending over and turned into his body. "Good, that'll give you air. Now, you're going to go ape shit." My nerves started to ease. "You're going to stomp my foot, hit the groin, elbow to the gut, just wail on me."

I pretended to stomp on his foot, hit his groin and gently tapped his stomach with my elbow.

"Now that I'm hurting, you're going to grab my forearm at your neck with both hands and move under my arm and back, twisting my arm as you slip my grip."

I did as he said. In the end, Isaac was bent over and I held him in an armlock.

"In this position, you can break my arm but I'd rather you kick the attacker, then push him away and run."

I did as he said. When I reached the other side of the mat I wasn't as shaky as before. This actually helped. I could get out of a choke hold now.

Isaac stood up and eyed me.

"How are you feeling?" Miles asked.

"Better. Less jumpy," I admitted, my voice going raspy. I walked over to the side of the mat and took a drink of my water bottle.

"Good, then let's stay with Isaac," Miles decided. No one argued. "If you're feeling alright, I'd like to get it into your muscle memory." I nodded and went to stand in front of Isaac again.

For over half an hour, Isaac worked slowly with me to make sure I got it down without triggering me.

When it was time for our next exercise, Miles sent Ethan and Asher a look. The two left the weight room without a word.

"Red, how are you feeling?" Isaac asked. I took stock. I actually felt better than I had at the beginning of the lesson.

"Good actually," I told them. Miles came to join us on the mat.

"Lexie, do you remember what position you were in when we broke into the cabin?" Miles asked gently, in his silky-smooth timbre. I thought about it, ran through my memories then shook my head.

"I remember the groin hit then trying to curl up but I couldn't. I remember how heavy he was. Then just..." I didn't have to finish.

"He was in an extremely dominant position." Isaac took a breath then told me. "He was between your legs with most of his weight on top of you while he had his hands around your neck." I looked away and nodded. Yeah, that sounded right. Isaac continued. "So, in order to teach you how to get out of that, I'm going to need-"

"To put me in that position," I finished for him. He nodded. I took a deep breath and let it out slowly. I could do this. It was Isaac. He'd pinned me before and I was okay. He'd make sure I knew it was him.

"That's why you sent the others out," I guessed.

Miles nodded. "I thought it would be easier without them watching."

I nodded as I bit the bottom corner of my lip. "Good call."

"So, when you're ready, Lexie," Isaac told me softly. I looked down at the mat and took several deep breaths.

When I was ready, I went to the center of the mat and laid down. Isaac cursed under his breath as he moved to my feet and knelt down.

"Lexie, we need you not to close your eyes and focus that this is Isaac," Miles began. "Focus on where you are and what's going on."

I took several deep breaths before I looked to Isaac. He was pale and looked vaguely like he was going to be sick. I sent him a reassuring smile.

"Let's do it," I said in a funny voice trying to make him feel better. Isaac gave me a half smile.

"Okay, we're doing this one part at a time," Isaac announced. "I'm going to scoot up until my knees are behind your calves." He waited until I nodded. Isaac knee walked closer, then shifted my legs so he was practically pressed against me. He stayed leaning back on his legs. I had the insane urge to giggle. Isaac's eyes met mine. "How are you doing?"

"I'm good." I barely managed to keep the giggle out of my voice.

"Alright, now, I'm going to put some of my weight on you. I'll hold myself off you so we can judge how you're doing."

I bit back a smile and nodded. I don't know why I found this so funny. Isaac leaned over me, bracing his arms by my shoulders while slowly lowering his weight against my lower body.

"What, no foreplay?" I asked, I couldn't help it. Isaac snorted. Miles didn't even crack a smile. "Oh, come on. That was funny!" Miles shook his head.

I looked back up to Isaac, who was fighting a smile. "Lexie, now, I'm going to rest my hands on your shoulders on both sides of your neck. You'll have my full weight then. I don't want to put my hands on your neck until we're going through the move." I nodded.

Isaac moved his hands like he said he would. His weight doubled, pressing me into the mat. I had a small flash; the memory of being pressed into the floorboards washed through me. I took several deep breaths focusing on Isaac's hair. That blue Cookie Monster hair. I bit back another giggle.

"Lexie, how are you feeling?" Miles asked.

"Like Isaac here owes me dinner and a movie," I threw out. Miles sighed as Isaac started laughing and I snickered. When I calmed down, I answered. "I had a flash but he weighs a lot less and so... not so bad," I explained in a surprised voice.

Isaac smiled. "Good. Now, I'm going to put my hands on your

throat. What you're going to do is grab my wrists hard. Then bring your legs up over my shoulders, locking your ankles behind me. You want my head locked between your knees. This is going to put me in a hold. Okay?"

I raised an eyebrow. "Is this legit? Because now, I'm starting to question this whole move."

"Yes, it's legitimate," Miles assured me as Isaac chuckled. When Isaac was calm again, I nodded that I was ready.

"One, two, three." Isaac put his hands on my neck, fear and the urge to swing filled me but I kept my eyes open and focused on that blue hair. I wrapped my hands around his wrists with a hard grip, then raised my legs until they were over his shoulders with his head between my knees. I locked my ankles tight and squeezed his head with my knees. "Good. Now thrust your hips to keep me down." I lifted my hips gently, noticing how he was forced down.

"Now you're in control," Isaac said. Isaac shifted, moving me over the mat in different directions to prove he couldn't get out. I focused on his voice.

"Now, don't do this hard. But you'd thrust your hips then you would yank my wrists to the sides as hard as you can. This can break my arms." I barely tugged at his wrists. "Good, now my arms are probably broken, brace one foot on the floor and shift to your side under me." I did as he said. "Now, brace your foot on my hip and shove me." I followed his instructions and got him away from me. "Now, if you need to, kick your way free, get to your feet and run."

I made the motions he said, scrambled to my feet and moved off.

I stood for a second with my back to them as I took deep breaths. Flashes of the cabin kept coming to me, but I kept my eyes open and focused on my breathing.

When I was ready and had control again, I turned back to them. They waited patiently, watching me. "Okay, let's go again."

THAT NIGHT, after filling Rory in on the cemetery, dinner and my shower, I laid down on my bed after shoving Hades over.

I had to get back to the Veil to make an alarm. I had put it off long enough. I pushed everything else from my mind and took a deep, calming breath. It was time to get to work. I closed my eyes, focused and dropped down.

The Veil was its usual shell of itself. Okay, time to build an alarm. I crossed my arms over my chest. How the hell was I going to do that? I looked around the Veil for a clue. I eyed the foggy, thick walls then looked up at the Way. An idea sparked.

What if I put up an additional barrier to the Veil? If I kept it paper thin then they wouldn't know it was even there. I liked the idea but what about the rest of the alarm? I tapped my fingers against my arm and tried to figure it out. I could make a string of will to the center and create an actual connection to an alarm there. But would it work? Only one way to find out.

I moved to the Veil's east wall. I closed my eyes and dropped my barriers. The Veil's energy moved through me. I visualized what I wanted to do then opened my eyes. I reached out my hand until I was almost touching the wall with my palm out and lowered my hand. My skin vibrated as energy moved through me, flowing down to the ground and up the wall until it barely touched the Way. To be sure, I gave the energy instructions.

"As time winds on, souls come and go. Allow all who would pass while letting me know," I whispered as I began to move clockwise. The gold light moved with me as if I was moving a giant curtain on a stage. I was completely focused on what I was doing. I kept whispering the incantation, concentrating on what I needed.

As I hit the three-quarter mark, I started to sweat. This was a marathon with focus; I had never held it this long. By the time I reached the east wall again, I was breathing heavy. Okay, I got that done. And that was just the start. I moved to the center.

Now for the alarm. I grinned as an image came to mind. I closed my eyes and focused. I pictured a stone pillar, standing tall in the Veil with a huge fog horn at its top. Energy flowed through me as the ground shook. I opened my eyes, still holding that image, to watch a circular, gray stone pillar burst from the ground and stretch halfway to the Way. I let go of the image as a large white and red fog horn appeared on top. I took a deep breath and let it out.

Okay, next part. I turned to the west wall, then focused on what I needed. A thick line of energy appeared at the wall, floating in the air until it reached the foghorn. I willed it to attach. Then let the image go. It stayed where it was.

"Yes!" I raised my arm in victory, smiling from ear to ear. I quickly did the same for the other areas, eight lines in all.

Now, how to connect it to me? A line? That would work, but I won't be here the whole time? What if I coupled that with an incantation? Huh, it was worth a shot. I conjured a line at the back of the foghorn then brought it to me.

Before I attached it, I said. "As is above, let it be so below. I bind this alarm to me. Mind, body, soul." Then I attached the line to my chest. I let the image go and the line still remained. I stepped back, testing the give of the line. As I circled the Veil I felt nothing. No tug, no pain. I was starting to wonder if this would work. Well, there was one way to find out. I smirked.

"Zahur!" I shouted. "I need a sec!" It was only a few heartbeats before she popped into the Veil. The foghorn went off, we both covered our ears as my bones shook. She eyed me as we dropped our hands.

"Your alarm, I take it?" she asked.

"Pretty neat, huh?" I said, looking back up at the pillar.

"Definitely clever," she admitted. I turned back to her.

"So, do you think this line will stay when I'm in the physical world?" I asked.

She eyed the line, then the connection, which required her to get more up close and personal than I liked. When she was done examining my connection she backed up.

"That's solid. If anything enters the Veil, you'll know it." She smiled at me. "Good work."

I made a dramatic bow. "Thank you!" She chuckled. Then raised her head, her face serious.

"I need to go," she stated a second before she popped out. That was interesting... With my work done, I pulled myself out.

I opened my eyes to my dark bedroom. Tired, I snuggled down into my blankets and fell asleep.

SCRATCHING WOKE ME UP. I stayed completely still as I opened my eyes. Hades wasn't in bed. Sitting up, I found him scratching at the door. A whine told me something was wrong. I got up and crossed the room. When I opened the door, Hades bolted downstairs. My heart slammed as memories surged forward.

The last time he'd done this Clay had been outside the house. I took a deep breath and stepped into the hallway. Light glowed up the stairwell from downstairs. I let out a deep breath. It was probably Rory. Wondering why he was up, I headed downstairs.

Only it wasn't Rory. Tara was on the couch, her knees pulled to her chest with her arms around them. Hades rested his head on her knees forcing her to look at him. She wiped her face then gave in and gave Hades' ears a scratch. It was impossible to resist that face he makes when he wants to help.

From the stairs, I could see her nose was red, her eyes puffy from crying. I went still. Tara and I didn't have the best relationship, but... she was my cousin. And she was crying. I couldn't just leave her alone.

I walked into the living room and sat down on the other side of Hades. Tara's head snapped up.

"What do you want?" she asked, her voice cracking.

"Are you okay?" I asked quietly.

She wiped her face again and focused on petting Hades.

I stayed put. Sometimes people didn't need to talk about something. They just needed to not be alone while they dealt with it.

It wasn't long before she said something. "Do you have nightmares?" Her voice was small, hesitant.

I stroked Hade's fur. "Every night," I admitted. "It's why the guys gave me Hades. He helps."

"The same one?" she asked quietly.

"Not always." I lifted my head to look at her. "The really bad ones I have over and over."

"How do you deal with it?" she asked, her voice thick.

"I don't know. I've had nightmares most of my life. I guess I'm used to it," I explained. "But my shrink says that once you figure out what your subconscious is trying to tell you, that nightmare will go away. Or at least happen less often."

She sighed. "I'll try that." She got to her feet and headed for the stairs. She stopped before going up. "Thanks, Lexie."

"No problem," I said, my voice turning raspy. I went to get a drink from the kitchen, by the time I came back she was gone.

I took Hades back upstairs and back to bed. While I waited to fall asleep, I wondered what kind of nightmares Tara had.

Ethan

RYAN WAS OFF AGAIN TONIGHT. *I cursed, stopped playing and turned in the garage to tell him so. Only I was alone.*

"Ryan? Oliver?" I called. No answer. The windows in the garage started fogging over.

"Eth." Sophie's voice had me spinning back around. Sophie stood there, looking exactly as she had the day of the car crash. "You need to let me go," she said firmly. She didn't sound like a little girl anymore.

"What are you talking about?" I asked as the temperature in the garage plummeted. Seriously, was it snowing outside? I moved to the windows but they were iced over.

"Ethan. You. Need. To. Let. Me. Go." Sophie's voice was hard this time. I turned back to her as my heart started to race. If it was snowing then Sophie needed a coat.

"We need to get home before the snow gets bad," I told her. Her face grew pained.

"LET ME GO!" she screamed.

I bolted up in bed, cold sweat running down my chest. Heart

pounding, I searched the room for what woke me. My breath came out in a fog. What the fuck...? A crunching sound came from the corner under the windows.

No... Taking deep breaths, I moved to the corner of my bed. My acoustic guitar was off its stand, on the floor and shattered into pieces. Fear tore through me.

This ghost was getting out of hand. I moved back until I was resting my back against the wall. I needed Lexie to take care of it tomorrow.

I watched the fog on the windows disappear along with the cold. I stayed put, trying to remember my nightmare until the sun came up.

CHAPTER 9

TUESDAY

I was cursing as I walked through the halls holding a tissue to my bloody nose. Why did I decide to try crossing twenty-one today? I grumbled at myself. I had been lucky not to pass out in the grass and only had a nose bleed and a splitting headache to deal with. Thankfully, my nose finally stopped bleeding before I reached the guys. I threw away my tissue as I passed a garbage can.

When I stepped out of the hallway I could see something was wrong with the guys. Every one of them was tense. Zeke's arms were crossed over his chest, Miles was tapping out that staccato rhythm on the table and Asher was rubbing the back of his neck.

I stepped up to our usual table with a smile. "What did I miss?" I asked, setting my bag down. I eyed each of them in turn. Ethan had deeper bags under his eyes today.

"That ghost needs to go, Lexie," Ethan announced vehemently. "It broke my acoustic guitar last night." My heart dropped. Oh, shit. I was going to have to tell them… I glanced to Miles, he met my eyes and made a slight shake of the head. Yeah, not now.

"Okay, we'll head over after school and deal with it," I offered in my normal voice. I don't know how I managed it but I did. My stomach knotted into one big knot. Ethan nodded as the bell rang.

"I'll walk Lexie to History," Miles announced. No one argued.

We were silent as we walked down a hallway until we were out of earshot of the guys.

"We have to tell them," I said, my lungs tight, heart racing.

"We'll tell them after school," he said calmly, his hand a comforting weight on my lower back. "There is nothing we can do until then." I wrung my fingers together as my classroom came into sight.

I nodded. He was right, I knew he was. But I didn't know if I could take the pressure in my chest until this afternoon.

Miles pulled me to a stop then tilted my chin up so I'd look at him. "It's going to be difficult. But we'll all be there. It'll be okay in the long run."

I nodded. "You're right. I know. It's just... nerve wracking."

He gave me a gentle smile. "I know. We're all feeling it too." He squeezed my arm before letting me go and stepping back. "One of us will be here when you get out of class."

I bit the corner of my lip and nodded before heading into class.

THE DAY SEEMED to drag on and on. That was until I was called to the office out of Chemistry. I walked through the empty hallways as I checked the slip again.

The counselor's office. The school had a counselor? I resigned myself to being questioned by someone I didn't even know as I walked into the office. I held up the slip to the woman behind the counter.

"Delaney to see Counselor Higgins," I announced cautiously.

She smiled a forced smile as she gestured to one of the office doors. "The door on the right."

I walked over and knocked. The door opened almost instantly, a short woman with brunette hair answered. She had on a pair of cat eye glasses that complimented her face. She gave me a friendly smile.

"Lexie?"

"Yeah," I muttered.

"Come on in and have a seat," she said, opening the door further. I stepped into her office.

It was clean, organized. Obsessively so. Even the books in her bookcase were color coordinated. I crossed the room to sit in one of the chairs across from her desk.

She walked around her desk with that same fake smile plastered on her face. Did it hurt to hold it that long?

"Lexie, I'm Mrs. Higgins, the school counselor." Her eyes ran over me and lingered on my forearms. "Do you know why I asked you to come in?"

I had an idea since she was still looking at my arms but I wasn't about to say so. "No, not really. I got the call slip and showed up," I said casually.

Her eyes met mine and the smile dropped. "What happened to your arms, Lexie?" She asked gently.

Oh, come on. I fought the urge to roll my eyes.

Her voice was serene as she added, "This is a safe place to talk about anything bothering you."

I took a deep breath and let it out slowly. "Look, I'm sure this is great for people who need help. And I appreciate the concern. But I just got cut up by a cat." Her hazel eyes ran over me before meeting mine again.

"A lot of teenagers say that when they want to hide that something is wrong," she said gently. I took another deep breath and reminded myself to be patient.

The office door opened behind me. I turned in my chair to find Mrs. Weaver, the Vice Principal, closing the door behind her.

Mrs. Weaver was a willowy woman with permanent frown lines. Her blond hair was back in a perfect French twist, her gray eyes ran over me with a slight glee in them as she moved to stand behind the desk next to Mrs. Higgins. This didn't seem to bother the counselor a bit.

"We just want to make sure you're safe," Mrs. Weaver said.

I snorted. The counselor, I believed. Mrs. Weaver? Not a chance. "I pissed off a cat."

"You were seen with a nose bleed this morning when you arrived on campus." Mrs. Weaver announced. I went still. Were they watching me? "Was that from a cat?"

I met her eyes. "No, that's because I picked my nose this morning and accidentally cut the inside with a nail," I said, my voice matter of fact.

Mrs. Weaver's eyes narrowed on me. "Is someone hurting you, Lexie? Your uncle perhaps?" Was she fucking serious?

"I got scratched up by a cat," I managed through my teeth. "Ask my friends if you don't believe me."

Mrs. Weaver leaned closer. "Why don't I believe you?"

I don't know, because you're an idiot? I bit back my reply by biting my tongue.

"Mrs. Weaver. This isn't how these meetings go," Mrs. Higgins chided the Vice Principal.

Mrs. Weaver leaned back and composed herself.

I was losing my patience. "Call Ethan Turner in if you don't believe me. It was his freaking cat."

Mrs. Weaver's face became a pleasant mask. "Speaking of your friends. They've been walking you to each class for a few months now, correct?"

"Yeah," I said, not knowing where she was going with this.

"This is making them late for class every day and it needs to stop," Mrs. Weaver announced. My stomach knotted as I gaped at her. What a bitch.

"I'm still having issues in crowds," I admitted. "That's why they walk me to class."

Mrs. Weaver's smile turned sickeningly sweet. "I understand that, but I can't have you making them late for every class. If they continue to do so then I will be forced to give each of them a suspension."

I glared at her. What the hell was she doing? Trying to use the guys against me? An idea sparked in my mind.

I gave her a polite smile. "Well, we wouldn't want that," I said calmly. "If my friends can't walk me to class any more then I'll have to bring in my service dog."

Mrs. Weaver's smile brightened. "That is an excellent idea. Just be sure to keep the dog quiet during class."

The bell rang. My phone in my pocket started vibrating.

I gave her a big smile. "Of course. He's very well trained."

"Good, now it's settled. You can go to lunch now." Mrs. Weaver dismissed me. Mrs. Higgins' mouth was in a tight line. I had a feeling Mrs. Weaver would get an earful after I left.

I picked up my bag and left the office. I stepped outside into the hall and pulled out my phone. The group chat was going crazy.

Ethan: Where are you?

Zeke: Where's who?

Isaac: Red. She got pulled out of class.

Zeke: And no one went with her?!

Miles: We didn't exactly have the choice.

Asher: If she got called out of class she's probably at the office. I'm the closest. I'll head over there now.

The last was seconds ago.

Alexis: I'm okay. I'm at the office.

Zeke: Stay there until Asher gets there.

Asher: Already on my way, Ally girl.

I put my phone away and waited as the hall grew crowded. A little too crowded. A guy I didn't know bumped into my shoulder.

"Sorry," he called over his shoulder as he kept walking. I took a deep breath and waited for the panic to hit me. When it did, it wasn't that bad. My pulse picked up and my palms started sweating. When nothing else happened, I took a deep, relieved breath. I didn't even have to do my mantra. Learning those moves really must have helped.

Asher stepped out of the crowd to my side. "Hey, how are you doing?" he asked instantly. I grinned up at him.

"I'm actually doing okay," I said, surprised at myself.

He smiled down at me. "Good, now let's get some food. I'm starving." We started down the hallway toward the cafeteria. "What did they want with you in the office?"

I explained as we walked, smirking the whole way. By the time I was done, he was laughing his butt off. He was still laughing as we reached the table.

"What happened?" Miles asked. I explained to them the reason I was pulled out of class. About the Vice Principal and her sudden appearance. I pointed at Ethan. "It was your cat who scratched me up, if she asks."

Ethan nodded. "Got it."

"Maybe we should get a cat," Isaac said thoughtfully, he turned to Ethan. "We can name it Isis or something, to match Hades."

"You might want to ask your mom first," Miles warned them before taking a bite out of his sandwich.

"As if she would say no," Asher said. "She'd adopt every animal in the pound if she could."

Asher held up his bag of chips and looked at Isaac. Isaac, with his mouth full, nodded and traded his bag of chips for Asher's.

"We'll have to ask tonight," Isaac agreed. "Of course, if we come across a stray cat before then…"

"Ask your mom first," I told him. The twins smirked and shared a look.

My smile dimmed as I thought about this afternoon. I was going to have to tell them. I set my sandwich down, my appetite gone. What was I going to say to them?

I was trying to find the best way to tell them when Zeke growled, "Lexie, eat." I blinked and looked up. He had his don't-argue-with-me look on his face. Which was nothing new really, but he was right. I picked up my sandwich and forced myself to finish my lunch.

I had just put my trash in my bag when my phone rang. It was Ryan.

"Hello."

"Hey, it's Ryan." His voice was uncertain.

"How's it going?" I asked cheerfully. I was acutely aware that the table had grown quiet and everyone was watching me.

"I was wondering if you'd meet me at the coffee house after school?" he asked. "I want to apologize for Friday night."

I got up from the table and walked just out of earshot of everyone but Asher. "You already apologized. You don't need to do it again."

"Yeah, I really do," he insisted. I sighed as I looked at the twins. There was no way I was bailing on them, even if I wanted to avoid that conversation.

"I actually already have plans this afternoon. But I can meet you now," I offered. The sooner this was done with the sooner I could focus on other things.

"Yeah, okay, um, I'll meet you by the picnic tables near the trailer class rooms?" he suggested, his voice nervous.

"Okay, I'll see you in a few minutes." I hung up the phone and went back to the table.

"What did Ryan want?" Asher asked.

"He wants to apologize about last Friday." I picked up my bag. Asher and Zeke got up and grabbed their bags. "Guys." They looked down at me. "I think I can go alone on this one."

That got everyone's attention. After all, going out alone at home was different than going through the crowded halls at school.

"Are you sure?" Miles asked gently.

"Yeah, I think so," I said. "I actually did pretty well in the hall waiting for Asher. I want to try a test run." Asher sat back down.

Zeke met my eyes. "You have a problem-"

"I'll call immediately," I promised. He sighed deeply then sat down. "I'll see you guys after school. And Ash, I'll see you before art class." There were murmured sounds of agreement before I walked away down the hall.

What the hell was I going to say to him? Apparently, he liked me, I could tell that much at least from the kiss Friday night. How did I not see that coming? I thought over my time with Ryan. At practices, at Vegabond, at school. I guess there were small signs here and there, but... I shook my head and walked out of the hallways towards the classroom trailers.

A few minutes later, I was waiting for Ryan on top of one of the picnic tables with a soda for him. I made the guy feel horrible the least I could do was buy him a soda.

Ryan came out from another hallway to the right. He spotted me then headed over with his hands in his pockets. There were heavy bags under his eyes. Guilt hit me hard, gnawing my stomach.

"I made sure not to wear my cologne," he told me when he got within ear shot.

"Thanks, I appreciate that," I said quietly before pointing at his soda on the table. "I didn't know if you liked Cola or Pepsi so I took a shot in the dark." He picked up the soda can and sat on the table next to me.

"You didn't need to do that," he said quietly.

"I made you feel bad," I said, looking down at the cement. "It's the least I could do to apologize."

He scoffed, "You made me feel bad? Damn it, Lexie." He took a deep breath. "You had a flashback. Because of me." He looked down at the ground, his face pained.

"Not because of you," I told him. "It was your cologne. Clay…" I sighed as I looked down at my hands dangling between my knees. I was trying to say the right thing here and it wasn't easy. "He hurt me, a lot and to do that, he had to be really close. And the whole time, I could smell that cologne." I looked over and met his eyes. "It really wasn't you."

His jaw clenched and unclenched. "Lexie, you didn't have a flashback until I kissed you."

I looked away to the hallways watching other kids walking by.

"You surprised me," I said quietly, peeling the label from the water bottle in my hands. "We learned over the last few months that I can't be touched by surprise. I have to see it coming or know who it is first." I looked back down at the ground. "I didn't expect it."

"Fuck, Lexie, what did he do to you?" he breathed with feeling. I turned and shot him an angry look. His face was pained and angry. He looked ready to kill someone. My anger melted away. He didn't realize what he was asking, how personal it really was. I looked back out at the people walking by.

"Not what you're probably thinking," I said quietly. "He beat the shit out of me. Gave me a skull fracture. Things like that." I shrugged, my thumb nail working at scraping off the label still.

He cursed. "I shouldn't have asked that. I'm sorry," he said earnestly, rubbing his eyes with one hand.

"It's okay. You didn't know." And it was okay. I realized I was talking about what happened to someone who wasn't one of my best friends, who wasn't my shrink, or Rory. And I was okay. I wasn't crying, I wasn't panicking, I wasn't ashamed or feeling dirty. I was okay. I held that to my heart. I was healing, it was taking time but it was a sign. I was healing.

"Is that why the guys walk you to class every day?" he asked.

"Yeah. I have trouble with crowded places," I admitted. "You know what the halls are like, everyone runs into everybody."

"Yeah, I get that," he said gently. "You hit me pretty hard though." He tried to make a joke of it. I winced.

"Sorry. I didn't know it was you, Ryan," I explained. "In that moment, you weren't you. You were *him*. I wasn't at the lake anymore, I was back at the cabin." I looked up to meet his eyes. He gave me a small smile.

"I'm sorry I surprised you." He looked back at the people walking by. "I... thought you knew that I liked you." My stomach knotted worse. This was the part I was hoping to avoid.

"I didn't," I admitted.

"Damn, I must have been too subtle." He shook his head before turning to look at me.

"Lexie, I want to take you out. You know, on an actual date."

I bit the corner of my bottom lip as I figured out what to say. I didn't want to insult him or make him feel bad. But I wasn't interested and I didn't want to lead him on.

"Ryan. You are a great guy. You're fun, sweet, cute as hell, and incredible on the drums." He looked down at the ground, crestfallen. I hurried to add, "Any other time, I would say yes and we'd go out and probably have a great time." He looked up and met my eyes. "But right now, with what happened, and where I am in dealing with that... I'm not even thinking of dating. I'm sorry."

He took a deep breath and let it out. Then he gave me that killer grin of his. "I figured that, but I had to try," he said. His face turned serious. "Whenever you do get to where you are ready, keep me in mind?"

I smiled. "I will." If I was over my best friends by then, sure. He really was a great guy.

He gave me a smile and got to his feet. "Alright, I'm going to take off. Thanks for the soda," he said, then pointed over my shoulder. "By the way, did you know Zeke is here?"

I turned and looked where he was pointing. In the hallway was Zeke's hulking figure leaning against the wall.

"Seriously?" I shouted. What the hell was I going to do with him? Busted, he headed towards us as Ryan chuckled.

"You didn't know?" He had a big smile now. "I'll leave you to yell at him. Bye, Lexie."

"Bye." Ryan walked off. I turned around on the tabletop to watch Zeke as he walked towards me. When he was close enough to see I wasn't happy I asked, "Zeke, what the hell are you doing?"

"I was making sure he behaved," he all but growled.

"Zeke."

"He kissed you Friday night," he bit out. "You had a flashback. I have the right to be worried." I went still. Did he have the right because he was my friend? Or because of our kiss?

"And why's that?" I asked, wondering if I was going to get an answer. He straightened and ran his hand through his hair.

"I'm dealing with my own shit right now, Lexie," he said gruffly. I went still. That sounded exactly like what I had told Ryan.

"Oh," I said softly as it hit me. My chest ached. "You could have just told me you thought it was a mistake."

His eyes flashed at me before he looked away. "That's not what I said," he said quietly.

"I just said the same thing to Ryan so I wouldn't hurt his feelings by turning him down, it's true, but it's the same thing," I told him as I climbed down off the tabletop. When I looked up at him again, he was scowling.

He met my eyes. "I say exactly what I mean to," he reminded me, his voice hard. "That is *not* what I said." My chest loosened under the fire in his eyes, my pulse picked up for the second time in months.

"Okay, that's not what you meant." I eyed him. "Do you want to talk about what's bothering you?"

He shook his head. "Not yet."

The bell rang.

"I'll be here."

His eyes were shadowed as they ran over me. "You have gym now, right?"

"Yeah." It wasn't a surprise that he had my class schedule memorized.

"Are you okay with me walking you? Or do you want to go on your own?" he asked, his voice tense.

I thought about it. "I could use the company," I hedged.

The corner of his lips twitched. "Come on, let's get you to class."

CHAPTER 10

TUESDAY AFTERNOON

The drive to the twins' house seemed like it took longer than it should have. It sure as hell didn't feel like five minutes. My stomach was knotted with dread as I walked into the house.

The twins were in the family room, sitting on the couch and pulling out their books for homework. I doubted any of us would get any done today.

"Hey," I said as I set down my bag next to the stairs. The twins looked up.

"Thank God, the Ghostbuster has arrived," Ethan said dramatically. "Do me a favor; when you cross this one, drop him on his head." Ooh, yeah, he was going to regret saying that.

I gave him a tense smile. "After the others get here," I hedged.

Ethan eyed me. "Why wait for the others? You're the badass with the dead," he said, pulling out his binder.

"I crossed twenty-one this morning, so, I don't know what the fallout will be," I explained. "And if Zeke wasn't here…"

"She's got a point," Isaac said.

"Yeah, but it would irk the hell out of him," Ethan muttered, looking down into his bag.

I smiled and stayed near the walk through. I crossed my arms over my stomach, hugging myself a bit. I started tapping my fingers against my arm.

The front door opened. Asher walked in, his face just as somber as I felt. He gave me a sad smile as he squeezed my shoulder before going into the family room. He took one of the overstuffed chairs as we waited.

I couldn't sit down. Not with the bombshell I was about to drop. I moved to the window and watched the traffic on the street. The world seemed like it had slowed down, or maybe that was wishful thinking because Zeke and Miles pulled up minutes later.

They walked up the walkway. When they spotted me, I gave them a small wave. They were stepping on the porch and then into the foyer.

I was really going to have to tell them.

My chest was tight as I moved away from the window to stand in front of the TV. My stomach hard as a rock.

Miles gave me an encouraging look as he passed me to sit next to Isaac on the couch. Zeke met my eyes before he sat in the armchair with its back to the foyer.

When everyone was seated, they looked to me. Everyone except the twins. They were bitching about homework.

I took a deep breath and let it out slowly through the tightness in my chest. God, help me say the right thing. I didn't know if I was praying or not. I just knew I'd take any help I could get right now.

"Ethan, Isaac," I said, my voice tense. They looked up from their homework. "Put the books down, we need to talk." Ethan looked around to see that no one else had opened their backpacks. They both set down their books.

"About what?" Isaac asked.

"It's about the ghost in your house."

Ethan's eyes narrowed on me as I twisted my fingers together. "What about it? It's a normal ghost, right? Not a rotted out one?"

"Yeah it's… the ghost told me on Friday it was wanting to cross soon," I explained.

Isaac gave me a confused look. "What's the problem? Go cross the sucker."

"It's not that easy." I swallowed hard as I looked at them both. With my heart pounding in my throat, I told them. "Your ghost... it's Sophie."

The world froze as the tension in the room jumped, the twins grew still. Ethan's face turned to stone. Isaac's had gone white. The only sound was my racing pulse in my ears.

"Sophie?" Ethan asked, his eyes storming.

"Yes." I took another calming breath.

"How long have you known?" Ethan asked through his teeth, his entire body rigid. His gaze was scorching, I fought to keep eye contact. He couldn't hide from this, neither could I.

"Since December," I answered quietly. Miles reached out and rested his hand on Isaac's shoulder. Isaac seemed shell shocked.

"So..." Ethan began, his voice shaking with anger. "Our little sister has been in our house for, how long?"

"Since the ghost stuff started happening," Zeke said as Isaac held his head in his hands, his fingers digging into his scalp. Miles started whispering to him.

Ethan got off the couch and moved towards the walk through, then turned back to us. His fists clenched, his body shaking with tension. "You all knew?" Ethan bit out.

Asher leaned forward. "Lexie told us, she didn't know what to do-"

"You all fucking knew," Ethan growled. "And you didn't say a fucking word!"

Isaac started shaking his head, he shoved Miles away, burst to his feet and headed for the foyer. "Cross her over." Isaac's voice cracked as he walked by. Miles got up and followed him. A door slammed open upstairs.

Ethan looked at us with disgust. "How could you fucking keep that from us?" His voice was full of pain. Banging continued upstairs.

My eyes burned. "There was nothing I could do at the time-"

"You could have fucking said something!" he shouted. Asher got to his feet and opened his mouth. Ethan pointed at him, his hand shaking. "Don't you even..." He growled then turned back to me. "Go cross her now!"

Heavy steps sounded on the stairs. Isaac came down with a duffle bag over his shoulder. "I'll be back after she's gone," Isaac called over his shoulder before he went out the door. Miles followed him. Zeke and Asher both went out after them. When Ethan turned back to me his eyes were wild.

I tried again through the knot in my throat. "I'm sorry."

"You're sorry? You have been lying to us for months!" he shouted. He shook his head. "I don't know you. The Lexie I know wouldn't have kept one of the most important people in our lives a secret." He turned around and headed for the front door. "Stay the fuck away from me and my brother!" he yelled before slamming the door shut behind him.

The silence was thick and heavy. I dropped into an armchair, tears streaming down my face. I couldn't breathe, burning pain tore through my chest. What the fuck was I going to do? I knew they wouldn't take it well, but I never expected...

My phone rang. It was Miles.

"Ethan left," I told him.

"I know, I see him heading to the car. Isaac's already inside," Miles said. "Are you alright?"

"Just follow them, Miles. Take care of them for me." I asked as I wiped my face. A car door closed in the back ground.

"I will. But... this is just shock, Lexie," he told me. An engine started. "You understand that, right?"

"Yeah." I sniffed and took a deep breath. "You can't talk and drive, just, all of you stay safe." That chill ran down my neck.

"We will," he assured me. I hung up the phone and went to the stairs, slipping my onyx bracelets on as I went.

Sophie was sitting on the steps, tears running down her face.

"It's just shock, Sophie." I tried to reassure her, but my own heart felt like it was breaking. How the hell could I help her? Sophie nodded.

"They'll come through," she assured me. "They always do."

"I'll go see what I can to do to help loosen his pull," I said. She was silent as I turned and left the house, locking it behind me. When I climbed into the Blazer I was ready to kill someone.

I needed answers and Serena better fucking give them to me this time or I was going to tear her apart.

Asher

"WHERE THE HELL DID THEY GO?" Zeke growled as he took the turn too fast.

"I don't know!" I snapped, pulling out my phone to call Miles. The twins had sped through a yellow light an hour ago, forcing us to stop while they moved on.

Our plan to keep our eyes on them had pretty much gone to hell right then. We'd searched the parks Sophie loved, the places the twins' liked to go to hide out. Even started calling their friends. We had nothing.

"Have you found them?" Miles answered his phone.

"No. We've looked everywhere!" Zeke barked at the speaker phone.

"What about the quarry?" Miles asked.

"Shit, I forgot about that one. We're right by there." I said as Zeke immediately took the road on the right that would run by the quarry.

"They have to be there," Miles stated.

"We're on it," I said before hanging up.

Zeke sped the jeep up the gravel road, I held on to the oh shit handle for dear life.

I can't believe we forgot the quarry. It was Sophie's favorite swimming spot. Zeke kept straight at the fork, speeding down the gravel path that would bring us out inside the old abandoned quarry. The deep pit had filled with water years ago and it was the only place to swim if you wanted to jump from heights. Sophie had loved it.

When we pulled out of the tree line, the twins' sedan was parked off to the side. Ethan and Isaac were at the water's edge. Isaac sitting in the dirt while Ethan threw rocks into the water.

We skidded to a stop, blocking their car in. We were both out in seconds and moving toward them, my heart pounding.

Isaac got to his feet as we came closer. Ethan turned and swung. I staggered from the blow, tasted blood. Isaac went after Zeke. Ethan tried to tackle me, I took him with me to the ground. I rolled him off me and gave him a small jab to his face. Chaos ensued in blood, knuckles, and cursing.

I focused on pulling my punches while Ethan focused on trying to hurt me as much as he could. I don't know how long we went on like that. I just remember tearing into each other.

A loud car horn echoed through the quarry, bouncing off the stone. I instantly covered my ears cursing; the sound was like an ice pick being driven into my ear. We broke apart and turned.

Miles was at his car which he parked across the road, cutting us all off from the exit.

"ENOUGH!" He shouted. Zeke let Isaac out of his head lock and wiped the blood off his face. Miles strode towards us. "Are you guys done?" Miles demanded in his ice-cold voice. We all nodded. I took stock. Several places hurt, but nothing felt broken. It didn't look like anyone else had broken anything either. But Miles wasn't done. "Because Sophie needs us right now, and you guys are acting like idiots."

Ethan glared at Miles. "Don't fucking talk to me about what she needs! You should have told us!" Ethan shouted. Isaac walked away to stare at the water. Miles moved through the group to his side.

"What would have happened if we told you in December?" Miles asked pointedly. Ethan opened his mouth to answer, Miles didn't let him. "Nothing. The Way was still closed. And Lexie hadn't even managed the link to the Veil yet. What could we have done? Let you two torture yourselves until she could cross?"

"She could have worked harder to get the link open!" Ethan shouted. Fury burned through me. All the torture, all the pain that Ally went through for Sophie and he…

I clocked him across the jaw with a right hook. Then I went after him. Arms grabbed me and pulled me back.

"You don't know what the hell you're talking about!" I snapped, straining against Zeke's hold. "She practically killed herself for her!" Zeke stopped pulling me back as Isaac turned and joined us. Ethan stood up and wiped his nose as he eyed me.

"What are you fucking talking about?" Ethan growled.

"Lexie! In December, she practically killed herself to reach the Veil," Zeke shot at Ethan. "Or don't you remember her being so sick she didn't realize she walked in the snow to the cemetery?"

Ethan grew still.

"That was for Sophie," I bit out. Zeke let me go. I stepped away from him, still seething. "She stayed with me that week. I saw what she went through. The nightmares she kept having so she could cross Sophie when she was ready."

"What nightmares?" Isaac asked, his voice thick. Everyone looked at me expectantly, moving into a circle.

She didn't….? I sighed. Of course, she didn't tell them.

"Remember the serial killer's memories? The ones that she had?" I asked. They all nodded. "While she was at my house. She could either work on the link to the Veil or get rid of them. But not both." I met Ethan's eyes. "Guess which one she chose?" Silence swept through the circle. "She'd wake up, thinking she was the one killing and… hurting those women."

Zeke turned away and took a few steps off, his hand running down his face. Isaac ran his hands through his hair, his fingers digging into his scalp.

"How bad was it?" Miles asked.

"Bad enough that she forgot who she was almost every night," I explained. "I had to tell her she wasn't the one doing those things. Some nights it took a couple hours to bring her back."

Everyone cursed. Ethan started twirling his rings, Miles started tapping a staccato rhythm against his leg.

Zeke turned back to the group. "She didn't tell us about the nightmares." Zeke caught Miles gaze. "Why didn't she say anything?" Zeke looked at me. "Why didn't you say anything?"

I sighed. Because I liked knowing something about her that you guys didn't. I couldn't tell them the truth, not right now.

"I thought she would," I lied.

"So, Lexie went through a great deal more than we were aware of," Miles summed up, his voice cold.

I nodded. "Yeah." I turned to Ethan. "So, don't ever fucking say she could have done more. She went through hell already for Sophie." Isaac turned his back, walked to the edge of the water and sat down again. He was still and quiet. That was never a good sign.

"Tell her to cross Sophie, now," Ethan said, his gaze on the ground.

"It's not that easy. She was pulled back here, by you," Miles explained. Ethan cursed. Isaac was still as a statue as Miles continued. "You have to deal with this, Ethan. She's not going to go be able to leave until you do. And she wants to go. She's ready."

The quarry was silent as Ethan turned away from the group and went back to his brother. He sat down next to Isaac. Without a word, the twins turned away from each other and rested against the others back. It was what they did when either of them was upset. Ever since we were kids, one would find the other and they'd sit that way.

My own heart heavy, I moved to Ethan's right and sat down in the dirt next to him. Miles sat next to Isaac's left. Zeke sat behind the twins.

We watched the water with them. If they thought we'd leave, they were wrong. We weren't going anywhere. Not as long as they needed us.

Lexie

THE DRIVE to Northridge was a blur. I barely remember parking the car or climbing the steps. When I walked into the store I didn't wait for her. I strode through the curtain at the back and found her in the kitchen. Two steaming cups of tea were already on the table. Serena put the kettle down then turned to me, her silver eyes assessing.

Serena was pretty woman with mocha skin and a lovely face. Her tight curls were pulled back into a bun at the back of her head.

"I felt you coming ten miles out," She said calmly. "You're hurting."

"No shit," I growled. "What can pull a ghost back after they crossed?"

Serena gave me a serene smile. "Why do you-"

"Because I just had to tell two of my best friends that their dead little sister is in their house," I snapped. "And she says one of them keeps pulling her back. Now, what can do that?"

Serena leaned back in her chair. "It depends on the situation-"

"Give me a list Serena," I bit out. Serena's eyes flashed mercury at me and I didn't give a damn.

"You're in a lot of pain, so I'm going to give you some slack." Her voice turned heated. "Don't hang yourself with it."

I took a deep breath and let it out slowly. "I need answers, not the run around," I told her. "You owe me."

Her eyes narrowed at me. "For what?"

"Mary Summers," I reminded her. "You held back information that could have saved her."

She was quiet for several heart beats. "Are you calling in that debt?" she asked in an oddly formal way.

"Yes," I all but hissed, my temper still boiling inside me.

"What do you want?" Serena asked in a neutral voice.

"I want the truth, not the run around. Nothing held back, all of it," I told her. She sighed as she looked over my shoulder.

When she met my eyes again, they were all business. "Just for today. Agreed?"

"Fine." I sat down across from her. "Now, what can call someone back after they have crossed?"

"Danger to a loved one, a family member holding on too tightly or as a messenger. Or even the soul watching over a family member," Serena stated simply. I was almost shocked that I had gotten a straight answer from her.

"And I'm thinking I can't cross her until whoever is holding her here lets go?" I leaned back in my chair, my anger fading from me leaving only a deep ache in my chest.

"Correct." She nodded. I moved on to my next question.

"There's no other way?" I demanded.

"Not unless you want to unmake her," she countered. I moved on.

"Why didn't you help back in October?" I asked, my voice turning raspy. I swallowed trying to fix it without drinking the tea Serena set out.

She sighed. "I had just met you. Magic is an extremely powerful force. I didn't know you well enough to give it to you."

"Why won't you give me the second book?"

"Because I haven't seen your control, I haven't seen how you work. I'm not about to just hand you what the Witches Council has been protecting for centuries and hope that you can handle it."

"Hmm. Good point," I said sarcastically. "Except, I don't work in the physical world. I work in the Veil. And I need to know more."

"I'm sure you think you've got it down-"

"I made an alarm within the Veil itself this week, anything crosses into it and I'll know," I stated. She blinked. Then I added. "Just the other morning I crossed a rotting ghost. You know the kind, like Mary Summers." Her face went white. I held up my forearms for her to see the scratches. "He fought the entire way, but once he hit the Veil the extra energy was taken from him and he was himself again." She lifted her mug and sipped her tea. "I can conjure anything I picture in the Veil. Now tell me again, that I don't have the control for the next steps."

Serena met my eyes. "I'll have to talk to the Witches Council. They'll want a meeting before they hand over the next book from the archives."

I scoffed, "So, you don't even have the information I need."

Her eyes narrowed on me. "You need to step lightly. The guardians of this world have pulled back, the Witches Council policies for magic users are law now. You're going to have to follow their rules." I grew still. That sounded like a threat.

"You said that before. You also said that Necromancy is a road that doesn't end well." I met her eyes. "Care to explain all of that?"

"This world's guardians kept the balance. Though, for the last four hundred years their numbers have dropped, so 200 hundred years ago they had to pull back. A Witches Council was formed. A deal was struck recently that allows Witches to police all Witches and magic users without them looking over our shoulders," Serena explained. "Our rules are simple. Harm none."

"And about Necromancy being a road that doesn't end well?" I reminded her. She wasn't going to slither out of this one.

She sighed. "Our records over the two hundred years show that Necromancers, more than any other kind of magic user, go rogue."

"Rogue?" I asked, my voice dead. Serena met my gaze.

"Bad enough to have to be dealt with," Serena said nonchalantly. My stomach knotted.

"They kill Necromancers?" I asked bluntly because I needed the truth.

"Only when they've crossed lines that should never be crossed," Serena explained.

"And who decides where the lines are?" I snapped back.

"The Council."

"And what's your version of rogue?" I asked, my temper spiking. "Is it one mistake? Two?"

Serena held my gaze as she answered. "Once a Necromancer raises the dead, they usually have to be dealt with."

"Why?" I asked directly.

"Because your abilities come from death. You're attracted to it, you live in it. You are surrounded by it." Serena leaned forward. "And it will twist you until you aren't you anymore. Once you raise the dead, you'll change."

I couldn't believe what I was hearing. This was... just... too much today. I eyed her. "Is one of the reasons you won't give me book two because you think I'll use it to work in the physical world?"

Serena's eyes didn't move from mine. "Yes." I nodded. Great. Prejudice among magic users. Figures.

"Now, the big question," I said. "Can I trust you?"

She blinked then met my gaze again. "Depends."

"On?"

"If you raise the dead or not," she said matter of factly. I had my answer.

"I'm trying to save the Veil here, I have bigger concerns." I got up and headed for the curtain.

"If you can already do everything from the book in the Veil," Serena began. I stopped at the curtain, "your abilities are strong and growing rapidly. By my guess, it won't be long before you're raising the dead from their graves." Her voice was cold with an edge to it.

I pushed the curtain aside and walked away from her threat. Because that's what it was. If I raised the dead, the Witches Council would come for me. Shit.

BY THE TIME I got home it was almost dark. I cursed as I looked at the house. The shadows crossing the lawn, the tall bushes hiding who knows what. I closed my eyes and told myself to nut up. I climbed out and walked up to the door with shaking hands. I went inside quickly. I took several deep breaths as I tried to get my calm back. Rory spotted me from the kitchen.

"Hey, Kid, how was your day?" he asked.

"Terrible bordering on catastrophic," I told him as I walked to the table and dropped into a chair.

Rory turned off the stove and came over with a dish towel over his shoulder. "What happened?"

I looked up at him, tears filling my eyes. "I had to tell the twins about Sophie today."

He cursed as he pulled out a chair and sat next to me. "Tell me what happened."

I did. I told him everything. Then I told him about my meeting with Serena, leaving out the Witches Council and her death threat. Rory wouldn't take well to that.

"So, there's nothing you can do if Ethan keeps holding on?" he asked, his eyes worried.

"Nope. Not a damn thing," I admitted quietly as I looked down at the table. He wrapped his arm around my shoulders and gave me a squeeze.

"It's going to be okay, Kid," he said gently. "They just need to get over the shock and process everything. Then they'll be able to deal with it." I nodded, hoping that he was right.

"I should have told them when I found out," I muttered.

"No, that wouldn't have made it any better," he assured me. "Sometimes not telling someone something important is for that person's own good."

"Like Tara?" I asked before I could think. He sighed. I turned to him. "Sorry, it just popped out."

"Yeah, like Tara," he said. "It's obvious she's not mine biologically, but she is my daughter in every way that counts." I left it at that. It was his story, he could tell who he wanted to. He met my eyes again. "The point is, it would have hurt those boys more if they knew their sister was there and they couldn't do anything about it." I knew he was right.

"It just sucks," I muttered.

"I know, Kid." He gave me another squeeze.

I looked up at him. "Want help with dinner?"

He grinned. "Sure. Come on."

I followed him into the kitchen to find him trying to bake chicken and make the fixings. Only he was way off on the potatoes and the green beans were already burnt. I showed him what to do and soon we had an edible meal.

Tara came in just as we were sitting down. She dropped her bag and joined us. Over dinner she kept shooting me smug, knowing looks. I ignored it because I had enough to deal with already without her adding her own crap to the mix.

"I heard a rumor today," Tara announced. I took a bite of my chicken and ignored her.

"What rumor?" Rory asked before taking a bite of mashed potatoes.

Tara looked at me smiling smugly. "That Lexie is sleeping with Asher Westfall," she announced.

I rolled my eyes and went back to my dinner. The silence grew thick around the table.

"Lexie, anything you want to say about that?" Rory asked calmly. I looked up from my plate to find his face blank.

"It's not true," I told him simply. "I'm not dating anyone and I'm not looking to right now." Rory seemed to believe me since he went back to his meal. Tara on the other hand….

"Oh please, Jessica Westfall saw you coming out of his room early in the morning in nothing but one of Asher's shirts."

I shrugged. "I went over to talk to Asher early in the morning, and I was fully dressed in my own clothes. The same way I arrived, thank you."

"Why'd you go over so early?" Rory asked.

"I was having a panic attack and couldn't remember how to make breakfast," I muttered as I started poking at my food with my fork.

"Which is how you ended up at Asher's," Rory finished for me. I nodded.

"How could you not remember how to make breakfast?" Tara asked.

I looked up to tell her to go to hell. Only she looked curious. I sighed. "During a panic attack, you don't think straight. Your mind is racing; you're swimming in fear and just trying to keep your head above the water. It's hard to think rationally."

"So, you ended up at Asher's how?" she asked an eyebrow raised.

"You're supposed to distract yourself to help stop an anxiety attack. I couldn't remember how to make breakfast and Asher loves to cook. So, I figured he could help me remember," I explained, my shoulders tense. I didn't like explaining this to her, but she didn't seem to be making fun of me.

Those blue eyes ran over me. "That sucks."

I blinked at her. "Yeah, it really does."

Tara turned to Rory and changed the subject. She went on and on about Student Council and their fund raisers over the next few weeks.

Was Tara... being nice? It seemed so.

My thoughts moved back to the twins. I wondered how they were. What the guys were doing. I was worried about all of them.

After dinner, I headed upstairs with Hades. I laid down and checked my phone. No calls, no texts. I need to know everyone was alright. I sent a text to Miles.

Alexis: Is everyone safe?

It was several minutes before I got a response.

Miles: Everyone is safe. Isaac is crashing at a friend's house while Ethan is at Ryan's.

I let out the breath I had been holding and relaxed into the mattress. My phone vibrated again.

Miles: Are you alright?

I smiled to myself.

Alexis: Yeah, just worried about everyone.

Miles: Everyone is alright. I promise. Get some sleep.

Lexie: Night.

I looked at my phone, debating what to do. Fuck it. I texted the twins separately.

Alexis: I love you.

I didn't get a response. I didn't need one. I just needed them to read it. I fell into a troubled sleep that night.

CHAPTER 11

WEDNESDAY

I cursed and grumbled as I made my way through the hallway. I had a shitty night where I couldn't fall asleep and when I finally did it was full of rotting Sophie dreams. Then, of course, Mr. Davis at the cemetery was a dick, demanding to know when it would be his turn. Not to mention my stomach was aching. Probably from stress.

The only thing that put a smile on my face was the way everyone got out of the way of Hades. My baby was rather scary looking, even with the service animal vest on.

I met the guys at our usual table, though Isaac and Ethan weren't there. As the guys greeted Hades I examined their faces. Zeke had a split lip, a black eye, and a bruised jaw. While Asher had a bruised jaw and a cut with bruising over his cheekbone. Miles was untouched.

"What the hell happened to you two?" I snapped.

Zeke shrugged. "After the twins left they needed a fight. So, we gave them one." He was so matter of fact that it left me speechless for a few heartbeats. Was this guy logic? Then again... I understood that need to hit someone. I looked to Miles.

"Tell me the twins aren't hurt?" I asked.

"The twins have minimal injuries," Miles assured me. "Zeke actually took the brunt of it." I shook my head and let it go.

"Since Hades is here, I take it we aren't walking you to classes today?" Asher asked with a grin.

I smiled. "Nope. She told me to bring my service dog. So, I brought my service dog." The guys chuckled.

Zeke turned to Asher. "Bet you ten she'll be in the office again by the end of lunch."

Asher chuckled. "Deal."

The morning bell rang.

"Well, we need to get to class," I said innocently. The guys chuckled again as I walked away. Feeling a little better, I headed for History.

I brought Hades into the classroom as if nothing was different. I sat down then told Hades to sit next to my desk. He took up the whole aisle between desks. Everyone kept sending looks my way, or at Hades. I couldn't really tell.

After the late bell rang, Mr. Matthews went to the podium then looked out over the classroom. His eyes settled on Hades.

"Lexie, who's idea was it to bring a dog into my class room?" he asked dryly.

I gave him an innocent smile. "Well, Mrs. Weaver didn't want my friends to walk me to class anymore."

He smirked. "Alright. Just don't let him eat any books."

My classes continued on like that for the rest of the morning until Math.

I was working at my desk when Laura leaned over the gap a little. "What kind of dog is he?" she asked. Laura was a pretty girl, when she smiled and stopped hiding in her long straight brown hair.

"He's a Neapolitan Mastiff," I said, looking back down at my work.

"So, he's going to be huge," she said.

I nodded then turned to her again. "Yep. He should reach my belly button by the time he's done growing."

Laura smiled. "I've got a dog at home. A terrier. She's nowhere near this big."

I smiled. "Maybe we should arrange a playdate for the dogs at your house," I suggested.

"He plays with Zeke's dogs but they are bigger than him. It'd be good to expose him to smaller dogs."

Her eyes grew wide, her face pale. "Um, I don't think that would work." She nervously looked back down at her notebook. "Your dog would probably scare mine to death." I eyed her. That was strange. I tried to shrug the feeling off as I went back to my work without another word. I kept trying to be friends with Laura but she was keeping me at a distance. Maybe I should stop trying?

"But at one of the parks might be a good idea," Laura offered. I looked up to find her smiling a tense smile. "That could be fun."

I nodded. "Sounds good to me." She smiled then went back to work. So, it wasn't me... Why would she have an issue with me going to her house? I ran over the scenarios until the bell rang. She hurried out before I could say good-bye.

I kept a good grip on Hades as we walked towards Chemistry.

"There she is," a voice said. "I told you she goes this way." It was the guys from the abandoned hospital, Travis and Keith. They were striding towards me.

"Hades, guard me," I whispered down to him. He instantly went into what Zeke called alert mode. His ears were up and he was against the side of my leg, looking around both of us. If someone got within two feet of me, he would growl.

"You're Lexie, right?" Keith asked as they reached me.

"How did you find me?" I asked as I kept walking.

"You're the only redhead in school," Keith pointed out.

"And Zeke Blackthorn isn't exactly easy to miss," Travis added.

I tightened my grip on Hades' leash as we entered the hallway. "This is creepy as fuck, did you know that?"

"We want to know what you saw that night," Travis stated emphatically.

I looked up at Keith. "You saw it. They were like shadows." I went to leave. Travis blocked my way. I instantly backed up a step taking Hades with me.

"I only caught a glimpse and that was after you saw something before anyone else." Travis pointed out. My hands clenched around Hades' leash but at the same time my temper sparked.

"No, I didn't," I told him clearly. He stepped closer. Hades growled, barked and lunged forward, I gave him more leash for him to make his point. Hades suddenly had Travis' attention.

He stepped back several feet. Everyone walking by glanced at us but didn't stop.

"If you're psychic, do you know how much good you could do in town?" Keith took a shot, moving to the side. "You could really help people."

"I'm not," I repeated. I didn't like the way they made me feel boxed in against the hall wall.

"Haven't you heard about the power surges around town?" Keith asked. "The rumors of ghosts have gone up over 100% in the last few months."

I had heard about the power surges. Hell, last week a transformer on our block blew and needed to be replaced. It was hard not to notice all the electric company trucks everywhere in town. But the sightings of the dead, that concerned me.

"What rumors?" I asked in a placating tone. I didn't want to give this guy anything that would increase his interest in me.

"Ghost sightings have been popping up all over town," Travis informed me. "It's getting weird out there and if you're a psychic, you can really help."

Okay, I wanted out of this conversation as fast as possible.

"I'm not, so leave me alone." I went to walk around Keith but Travis was faster than I thought. Hades growled again.

"You're seriously not going to help us?" Travis snapped.

"You're about five seconds away from me loosening my grip on my dog," I growled at him quietly.

"Lexie?" A familiar voice called from down the hallway. Morgan started walking towards us, frowning at the boys blocking my way.

"Hey, Morgan," I said. I'd never been happier to see that shaggy dark hair and those dark, heavily-lidded eyes. Morgan was taller than both Travis or Keith. But don't let his lean body fool you. He had some serious strength in those lean muscles.

"Why are you blocking her way?" Morgan asked Travis and Keith. "If a girl wants to leave, you don't stop her. And you certainly don't block her in." Keith's cheeks turned red, Travis just scowled.

"We were having a private conversation," Travis announced.

"And I was trying to leave so I could go to class," I pointed out. Keith grabbed Travis' shoulder and got him moving.

"Come on, we'll be late," Keith muttered while keeping his friend moving.

I turned back to Morgan. "Thanks, I was about let Hades loose on them."

He grinned. "You're welcome. Nice dog." Morgan started walking again.

I didn't tell Hades to heel, which was the command to stop guarding me, until I reached the class room.

Mr. Turner took one look at Hades and smiled. "What's with the dog, Lexie?" I explained the situation to him quickly. He was laughing as he waved me to my group. My attention immediately went to the twins. Isaac had a split lip and a bruised jaw. Ethan had a black eye and a bruise on his chin.

"Damn," I said softly. "Are you guys okay?" Isaac continued looking down at the table, his eyes unfocused. Ethan clenched his jaw and didn't answer. It felt like a blow to the stomach.

My eyes burned. They weren't talking to me. I sat down slowly then looked to Miles. He gave me an understanding smile as he reached over and ran his hand up and down my back comfortingly. Hades left my side to go to Isaac's. Isaac reached down and scratched Hades' ears.

During the rest of class it really started to get to me. If I could just talk to them… and what Lexie? You lied to them for months, and now they are hurting because of it.

We did the lab in silence. I hated this. My stomach started aching more and more. Cursing my luck, I made a mental note to stop at the bathroom once class was over.

When the bell rang, Ethan and Isaac all but ran out of class. Not able to take it anymore I followed them around the corner.

"Guys," I called. Ethan stopped, his gaze on the ground as he clenched his jaw. Isaac kept going. I went to Ethan's side. "I know you're mad at me, and I deserve it-"

"I'm not mad at you," he growled. I went still. Ethan took a deep breath and let it out slowly before he looked at the wall. "I'm just mad. And I'm going to be for a while. So, just... leave me alone."

"And not talking to me is a part of it?" I asked carefully.

He nodded. "Isaac hasn't said a word since he left the house. He's not talking to anyone. Not even me." He turned and walked off. Tears filled my eyes. Isaac wasn't talking to anyone?

That wasn't good, that so wasn't good. Wintergreen reached me before Miles stepped next to me and held out my bag. I must have left it inside.

"Thanks."

"You're welcome," Miles said gently in that silky-smooth timbre I loved. "This is their process, Lexie. When they are angry they break off and don't talk to anyone."

"Seriously?" I asked.

He nodded. "When they are ready to deal or talk about it. They'll come back." I bit the corner of my bottom lip as I looked at the direction they went. I didn't like it.

My stomach cramped hard, bringing me back to my current situation. "I've got to hit the restroom," I told him.

"I'll hold on to Hades outside," he offered.

"Thanks." We walked to the nearest girl's bathroom. I left Hades with Miles and went in alone. I quickly checked my makeup in the mirror before going into a stall.

Sure enough, my period started. I cursed. As if I didn't have enough problems right now? I dug into my backpack then cursed a long blue streak. I was out of fucking tampons. I wanted to punch the stall wall. And the bathrooms didn't carry the dispensers. Fuck! I made a makeshift pad and hoped it would hold until I got home.

After washing my hands and checking my shoes for trailing toilet paper, I walked outside to find that Zeke and Asher had found us. Great.

"I- I need to head home real quick," I said cryptically as I slung my bag over my shoulder. Asher opened his mouth then stopped as understanding filled his eyes. Yeah, he had a sister, he'd get it.

"Why?" Zeke demanded. Both he and Miles looked confused.

"Because I do," I told him.

Miles was looking at the bathroom door, probably figuring it out when Zeke growled, "Why do you have to go home?"

Completely irritated, I snapped. "Because my period started and I don't have any tampons in my bag."

Zeke's brows darted up. "Oh." The shock on his face was almost comical.

"Zeke, you're so dense sometimes," Asher told him as he fought back a smile.

Zeke shot him a look. "Well, I don't have to deal with this shit. Sylvie's in menopause or whatever it's called." My face was burning when Miles brought his backpack around his shoulder.

"Okay, now that everyone knows, I've gotta go," I announced quietly.

"Don't they have dispensers? Like the condoms in the guy's bathroom," Zeke asked. My face felt like it was on fire.

"No, they don't," I said pointedly. "Hence, why I have to run home." I wanted to disappear out of this conversation. I might not even come back to school today after this.

Miles opened the front pouch on his backpack and pulled out a tampon still in the wrapper. "Here." He held it out to me. I gaped as I barely took it from him. I was speechless.

But the guys weren't.

"Why do you have those in your bag?" Asher asked, holding back a laugh. Zeke was looking at Miles as if he was from another planet.

Miles shrugged, his ears turning pink as he closed his backpack. "I read an article about how if you're friends with a girl, you should carry a couple for emergencies." he admitted.

Zeke and Asher burst out laughing. I was just stunned. Then I was hugging Miles tight.

"Thank you so much, sweetie," I said before pulling back and kissing his cheek.

"You're welcome," he muttered, his face red. The others were doubled over when I walked back into the bathroom.

When we got to our usual lunch table the guys had finally stopped laughing. I told them what Ethan had said to me.

"That is their usual reaction," Zeke admitted.

"Don't take it personally Ally, it's just the way they are," Asher said as he pulled out his lunch.

I pulled out my lunch bag. "I'm still worried about them," I muttered.

"We are too," Miles admitted. "We can only wait now." I had just taken a bite out of my sandwich when the P.A. system crackled to life.

"Alexis Delaney, please report to the Office. Alexis Delaney." The female voice announced. I growled before handing Hades half my sandwich to eat as I put the rest of my lunch away.

"That's probably about Hades," Zeke said before turning to Asher. "Pay up."

Asher was digging in his wallet as I stood up.

"I'm not in the mood for this shit today," I grumbled as I picked up my bag. The guys chuckled.

"Don't get suspended, Lexie," Miles warned.

"Fine, what about a write up? Can I get a write up?" I asked impishly. Miles shook his head. I grumbled dramatically as I walked away with Hades.

It didn't take long to get to the office.

"Delaney as requested over the P.A.," I said sarcastically. The woman at the counter frowned at me. Okay, maybe I should pull in the attitude a bit.

"Mrs. Weaver will see you now," The woman said pointing to the door behind the counter. I walked around the counter with Hades and went to the mostly open door. I knocked.

Mrs. Weaver looked up then her gaze went to Hades.

"Lexie, have a seat," she said politely. I came in and sat down in the chair across from her desk. Hades sat on the floor next to me, panting away. I scratched his ears as Mrs. Weaver eyed him. "We seem to have had a miscommunication."

"We have?" I asked dryly. Her gaze darted to me and she wasn't amused. Yeah, I should pull it back.

"When I said you could bring your service dog I assumed it was a lab, or golden retriever. One of the dogs mostly used for service animals. I did not expect you to bring a guard dog," she said.

I raised an eyebrow at that. How did she know he was a guard dog? Hades had only growled at someone once today.

"You told me to bring in my service animal, I brought in my service animal. The fact that you thought I had a different breed of dog isn't my fault," I pointed out.

"Alexis, I'm getting very tired of having you in my office," she said. Great, I was tired of being in her office. "So, I'm going to make myself clear. You will leave the dog at home."

I bit back a grin. What she was telling me was very illegal. You couldn't stop someone from bringing a service animal into a school or anywhere for that matter. Thankful to Rory, who had insisted I memorize the laws about service animals, I leaned forward.

"Alright," I waited a heartbeat for her to get that smug look on her face. "But of course, that means my friends will be walking me to class again."

She sighed wearily. "No, Alexis they won't. If they are late one more time I'll suspend them."

"Then I'll be bringing in Hades tomorrow," I said instantly. She all but slammed her hands onto the desk.

"Alexis, I understand you're afraid," she said, trying to sound soothing. "But it's about time you get over it. What happened to you was awful but you've healed-"

"Excuse me," I bit out. Anger boiled in my veins. "But did you just tell me to get over it?"

She seemed to realize how that sounded. "Yes, what I want to see-"

"What *you* want to see? You're not my shrink," I snapped, my voice getting louder and louder as I continued. "You don't get to tell me how to deal with what happened. I'm not going to recover on your schedule. I'm going to go at *my* pace. It's going to be painful and terrifying but that's what it is. I'm dealing the best way I can. The way that works for me."

"I understand-"

"No, you don't. Otherwise, you wouldn't be telling me to leave my service dog at home or that my friends can't walk me to class. You're trying to take away my coping mechanisms. So, no. It's very clear that you do *not* understand a fucking thing," I growled.

Silence filled the small office, phones out in the main office went unanswered. I felt better. As if I had let something out that had been festering inside me for months.

Mrs. Weaver's face was hard. "Go sit outside in the main office," she ordered. "I'm calling your uncle to come in for a meeting."

I scoffed. "Be my guest." I got up and took Hades out into the main office. Sure enough, the women in the office quickly made themselves look busy.

I dropped into a chair and pulled out my phone then opened our group text.

Alexis: I won't be back for lunch.

My phone instantly started vibrating.

Zeke: Where are you?

Asher: What happened?

Miles: Are you alright?

I smiled down at my phone.

Alexis : I'm fine. I'm in the office waiting while the Vice Principal calls Rory in for a chat.

Miles: What happened?

Alexis: I might have yelled at her.

The door to the office opened. Asher walked in, followed closely by Zeke.

"What the hell happened?" Zeke snapped. I started to explain when Miles came through the door and joined us. By the time I was done, Miles was sitting next to me and Asher was in the chair on the other side. Zeke stood across from me, his arms crossed over his chest.

"So, in short, I kind of lost it in there," I admitted. The guys shared looks, then they all started chuckling. "What?"

Asher shook his head while Zeke walked over to the chair by the window.

"We're just thinking about what Rory is going to say when he hears that she threatened you," Miles explained. My fingers twisted in my lap.

"You don't think I'll be suspended?" I asked hopefully.

"She can't," Asher said. "She tried to keep a service dog out of the school and she tried to blackmail you."

"Rory is going to screw her to the wall," Zeke offered with a smirk.

The bell rang for the end of lunch. The guys didn't move.

"Guys, class," I reminded them.

"Forget it," Zeke muttered.

"I'm not moving," Asher said as he made himself more comfortable.

"I've already memorized the chapter for the week," Miles announced. I smiled to myself.

I loved these guys. I just wished the twins were here.

It wasn't much longer before Rory stormed into the office still in uniform. His hard eyes went to me as he strode over.

"Explain," he demanded. I did, as quickly as I could. I even told him about the cat excuse. When I was done, his face and eyes were furious.

"I know I shouldn't have yelled at her, I just...couldn't seem to stop," I admitted.

Rory looked to the guys. "You boys staying with her?" There was a mix of yeah and yes.

Rory nodded, then went to the counter and the woman standing behind it. "Rory Delaney for Vice Principal Weaver," he said calmly. Mrs. Weaver came out of her office just then.

"Ah, you must be Alexis' uncle." She smiled politely until she saw the boys. "Boys, the bell rang, get to class." They ignored her. "If you boys aren't in class by the time I'm done with this meeting you'll each be suspended, again." The guys continued to ignore her as she led Rory to the office. I started bouncing my knee.

Rory

FURIOUS, I kept a lid on it until Mrs. Weaver was behind her desk and I sat in the little chair across from her.

The woman had to be in her late forties, early fifties. By the way she was dressed, not a hair out of place, everything pressed and perfect, I could see how Lexie would annoy her. It was obvious she was all about control and order. And Lexie... well, she was not. Still, that didn't matter.

She turned to me with a pleasant smile that was as fake as her capped teeth. "I'm having some difficulty communicating with Alexis. She continually curses. I also believe she is having more trouble than she's admitting to and when we tried to discuss it with her she wasn't honest about it."

"Really?" I asked, keeping my voice neutral. I was well aware of how much trouble Lexie was having, and I highly doubted this woman had a clue. I wanted to see how deep of a hole this woman would dig for herself.

"Yes, first there are the cuts on her arms," she said with a concerned look on her face, though the light in her eyes told me she was enjoying this.

"The ones from the cat?" I asked.

Her eyes filled with sympathy. "I doubt it was a cat, Mr. Delaney. I believe Lexie is hurting herself."

I raised an eyebrow. "I was sitting in the living room with her at the Turner house when Ethan's cat got angry and scratched my niece. So, I think we can lay that one to rest."

Her eyes narrowed, growing hard. "She's also causing her friends to be late to class. They are on the verge of suspension because of it." She leaned forward over her desk. "When I told her this, she agreed to bring in her service animal. Which I thought was a wonderful idea." She leaned back with an exasperated look on her face. "Unfortunately, the dog is not well trained. He's been disruptive in every class Alexis has been in today. He's even growled at several students."

Now that was an out and out lie. Hades was extremely well behaved and the only time he'd growl would be to protect Lexie. I'd seen it myself. I kept listening, waiting.

"When I brought your niece in here to discuss it she started yelling and cursing." She continued.

"Making a ruckus?" I offered. She latched onto that like a life preserver.

"Yes, she must do it at home as well. I don't know how you deal with that girl," she said.

I looked over her shoulder and counted to ten before meeting her gaze. "It's rather simple to deal with Lexie. You tell her what you expect and she'll do what she's supposed to," I said, keeping my voice calm.

"Well, we're not seeing that here," Mrs. Weaver said. She was really digging in on this one.

"I do have a question about this incident." I leaned forward so I would have her complete attention. "Did she start yelling and cursing before or after you told her to 'get over it' in regard to her PTSD?" Her face paled under her makeup. "You see, I spoke to Lexie before you came out. And she told me exactly what happened." I pointed at her. "You threatened to suspend her friends if they didn't stop walking her to class. You threatened a traumatized seventeen-year-old girl, by taking away the people who help her feel safe. Then when she brought in her service dog you told her she couldn't have that either."

"Those boys are late to every class every day," she stated.

"No, they're not," I replied. "One of them is late maybe twice a day. And who that is changes every day." I leaned back and met her gaze. "When Lexie came home from the hospital we worked together to find a way to get Lexie back to school as soon as she healed up enough and felt up to it. I'm very aware of what those boys have been doing and I am extremely grateful to them for it."

"If you care about those boys then you know they need to get to class on time," she tried again.

"What I know is, you told my niece to 'get over it' and told her she couldn't bring her service animal into school." I met her gaze again. "You can *not* deny a service animal. It's against the law. I can bring you up on charges." She stared at me slack jawed. "So, now that you're done lying, perhaps we can get to the root of this issue."

"Excuse me?" she said, shocked.

"My niece is stubborn, loyal, foul mouthed, and when she's on her game, she's a force of nature," I informed her. "But right now, she's limping. She pushes herself every damn day to get back to normal. She doesn't know I see it, but I do. And she's making progress. It's slow, but it's progress."

"The dog is-"

"Extremely well trained. He won't make a noise unless something is wrong with Lexie or someone threatens her." I took a breath and let it out slowly. "That is her service animal and you can't refuse to have him here." She looked embarrassed and furious all at the same time. "So, I'll make you a deal." She raised an eyebrow. I continued. "If you show her some compassion, stay off her back, stay off the boys' backs until the end of the school year. Then I won't bring this conversation up at the next school board hearing."

Her jaw clenched. "Alright. I'll give her a little more leeway."

I bowed my head in thanks. "I appreciate it."

Lexie

I WAS STILL BOUNCING my knee when Rory strode out of the Vice Principal's office. How mad was he? He gestured at us.

"Outside," he ordered. No one argued, we grabbed our bags and left the office. When we were outside Rory stopped and turned to us. "Here's what's going to happen." He looked at the boys. "You guys will continue to walk Lexie to class." He turned to me. "You will leave

Hades at home and try to stay under this bitch's radar for the rest of the school year. Understood?"

Everyone said yes. He nodded. "Good, now get back to class."

"Sorry, Rory," I said.

"This wasn't on you, Kid," he assured me. I gave him a small smile before heading to gym.

CHAPTER 12

WEDNESDAY AFTERNOON

I walked into the house after doing my homework at Miles'. It hadn't been the same without the twins. I let Hades off his leash and hung up my hoodie.

"Look who's here," Tara said cheerfully. I turned and instantly wanted to walk right back out the door. Tara's friends were over, along with Jessica. Great.

"Hey, Tara," I said before turning to head upstairs. There was no way I was going to stay down here with those bitches.

"I heard that a couple of your friends aren't talking to you anymore," Tara taunted. I turned back to see the smirk on her face.

"Mind your own business," I warned her.

Her smile didn't go away. "I told you those guys wouldn't stick around." It felt like a kick in the gut. And way below the belt.

My heart ached as I met her eyes. "How's trying to get into Asher's pants going? Or is it Zeke's this week?" I asked coldly. Her eyes grew wide, her mouth dropping open. "It's not going to happen, Tara. Don't you get it? Zeke and Asher want nothing to do with you. So, stop chasing them like a bitch in heat."

I turned around and took the stairs with Hades. I closed and locked the door behind me then sank to the floor as tears fell down my face. Tara had hit too close to the mark right now. With the twins not talking to me or the guys, I didn't see how this was going to end well. I wrapped my arms around my knees and rested my forehead on them.

Someone slammed on my door making me jump. "You bitch," Tara hissed. "You're nothing to those guys. Just a piece of ass." She hit the door again. "Do you really think they care about a piece of trash like you? Your own mother didn't even want you!" Tara stomped down the stairs.

Tears fell as Hades nudged his head under my neck forcing my head up. I gave him a watery smile and hugged him tight. They weren't going to leave me. They weren't. I held tight to Hades while I tried to remind myself that they cared about me.

***

Zeke

THE DOGS WERE GOING CRAZY. I walked out the back door with their food. Whistling before setting down their bowls in their assigned spots. They didn't come. I whistled again.

The dogs growled and snarled further back on the property. Striding toward the sound I almost jogged to see what had them so worked up.

"Tank! Kita!" I called. The dogs were backing away from the fence, their fur up and teeth bared. That wasn't right. "Tank! Kita! Come!" I ordered. They continued to back up to my side.

They kept growling. Something wasn't right. I looked out in the fading light, wondering if a bear was on the property on the other side of the fence. I searched but found nothing.

I touched their backs, they were both trembling. "House," I ordered. The dogs didn't move until I backed up. They moved between me and whatever they saw. This wasn't normal. I pulled out my cell phone and called.

"Hey," Lexie said in her tired, raspy voice. She had my complete attention instantly.

"What's wrong?" I asked as I kept backing toward the house, taking Tank and Kita with me.

"Nothing, I just had a run in with Tara," she muttered. She took a drink, probably from her water bottle.

"Shit."

"Yeah, that was my thought too," she admitted, her voice back to normal. "What's with the dogs?" I kept backing up, the dogs keeping pace with me. Still growling, still baring their teeth.

"Something strange is happening," I told her. "The dogs are acting like there's something here and I can't see it. It could be a bear or mountain lion out in the woods but I'm heading back to the house with them and they aren't letting up." She started moving instantly.

"You think there's a soul out there?" she asked, then moved her mouth away from the phone and called for Hades.

"Maybe," I said. "I've never seen this behavior before unless a bigger predator was around."

"I'm on my way."

"Thanks."

"No problem," she said before hanging up. I brought the dogs back into the house.

They kept pacing and growling. I looked out the back windows expecting to see a bear or mountain lion somewhere. I couldn't see shit. I was going to have to wait for Lexie.

Lexie

I PULLED up to Zeke's house. This time it had only taken me ten minutes to get across town.

Zeke's house was a mix of cabin and bungalow. There was a small wrap around porch that kept some of the yard tools out of the weather. I personally loved the house, but that didn't matter right now. The dogs inside were going bonkers.

I hurried to the door with Hades. Zeke opened it before I could knock.

"Get in here," he grumbled, reaching out and taking my arm. He all but dragged me inside.

"I'm in, I'm in," I said, surprised at his grip on my arm. Zeke had never grabbed me that hard before. "What's with you?" He was looking out the window again, frowning.

"There might be a mountain lion or bear outside," he reminded me, his fists clenching and unclenching at his sides. Okay, that made sense.

"Well, I'm going to need to go outside to look around." I pointed out. He led me through the kitchen to the back door. There he picked up his shotgun.

"Do you really need that?" I asked as I slipped on my bracelets.

He looked out the back window as he answered. "That fence is eight feet high, mountain lions can jump fifteen up into a tree."

"Yep, taking the shot gun with us," I said immediately. He grunted as he opened the door and walked outside first. I followed closely behind him.

"I'll show you where they were barking," he said, the gun braced against his shoulder, the muzzle pointed at the ground. He reached back, took my hand and brought it to his belt at the back of his waist. Directly above his butt. I focused on holding onto his belt. "I want to know where you are, so don't let go," he ordered.

I didn't say anything as I followed Zeke to the back of the fenced in area. We were halfway there when that chill ran down my neck like a lick of fire. I hissed and slapped my hand against my throat.

"Relax, it's a ghost," I told him, wincing. He lowered the shotgun and clicked the safety on. He began unloading it as I waited. I'd been to the range enough with Rory and Zeke in the last few months to know you never walk in front of a barrel, even with the safety on. I did it once and Zeke about ripped my head off. Rory quickly followed with his own lecture on gun range safety. I never did it again. Zeke put the shells in his pocket before pointing the barrel at the ground again.

"Clear," he said. I stepped around him and started looking for the soul. I walked along the fence line with Zeke right beside me.

I eventually found him in the south corner of the fenced in area. He was wearing snow camo, an orange vest, gloves and a beanie.

He must have been a hunter. When he turned around my mouth dropped. He had a deep hole in his chest, deep enough that his ribs were visible. His face was dazed, his eyes unfocused. He seemed confused.

"Found him," I told Zeke before walking towards the ghost. When I was close enough I spoke to him. "I see you."

He turned, his face white, his eyes wide. "Wh-what the hell is going on?"

Shit. He didn't know. "What's your name?"

He swallowed hard. "Alex, Alex Osburn. I need to get home. My wife..."

"Alex," I said gently, "you're dead."

His eyes filled. "No, no, I'm just lost."

My heart ached for him. "Look at your chest."

He looked at me as if I was insane before looking down at his chest. "Holy Mother!" His hands started shaking as he reached up to touch one of his ribs. That was kinda gross. Tears ran down his face as he looked at me again. "My wife... she's pregnant. She needs me..."

Judging by his clothes, he had been dead for a while. "What's her name?"

"Meredith," he breathed as tears continued to fall. My eyes filled as well.

"You can't stay here. If you go to the cemetery in the morning, there are others waiting to cross over. They can explain everything. If you do that, I'll find out about your wife."

"You promise?" he pleaded.

"I promise."

He nodded, tears still falling as if he didn't notice it. "Okay, the cemetery. The one on Walnut?"

"Yeah, just follow the driveway to the highway and head back to town," I said gently. He nodded again as he turned and walked through the chain link fence then along the fence towards the driveway.

"He's gone," I called to Zeke as I wiped my face. "His wife was pregnant."

"Shit," he bit out. I nodded, that just about covered it. We headed back towards the house. "You okay?"

Was I okay? I shrugged. I was tired. Tired of the dead and their tragic stories. Tired of crossing them, tired of being the only way into the Veil. Tired of Tara's bullshit. I ran my hand down my face.

"Yeah, I'm fine," I lied. Zeke had his own problems to deal with. He didn't need mine. His calloused hand wrapped around the back of my neck, comforting me. Making a part of me relax. "I have to find out what happened to his wife and baby." I shook my head. "I'm just hoping they are both alive and doing okay."

"I'm sure they are," he said gently.

I scoffed, "Sure, they are." I could feel his worried gaze on me. "Because everyone gets a happy ending." I took a deep breath, wiped my face and gave him a strained smile. "I'm fine, just a little tired of sad endings."

I opened the back door and was greeted by the dogs. They were calmer and back to their normal selves. I put a leash on Hades.

"No, not everyone gets a happy ending," Zeke admitted as he walked me to the door. I turned and met his eyes. "But that doesn't mean they don't exist."

I gave him a small smile. "Well, if you're going to bring logic into my pity party," I countered. He chuckled, the sound making me give him a real smile. "I'll see you tomorrow."

"Thanks, Lexie," he said as I headed toward the Blazer.

I waved without turning around. "No problem, it's what I do," I said tiredly. Hades jumped in and I followed. Zeke had his worried face on as I turned to go down his driveway.

My thoughts just got darker as I drove away. I had to find Osburn's family. What if they were dead? What if the baby didn't make it? I pushed those thoughts away as I tried to focus on driving. He had a baby on the way. It wasn't fair that he never got to meet his kid. Out of all the fucked-up stories I've heard over the years, this one was up there in the top five.

I was still grousing when I pulled up to the house. The sun had set while I was at Zeke's.

Rory's truck wasn't in the driveway. Neither was Tara's car. I took deep breaths as my chest tightened. The shadows in the yard seemed to grow. Snow flashed through my mind. Then the arm around my throat. I was taking heavy breaths as tears fell.

Come on, Lexie. You can do this. I rested my forehead on the steering wheel as I cried. I didn't want to fight this time. I just wanted to be able to go inside without a problem for once... I took deep gasping breaths as my chest tightened, my heart raced. I needed help tonight. I couldn't... I was tired... I pulled out my phone and called the first person I could think of. He answered.

"I need you," I said immediately, my voice thick with tears. "I can't... I can't make myself walk into the house alone. Please?"

The line went dead. He hung up on me.

I kept crying, not knowing if he was coming or not. I could do this…. But I was tired of pushing it today. I just wanted my bed, my dog and sleep.

I was contemplating just staying in the car until someone got home when my door opened. Isaac's eyes ran over me before he reached in and pulled me out of the Blazer. Hades hopped out after me. He took my hand and led me up to the house. He used his own key to open the door then switched on the light.

I stepped inside, the pressure in my chest easing. I quickly turned off the alarm. When I turned to Isaac he was looking out the door.

"I'm sorry. Thanks for coming." I sniffed, feeling ridiculous. He met my eyes and nodded. Those amber eyes were haunted as he stepped closer, kissed my forehead, then walked out the door.

He hadn't said a word to me. My heart took a big kick. Damn it.

CHAPTER 13

THURSDAY MORNING

*S*hit! My alarm hadn't gone off this morning so I had to skip the cemetery and rush to school. I hadn't even had time to brush my teeth. I hurried into second period in the last ten minutes of class.

Mrs. Hayes sent me a censoring look. I shrugged apologetically as I sat down. While everyone else talked our teacher came over to me.

"Lexie, what happened?" she asked.

"Power went out last night and my alarm didn't go off," I lied. The truth was I used my phone for an alarm and I had such a hard time sleeping last night that when I meant to hit snooze I turned it off.

She sighed. "We've had a lot of issues with the power going out lately." She pointed at me. "I'll let you off this time, I suggest using your phone for an alarm."

"Yes, ma'am," I said instantly. She gave me the assignment for the day then headed back to her desk. I leaned back and sighed. That was close. I pulled out my phone and used the group text.

Alexis: I was majorly late today.

It wasn't long before I got an answer.

Zeke: No shit.

Asher: I'll take you to Math. Miles, can you take her to Chemistry?

Miles: Of course.

Alexis: Thanks guys.

The bell rang and I picked my bag back up then went to wait in the hall.

Eric started down the hall then turned back.

"I could walk you to class if you want," he offered.

I eyed him. That was new. "No thanks, Asher's coming to get me." He turned and walked away. Why wouldn't he leave me alone? It was starting to get creepy. Then again, I was more sensitive to the creep factors lately.

Asher stepped out of the crowd with a grin. "What happened this morning?"

I pushed away from the wall and started walking with him towards my Math class. "Hit off instead of snooze on my alarm."

He chuckled as he shifted his bag around to his front and pulled out a couple pieces of gum. "Here."

I took them gratefully. "Is it that bad?" I teased. I popped them in my mouth and enjoyed the minty freshness.

"No, but I know you," he said with a grin. I shrugged. "Did you sleep alright?"

No, but that wasn't anything new. "The same as usual," I muttered as I stepped around a couple in the hallway who seemed to think they owned the whole thing. We reached my classroom. "Thanks, Ash."

"No problem, Ally girl." He waited until I was inside before taking off.

I took my seat next to Laura and took a deep breath. Laura's eyes ran over me. "Are you alright, Lexie?"

"Yeah, just... too many balls in the air and I'm running out of hands." I muttered as I pulled out my text book.

"Sounds exhausting," she said as she pulled out her own book. "Maybe you should let something drop?"

I shrugged. "Maybe." Class started while I thought about what she said. What could I drop? I couldn't drop the dead, I couldn't drop the Veil, I wouldn't drop the guys, I couldn't drop homework and school. All that was left was MMA training, rock climbing, and the job I wanted to get. But that was the only stuff I wanted to do, besides hanging out with the guys.

I rubbed my eyes wearily. There was nothing I could drop. Maybe I shouldn't try to get a job... I was stretching myself too far already, and I couldn't stop.

I decided to focus on class instead. One day at a time, that's all I can do.

THE CLASS WAS HALF over when the overhead lights grew bright.

"What in the world..." Mr. Hatter said. The lights went out, plunging the room into dim light. I stayed still as that chill ran down my throat like a hot poker. Shit. I slid my bracelets on quickly and tried to look like every other girl in the room. Only they couldn't see the ghosts walking through the walls and into the room. I cursed under my breath as Mr. Hatter got on his cell to the office.

The ghosts, led by Mr. Davis, started yelling. I closed my eyes and took a deep breath. The room started to get chilly. People started talking. Girls started pulling on their hoodies. I opened my eyes to meet Mr. Davis'. My will was a pressure in my chest that kept building. I mouthed 'get out' and let it fly. A silent blast of gold light shot out from me in a wave knocking every soul back through the wall. Every bulb in the ceiling shattered. Girls screamed. I sagged over my desk, taking deep breaths as my head exploded and stomach lurched.

I closed my eyes, fighting to stay put. When my stomach cramps eased a little I realized my nose was bleeding. I reached into my pocket and cleaned up my face. I raised a trembling hand.

Mr. Hatter spotted me. "Lexie?"

"I'm not feeling so well, I think I need to hit the nurse's office." I managed as my stomach tried to decide if I would be sick or not.

He eyed me. "Go ahead." He turned to the rest of the class. "In fact, everyone, it's a half day. A transformer blew, and it looks like the back-up generator is fried. School is out until Monday."

Everyone cheered. I just grabbed my bag then hurried out of class, still holding tissues to my nose.

I didn't go to the nurse's office, I went to the girl's bathroom and the first empty stall. I sat down with my back against the tile, hoping I wasn't going to be sick. What the hell did I do in there? I'd never done that before, not out of the Veil at least. What the fuck was going on?

The pain in my head increased, my stomach lurched. I moved to my knees just in time to be sick into the toilet. I dry heaved again and again. I had nothing in me to start with. When it finally stopped, I noticed my tissues were soaked. I dropped them into the toilet and grabbed more.

The cold tile against my back helped. I sat there in misery.

Miles

I HURRIED AWAY from Lexie's Math class and put my phone to my ear.

"What?" Zeke answered.

"I can't find Lexie," I said immediately. "Her teacher said she got a bloody nose and went to the nurse's office." I headed for the hallways.

"Fuck." Zeke snapped. "At least we know she's not at the office."

I moved through the crowd quickly. "If she was at a two then she'd hit a bathroom."

"Shit, we need a girl," he growled.

"Get Tara," I ordered.

"What?"

"Asher probably knows where she is. We'll send her into the bathrooms to look for Lexie," I explained, moving to the side of the hallway so I could stop. "Unless you want to wait until enough people clear out so we can go into the girls' bathrooms?"

"I'll call Asher," Zeke growled before hanging up. I looked down at my phone. Hurry.

Something had happened here and I had a good idea that Lexie was at the center of it. What the hell was going on?

Lexie

EVENTUALLY, the door to the bathroom opened. Light footsteps echoed off the tile.

"Lexie?" Tara's voice echoed off the tile.

"Here." I croaked. Why was she looking for me?

"She's in here and it's empty," Tara called, the sound grating on my ears. Heavy footsteps moved over the tile.

"Lexie?" Miles' soothing voice eased my stomach a bit.

I opened my eyes. "I'm fine, just..." What was I going to tell them?

"Thank you, Tara, we can take care of her from here." Miles announced.

"Fine, don't tell me what's going on." Tara bit out before walking out the door.

I opened my eyes. Miles was kneeling beside me. Zeke was just outside the stall with Asher. All of their eyes were full of questions. Shit. "I'm okay..."

"Did you use your kit?" Zeke demanded. Fuck...

"I forgot," I admitted. My barriers had been stronger than ever, I hadn't had to use them for weeks. Miles began to dig into his bag then pulled out a kit.

"What happened?" Asher asked. I sighed. What was I going to tell them?

"Some ghosts showed up in class," I said, my voice raspy. Where was my water bottle? Oh, I don't care. "I made them leave and here I am." There, that wasn't a lie...

"How?" Miles asked gently as he handed me two nausea tablets.

"I... I'm too tired to explain it right now." I hedged before popping them into my mouth. They seemed to take that at face value.

"Come on," Asher said. "You can get some sleep at my house. Jess won't be home till nine tonight."

That sounded like a great idea. I didn't want to be alone right now. "I just need a couple hours." I said as I checked my tissues and found my nose had stopped bleeding. I tossed them into the toilet and flushed. Miles helped me up. When I caught sight of my reflection, I winced.

My face was white as paper and covered in blood. I quickly washed my face before leaving the bathroom with the guys.

When we reached the parking lot, Zeke held his hand out. "Keys."

I didn't even argue, I just handed them to him. Asher guided me to his truck, then made sure I was buckled in before closing the door. They were talking about something out there, but I couldn't care right now. I leaned my head back and slipped under.

CHAPTER 14

THURSDAY EVENING

I woke up to the smell of vanilla and cinnamon. Opening my eyes, I recognized Asher's room in the dim light coming through the blinds.

I rubbed my face, trying to remember how I got here. I remembered the bathroom, getting into the truck, then nothing. Asher probably had to carry me upstairs. Debating whether to get up or not, I rolled over. There was a post-it on the nightstand. I reached out and picked it up.

'I'm sorry I had to leave. But when you wake up, you better head straight home. Rory wants to know what happened. - Asher'

I was going to head home, but I had something to take care of first.

When I sat up Hades moved from the end of the bed to my side. I smiled. They even remembered Hades. I searched Asher's room until I found my shoes by the door. I slipped them on. Hades' leash and my keys were on his desk. They really thought of everything. I put Hades' on his leash and left Asher's, making sure to lock the door behind me.

By the time I reached the cemetery I was fuming. I skidded the Blazer to a stop in the gravel. Holding on to my temper by my nails, I climbed out of the truck and strode towards them.

"Those of you who came to the high school today," I took a breath and let my temper fly, "what the fuck did you think you were doing?" I shouted. Several spirits flinched but others glared back. Including Mr. Davis.

"You didn't show up!" Davis shouted.

"I slept in, you fucker," I snapped. "I was going to come by after school."

"As if we're supposed to know that!" Davis shot back.

"For the last few months I've shown up six days a week," I growled. "I show up when I'm sick, I show up when I'm tired. If I don't show in the morning, you can damn well bet that I'll be here in the evening."

"You need to take more of us at once. We need to cross," Davis snapped.

That's it. I've had it.

"Enough!" I shouted. "Here's the way things are going to go now. First, stop running around town in groups. You're killing the transformers and being seen. Second, you will not go looking for me. The rest of my life is off limits! If you can't follow those rules, go find another way into the Veil!"

"Your job is to-"

"This isn't a job, this is my fucking life!" I shouted back. "And because of the shit you just pulled, no one's crossing for the next couple of days. You guys can just deal with it." I turned to walk away.

"You can't do that!" Mr. Davis shouted.

I turned back. "Oh, yes, I can. You see, I'm not dead. I have options." My eyes ran over the group, I wanted them to understand exactly whose fault this was. "And no one is crossing for one reason." I met his hate filled gaze. "You. And your actions." I turned away and ignored the souls yelling at Mr. Davis.

I climbed into the Blazer and drove out of the cemetery. That had felt good. Really good. Hell, a reality check had been overdue. I looked down at my portfolio and resume that I had put together for the tattoo shop. I had been carrying it around hoping to have time to go and apply. That's when it sunk in. I didn't have the time to have a weekend job. Especially if I didn't even have the time to go apply. I shook my head as I started for home.

My heart was heavy as I pulled onto my street and noticed the guys' cars were there. What the...? I pulled in front of the house to see them in the driveway, leaning on Rory's truck. But that's not what caught my eye. I shut off the truck and slowly climbed out.

The front of the house had changed. Instead of sage, the house was white. Instead of the normal white door there was a brand-new blue one in its place. With four small windows in a line across the top. But the biggest change.... The bushes where Clay Ordin had hidden had been torn out. Instead, the bed was just dark dirt with the start of some plants here and there.

My eyes burned as I realized what had happened. I looked over at them, my eyes watering.

"How did you know?" I asked quietly.

Rory moved to my side and hugged me tight. "Isaac texted Miles last night. Why didn't you tell me you were having trouble coming into the house?"

"I thought I'd get through it," I rasped. I quickly took a drink of water. "It was only at night."

"You didn't have to deal with it alone," he reminded me. I nodded. When he pulled away I wiped my face.

I looked at the house and for the first time in months, I didn't have a flash of being grabbed off the porch. Tears fell down my face as I looked at the work the guys had put in.

"Thank you," I said softly. My throat had a knot making it hard to talk.

"Oh, that's not all," Asher announced. He hurried to just inside the door and flipped a switch. The front yard lit up with floodlights. It took a second for my eyes to adjust, but when they did I was smiling again. The yard was bright as day. There were no shadows for someone to hide in, there was nothing to hide behind. Tears fell faster.

"Thank you." I looked at the guys and moved. I hugged Miles because he was the closest.

"You needed to tell us," he whispered to me. I nodded.

"The neighbors are going to be so pissed about those lights," Zeke said dryly.

169

I laughed as I moved to Zeke. I really wanted to hug Zeke and he knew it. He reached out, I took his big, dirty, calloused hand and squeezed it tight.

Asher joined us and wrapped me in a hug. I squeezed him back. When I pulled back he kept his arm around my shoulders.

"You guys... thank you so much," I said again, still stunned by everything they'd done.

"Well, just don't look at the back half," Miles said. "We only had time to paint the front today." Everyone chuckled.

"Come on inside and get cleaned up boys, the pizza should be here soon." Rory announced.

Zeke checked his phone. "I can't. I have to go to work." Everyone complained. He ignored it as he tucked his phone away. "I'll see you guys tomorrow."

Zeke headed for his Jeep without another word. He started the Jeep, then glanced over and met my gaze. With shadowed eyes, he turned away and pulled out onto the street.

I watched as he drove off, leaving my stomach in knots and my heart full of dread. The night grew quiet as Asher and Rory headed inside. Miles moved to my side.

"He doesn't have to work tonight, does he?" I asked quietly.

Miles sighed. "No, but I think he needs to."

I looked down at the grass. "Is he going to start avoiding me too?"

Miles' hand went to the small of my back. "No, he's avoiding his own issues right now."

His thumb began to rub circles on my spine. "Your issues have just brought up some of his own."

I slowly started walking towards the door. "Is there anything I can do to help?"

"Not until he's ready to talk to you about it," Miles told me quietly. I nodded. I got it. It hurt but I understood.

We joined Rory and Asher as a vote for a movie started. I didn't care. Two of my guys were here, and I could come home at night without issues. The night went on without Zeke, Isaac and Ethan. But without everyone there, it wasn't the same.

I WAS LYING in bed exhausted, but my brain kept going around in circles. Asher, Rory and Miles had asked about what happened today. I kept it vague. I didn't have an answer for them.

In theory, I knew what happened. I'd shoved the ghosts away. But it had never happened that way before. Serena might be right; my abilities were growing. What were they growing into? I don't think I wanted to know.

After the guys left I sent Isaac a text.

Alexis: Thank you. I miss you.

I hoped for an answer but my phone stayed silent.

Now I was trying to sleep, but to no avail. Questions kept running through my head. I checked my phone. 11:47pm. Shit. Okay, let's try counting sheep. I started counting. When I reached 100 I knew it wasn't working. My phone rang. I answered it as fast as I could.

"Hello?"

"Hi." Miles' voice filled my ear.

"Hey, what's going on?" I asked, laying back down.

Miles sighed. "I can't sleep. The house is too quiet. With everything that happened today and tomorrow…"

"I know what you mean," I admitted. "I can't sleep either."

"I wonder if anyone is sleeping tonight," he said absently.

"Probably not. Do you want some company?" I asked, hoping he'd say yes. Hell, I wanted company right now and Hades was just hogging the bed.

"No, it's alright," he said instantly. "I've got that competition tomorrow. I'll try some tv or something. Try not to worry, everything will work out. Get some sleep, Lexie."

"Night," I said before he hung up. I put my phone down and looked up at the ceiling.

I was only in bed for a few more seconds before I gave up. Then I was up and pulling on my sneakers. Miles calling in the middle of the night was strange enough, but after everything that's happened lately? With the State Championship tomorrow? I couldn't not go over.

I opened my door and headed downstairs, Hades following close. I put a leash on him, left a note for Rory and was out the door in minutes.

It wasn't long before I pulled into Miles' circular driveway. I hurried out, ignoring the slight chill in the air. I unlocked the door with my key and quickly punched in the combo to the security system.

After shutting the door, locking it and arming the system again, I let Hades off his leash. He followed me up the stairs and down the hall. Miles' bedroom door was closed.

I knocked twice before I opened the door and peeked around it.

"It's just me," I said. Miles was sitting up in bed wearing a white undershirt and a pair of green flannel pajama bottoms. When he saw it was me he put his book down.

"Lexie, what are you doing here?" he asked, "It's late."

I opened the door and came in. Not waiting for an invitation, I toed off my shoes and climbed into the empty side of his bed.

Hades joined us at our feet. As I made myself comfy by pulling his blankets up over my shoulders, Miles looked down at me like I was crazy.

"You couldn't sleep, I couldn't sleep," I said. "So, I came over." He smiled that smile that showed how handsome he was. Butterflies took off, and for the first time I didn't mind. I hadn't felt them that strong in a long time.

"Rory's going to be angry," he warned.

I shrugged. "I left a note." He smiled down at me. "What are you reading?"

He held up the paperback. "Twenty Thousand Leagues Under the Sea."

"Jules Verne? Nice." I smiled up at him.

"You've read it?"

"Years ago," I said. I met his eyes. "Read to me?" I asked quietly. Miles smiled and picked up the book. He went all the way back to the beginning. I scooted closer so I might see the print. Miles adjusted his pillows so I could.

His silky-smooth timbre relaxed me like nothing else could. I laid in his bed as he read several chapters out loud. During that time, I was at peace. My mind was quiet and the world was far away.

When he stopped to get a drink from the bottle of water on his night table, I had to ask. "Miles, why are your walls black in here?" He set the bottle down.

"It's for the fiber optics," he said as he opened the book again.

"What fiber optics?"

He grinned as he set down the book and picked up a remote. He shut off the lamp, plunging the room into darkness. My heart raced.

"Um, Miles?" I asked, wondering again if he liked me. Little lights in the ceiling turned on, the glow filled the room with soft light. I looked up and smiled. It looked like the night sky was on his ceiling. "Wow."

Miles laid back down next to me, his shoulder touching mine. "I had them installed a couple years ago. It works better with black walls."

"It's beautiful," I told him. "How can't you fall asleep with that on the ceiling?" Miles grew quiet.

Eventually he answered. "My mother always had music going. In her room, the kitchen, the conservatory- it didn't matter. Wherever she was there was music. The only time the house ever got this quiet was after my father beat her." I turned to him. His gaze was on the ceiling. "He'd shut off her music and that'd be it. Silence for the rest of the night."

I reached over and took his hand. He gave mine a small squeeze.

"I'm sorry," I said softly.

He turned to me. "You didn't know."

Wanting to make it better, I raised an eyebrow. "So, does snoring count? Cause I can do that." He chuckled.

"As I've learned from the others, yes," he smiled at me, "snoring counts."

I smiled to myself. "Good." We were quiet as we looked up at the 'stars.' "Are you nervous about the tournament tomorrow?"

"A little, I've been State Champion for the last two years. The coach expects me to keep pulling it off," he admitted.

"Do your best, that's all anyone can ask," I told him.

He squeezed my hand. "I know. If I lose, I lose. If I win, I win. There's no good coming from worrying about it right now." The room fell into silence. I peeked up at him.

"Can you still read to me?" I asked in an innocent voice. He chuckled softly, then picked up the book and started reading to me again.

I watched the 'stars' above as his voice slipped through my ears. I vaguely remember moving closer and snuggling into him as he read. There were lips on my forehead just as I slipped under.

CHAPTER 15

FRIDAY MORNING

I woke up slowly. I was warm, safe and comfy. Wintergreen filled my nose as I rubbed my face against his skin.

I never got to cuddle with Miles. I was going to enjoy this as long as I could. That's when I realized where I was. I was laying *on* Miles.

At some point in the night I had rolled over onto Miles, my stretched-out legs were between his. One arm was resting over his shoulder, my fingers in his hair. My other arm was over his other shoulder and buried in the pillow. The poor guy was stuck. His arms were around me though, and he didn't seem to mind.

His lips rested against my forehead and his breath moved through my hair. His fingers trailed down my spine then back again.

"Curium. Berkelium. Einsteinium..." he breathed. I grinned. He was awake and listing the table of elements.

"What time is it?" I grumbled. He smiled against my skin.

"Around eight," he told me softly. I groaned. I had to get up.

"I don't want to get up," I mumbled. "You're comfy." He chuckled quietly.

"Then go back to sleep."

I pulled back a little and looked up to meet his warm emerald eyes.

"Don't tempt me." I warned him. "That's the best night of sleep I've had in a while."

His eyes grew concerned. "Bad dreams?"

"Yeah, all cabin ones," I admitted quietly. Not to mention all the ghost crap I was trying to deal with. He reached up and brushed some of my hair gently out of my face.

"I'm sorry we didn't get there sooner," he said softly. I blinked up at him.

"It's not your fault, Miles," I told him. "It's his."

He nodded sadly.

"Did you sleep?" I asked.

His ears tinged pink as he answered. "I fell asleep shortly after you did."

"Good." I moved to get up, Miles dropped one of his legs so I could move out from between his. I moved to my back beside him.

"So, how did I totally pin you last night?" I asked, making a joke of it.

He chuckled. "I don't move much and I'm usually a back sleeper."

I stretched. "Sorry, I'm a cuddler." My voice turned raspy. I looked for my water bottle and didn't see it.

"You didn't bring a water bottle. Feel free to use mine," Miles said as he stretched.

I grabbed his water bottle and took a drink then laid back down. "What time does the tournament start?"

He had a small half grin on his face as he reached over me and picked up his glasses from the night stand. "It's already going, but my division doesn't start until ten. You don't have to come to the first part," he offered, laying back down and putting on his glasses. "The last race is scheduled for one this afternoon."

I rolled onto my side, braced my jaw on my hand and smiled at him. "Well, that will give me time to get dressed and get some drawing done."

He scratched his jaw. "That's a good idea, you haven't really drawn lately." Then his eyes met mine. "Lexie, what happened yesterday?" My stomach knotted as I remembered.

"I got the ghosts to leave," I said, repeating my answer from last night.

His eyes narrowed at me. "Then why were you sick?"

I sat up and put my back against the headboard, buying time. "It was just a two, Miles," I lied. But I didn't want to tell them. I needed to keep this ghost shit from touching them. His gaze ran over my face. I changed the subject. "I'll be there in time for the lunch break and I'll even bring you lunch," I offered.

He smiled. "I would appreciate that. It needs to be light. Could you pick me up a salad, please, with-"

"Half romaine and half spinach, grilled chicken, tomatoes, cucumbers, and Italian dressing." I recited his usual swim day lunch. He raised an eyebrow.

"You remember what I eat on race days?" he asked quietly. My face grew warm.

I shrugged nonchalantly. "You have the same thing every time," I hedged before I moved to the edge of the bed and started looking for my shoes. I found them, then focused on putting them on until my face stopped glowing.

I hurried to my feet and grabbed Hades' leash. "I'll see you at the meet," I said cheerfully as Hades followed me out the door.

In the hall, I took a deep breath and let it out slowly. Damn it, Lexie, stop flirting. And why the hell were you practically laying on him this morning? You know better than that!

I berated myself the whole way home.

Miles

I LISTENED to Lexie walk down the hallway, my mind troubled. She was lying about yesterday. I sat up and rested my back against the headboard as I ran through yesterday in my head, again. We'd all seen her have a two, and that wasn't a two.

Something else happened to make her sick. And something fried the backup generator at school. I tapped against my knee. It had to have something to do with the dead, it's one of the only things we didn't hear about anymore.

In fact, she's been eerily quiet on the subject for the last couple of months. Except for suggesting that the ghosts might be responsible for the transformers around town...

How many ghosts would it take to knock out a transformer or cause the power surges that had been showing up around town? I could only assume a large number.

Something was definitely going on with Lexie and she seemed determined to keep it to herself. I picked up my phone and called Zeke. He picked up on the fourth ring.

"What?" His gravelly voice was still half asleep.

"You were right," I admitted. "She's not telling us something."

"Told ya," he grumbled. "It has to be that Necromancy shit."

"I believe so, she's been oddly quiet about it for awhile," I told him, looking at my closed bedroom door.

"When she got that ghost out of here the other day, she looked tired. Bone tired," he informed me. "She needs to start talking."

"I agree, but right now is probably not the best time. Not with Isaac and Ethan trying to deal with the fact Sophie is here."

Zeke cursed. "We're going to have to watch her more."

"How she's acting, how much sleep she's getting...." I began making a list.

"She's been coming to school with nosebleeds for a few days now," he informed me. It shouldn't surprise me that Zeke noticed and I didn't.

"That's not a good sign," I said. "But until Sophie's crossed, I don't want to push her."

"I'll fucking do it," he snapped.

"Zeke," I chided. "We want answers, not her pulling away."

He sighed. "Yeah, yeah. I know."

"I have to get going. I'll see you at the meet."

"Good luck."

Lexie

I stopped the Blazer far enough away from the crowd of ghosts that Hades wouldn't start barking. After my morning to myself, I wouldn't even be here if it wasn't for a damn promise I made.

"Mr. Osburn!" I called into the large group. Mr. Osburn made his way to the edge of the group, his face hopeful.

"Did you find them?" he asked.

"Thanks to my uncle, yeah," I said. "Your wife gave birth to a healthy boy. She lives in a nice part of town and is doing fine." He all but deflated as he dropped to his knees.

"Thank you," he said softly.

"No problem," I said. I turned away and headed back to my truck.

"That's it?" Mr. Davis snapped. I turned and crossed my arms over my chest. The ghost was furious. "You're not crossing anyone?"

I smiled sweetly at him. "No. I'm not," I stated. "I'm taking the day off. And it's all your fault."

The ghosts started shouting at Davis again as I grinned, climbed into the Blazer and got out of there. Davis had to answer to the other souls, not me.

Thirty minutes later, I was pulling into a spot at the city's indoor pool. It was the only Olympic sized pool for miles around. The place was packed with people.

I grabbed Hades' leash and the bags of food before heading towards the gates. The guys, after hearing that I was getting Miles' lunch, instantly put in their orders.

"Hades, guard me," I whispered the order to him. He instantly went into alert mode. If someone got within two feet of me, he growled until they backed up. When I stepped up to pay my fee they hesitated.

"No dogs allowed," the tall woman snapped.

I gave her a smile. "Service dog."

The woman ran her eyes over Hades, then looked to me again. "I don't buy that. Where's his vest?"

I sighed, dug into my wallet and pulled out the card that Rory made sure to fill out for me at the station. She read it, frowned, then handed it back. Then she took my money.

"Complete bullshit," she mumbled under her breath as she made change. My temper spiked. A couple weeks ago I might have let that slide. But I was sick and tired of letting people and ghosts walk over me. I took my change and ticket, then met her eyes.

"What was that?" I asked politely.

She smiled. "Oh, nothing."

Yeah, that wasn't going to fly with me. "No, I believe you said, 'Complete bullshit.' Right?"

Her face turned pink. "Perhaps I did," she admitted. "But it's people like you who abuse the system-"

"Would you like to know why I have a service dog?" I asked directly. The woman blinked. She couldn't ask that and she knew it. I told her anyway. "In January, this psycho stalked me, kidnapped me, then almost killed me." I told her matter-of-factly. Her face grew pale.

"Now, I have issues going into crowds."

"That was you? The girl the Ordin's boy-"

"Yeah, that was me. So, thanks for the ticket and fuck you very much," I snapped and walked past her, fighting the urge to turn back and go at her more.

A person says service animal, you had to allow it whether you believed it or not.

I made my way through the foyer and into the pool area. It was huge, and packed. Trusting Hades to keep people away from me, I searched for the guys. I couldn't spot them. A race was still going so I stayed to the side of the bleachers, still looking for the guys. You'd think Zeke would be easy to spot even in this crowd.

"Lexie?" A girl's voice caught my attention. I looked for the owner. Laura was sitting a couple rows up the bleachers. I smiled up at her.

"Hey," I said, moving closer to the bleachers.

"Where are your friends?" she asked, tucking some hair behind her ear.

I looked back out at the crowded bleachers. "I don't know." I turned back to her. "Who are you here for?"

Her face turned crimson. "Michael is on the team."

Hades began pulling on the leash, I kept him at my side. "Really? And how's that going?" I asked mischievously. She smiled and looked away while scratching her arm. Her scratching lifted her long sleeve shirt, flashing burn scars along her arm. I looked at the race going on. The burn scars were deep and completely healed.

I kept my mouth shut as Hades gave another lurch. I pulled him back, telling him no.

A giant figure moved out of the crowd. Hades started pulling harder at his leash.

"We're on the far side. There's one more race and then the lunch break," Zeke said as he scratched Hades' ears.

I turned to Laura. "I'll see ya, later." She nodded shyly. I followed Zeke around the pool to the far side near the starting blocks for the swimmers. Asher was waiting in the bleachers. He was alone.

My heart dropped. "Where are the twins?"

Asher gave me a tense look. "They're here. They aren't sitting with us, though." I sat down next to Asher, my chest tight. They should be sitting with us, cheering for Miles. This wasn't right.

"Look," I handed Asher the bags filled with everyone's lunch, "I'll go sit with Laura so the twins will come back."

When I went to get up Asher took my arm and stopped me. "It's not just you, Ally. They don't want to talk to anyone right now."

"Sit down, Lexie, they're dealing with their shit," Zeke growled as he sat down on my other side. I sat back down as the race ended. Hades settled on the bench in front of me.

An announcement of numbers came over the P.A. Swimmers climbed out of the pool while others came out of the locker rooms. I spotted Miles.

Holy shit. Sweet Miles, who was always properly dressed... was wearing only a dark green Speedo. I swallowed hard. His tall, lean body showed every ripped muscle. I made a point to make sure my mouth was closed as my eyes ran over him. From his strong shoulders, down his muscled pecs, even further to what I swear was an eight pack, but his Speedo hid the last of the view. His legs were just as ripped as his upper body.

I had been laying on that all night? Dear God.... I reminded myself to breathe. Miles must have had his contacts in since he was only carrying a pair of goggles in his hand. He was talking to another swimmer, but I honestly couldn't tell you who it was or what he looked like. I needed to stop staring. I looked away to the pool and focused on petting Hades. Rule One of being friends with guys: don't get caught drooling.

"So, which race is this?" I asked, hoping to keep my eyes from drifting back to Miles as he lined up behind his starting block.

"The second semi-final. Everyone in this race has beaten out everyone else on one side of the bracket," Asher explained. "The top three here will go on to join the final."

"So, I got here just in time," I muttered.

"Yeah," Asher answered. The swimmers climbed onto their blocks and got into position.

Everyone bent over and placed their hands on the edge of the block. My knee started bouncing as the entire building grew silent. A buzzer went off. The swimmers were instantly in the water. My heart raced as Miles came up and started moving. He wasn't the fastest.

"How many laps?" I asked nervously, scratching Hades' ears.

"It's 200 meters. So, four laps." Asher pointed towards the guy in the first lane. "That guy is going to wear out fast. This is an endurance race." I nodded as I watched Miles and the leading group dive under the water, turn and push off the wall. Miles started picking up a little more speed. The guy in the lead was starting to lag behind. They hit the other end of the pool and shot back down the lanes. I twisted my fingers together. Half way through the third lap, Miles and four others started pulling ahead.

"Here it comes," Asher announced. Asher stood up and he wasn't the only one. Everyone stood up, blocking my view of the leaders turning at the wall. I stood up and could still barely see. I cursed and stepped up on my seat.

Zeke reached out and steadied me with his eyes still on the race. Miles was pulling ahead with two others. They were close, I couldn't tell who was ahead. Then halfway through the last lap, Miles and two other swimmers pulled ahead. I bit the corner of my bottom lip. Miles and two others hit the wall. The crowd went crazy. We cheered as the three winners hung on the dividers and got their breath back.

"Go Miles!" I shouted. The guys whooped. Miles looked up and spotted us. It wasn't hard, Zeke was huge after all. He waved with his goggles in his hand, still trying to catch his breath. We stopped making noise and sat back down.

The crowd started to break up and head for the doors while we stayed put. Miles and the others climbed out of the pool using the block to get out. Soaking wet Miles was... yummy. My mouth went dry as he grabbed a towel and dried off. He talked to one of the other swimmers while they walked back into the locker room.

I pulled my eyes away from him and looked around at the remaining crowd. I spotted the twins on the other side of the pool.

"I picked up the twins' usual sandwiches too." I went to stand up. "I'll take them their lunch really quick."

Asher's hand grabbed my arm, stopping me. "You don't want to do that, Ally girl." He warned. He took the bag from my hand and tugged me back down to my seat. He looked past me to Zeke. "Are you coming?"

Zeke sighed. "Yeah." He heaved himself to his feet and followed Asher down the bleachers. That was strange. I watched them go over and hand the bag to Isaac. Smart, he'd always been more food driven. My shoulders grew tense as I watched the guys try to talk to them. Ethan was doing a lot of gesturing. Isaac opened the bag and pulled out his sandwich.

I was still watching them when Miles came out of the locker room.

"Hi." Miles' voice pulled my attention from the others. He was wearing a white shirt, a pair of dark track pants and sandals. His wet hair wasn't dripping, but it wasn't brushed either.

I gave him a smile. "Hey, you kicked ass out there." Really, Lexie?

You just saw him in almost nothing, and that's all you could come up with?

His ears turned pink as he sat on the bench below me. Hades moved to the side a little when Miles scratched his ears. "Thanks, we're almost done. Just one more race." He sighed. I opened the bag next to me and handed him his salad and plastic utensils. "Thank you for lunch. I really appreciate it."

I shrugged. "No problem. It's the least I can do after hogging your covers all night." He grinned as he opened his salad.

"You didn't hog the covers," he told me quietly, pink tinging his cheeks. He was right, I had climbed on top of him. My face burned. I dropped the subject as I pulled my sandwich out of the bag. "So, the twins are here," he told me.

I licked my lips. "Yeah, I brought them lunch. Asher and Zeke took it over. I'm hoping they'll at least eat the lunch I brought."

He reached out and touched my knee, getting my attention. "They're still processing everything," he said gently. "It's not going to happen overnight."

"I know, I just miss them," I admitted. He squeezed my knee gently.

He took his hand off my knee and went back to his lunch. "So, what did you do this morning? Have you gone to get that job yet?"

I looked away to the pool. "No, I... changed my mind."

Miles turned on the bench giving me his full attention. "Why didn't you?"

I looked down at Hades. "I ... I realized that I don't have the time for a job right now. Even a once-a-week one."

"What's stopping you? Maybe we can help." he offered.

I gave him a sad smile. "It's just not going to work right now." Miles met my eyes and waited. I turned away in time to spot the guys coming back.

"Yeah, they aren't talking much," Asher announced. Zeke sat next to me, Asher sat on the same bench as Miles. I handed them the bag. Everyone got their sandwiches out.

"What did we miss?" Asher asked as he opened his sandwich.

"Lexie didn't apply for that job." Miles announced.

"Why?" Asher asked, frowning. My shoulders grew tense under their eyes.

"Because I don't have enough time," I muttered as I pulled my sandwich out of the bag.

"Then just work weekends." Zeke suggested.

"That won't work right now," I mumbled before taking a bite. Zeke and Miles shared a look before changing the subject.

As lunch went on we talked about the next race as if there was no one missing. I looked across the pool at the twins. Neither one of them was talking. Ethan was looking down at the water, his face pensive. Isaac was looking at the cement floor near the pool.

People started coming back from lunch. A cop in uniform made his way through the returning crowd. I smiled as Rory walked over to the twins and sat down.

"Rory's here," I announced. Everyone turned to see him.

"Maybe he could help," Asher muttered. It didn't look like he was. Ethan wasn't talking, he was just staring at the water.

"It doesn't look like it," I mumbled.

"They'll come around," Miles reassured me.

"So, what's everyone doing this afternoon?" Asher asked.

I shrugged. "Nothing planned."

"Busy," Zeke muttered.

"I'll probably be napping," Miles admitted.

I turned to Miles. "We're still doing your party tonight, right?"

Miles met my eyes and smiled uncertainly. "If you guys really want to…"

"Sounds good to me." I looked across the pool, wondering if the twins would come. I rubbed Hades' ears and turned back to Miles.

"Want us to bring snacks?" I asked.

Miles shook his head. "We can order in."

Asher scoffed, "No, we won't." I smiled at the indignation in Asher's voice. "I'll make snacks this afternoon and bring them over."

Miles shook his head. "You guys don't have to-"

"Oh, yeah, we do," I countered. He turned back to me and I gave him a big shit-eating grin.

He smiled and shook his head. I looked up in time to spot Rory walking around the pool.

Asher nudged me gently. "Do you want to come help make snacks?"

"Sure. As long as you make cookies too," I suggested.

"Alright, but we'll make Miles' favorite," he stipulated.

I held my hand out. "Deal." We shook on it.

"So, I assume you made it to the final," Rory announced as he reached us.

"Yes, we have the last race in fifteen minutes," Miles said awkwardly.

Rory sat down on the other side of Hades. "How's the competition?"

Miles looked down at the floor. "Um, it's stronger than last year," he admitted before looking at the pool. "This next race won't be easy. There is one former State Champion still in the race. It's his last year and he's rather determined to win his title back."

"That's Eric Johanson, right?" Rory asked. Miles nodded. I smiled to myself as I listened to the two of them talk about the competition. It seemed Rory had adopted Miles too.

Soon enough, Miles was heading back into the locker room.

The bleachers started filling up.

"Rory, do you care if I go over and help Asher with snacks for a video game marathon tonight?" I asked, scooting over a little to give Zeke more room. He was glaring at the guy next to him, and the poor guy might have a heart attack. Zeke took the room, sliding over until his thigh met mine.

"Sure, no problem, just be home by eleven tonight," Rory told me. I nodded as the announcer called for the swimmers to come to the pool, the sound echoing through the building.

I was more prepared for Miles in a Speedo, but I still had to make sure I wasn't drooling. There was no talking among the swimmers this time. Everyone had their game faces on and were ignoring the others.

"Swimmers, to your blocks." The announcement rang through my ears.

All six swimmers moved to their lanes. Miles went to lane five and climbed onto his block. My knee started bouncing. It only lasted a few heartbeats until Zeke put his large hand on my knee, stopping me. I glanced up at him. He shot me a look.

I rolled my eyes and started bouncing my other knee. Asher didn't mind when I bounced my knee.

Too soon for me, the buzzer sounded and Miles was in the water. The race started like the last one, only no one pulled ahead on the first lap. The same for the second. Half way through the third the swimmers picked up the pace.

Everyone stood up again. I stood on my seat so I could see, with my hand on Zeke's shoulder and Asher's hand on my waist keeping me balanced. I kept my eyes glued to Miles' lane. He moved through the water like a machine, slicing through it easily. They hit the turn. Somehow in the turn four of them took the lead, including Miles.

"Come on, come on, come on," I muttered, practically bouncing in place. My heart pounded as the swimmers went all out. Miles and another swimmer pulled ahead easily.

They were neck and neck. Then at the last quarter Miles really put on the speed. They hit the wall almost at the same time. I couldn't tell who won. The crowd went crazy. I shouted along with them. Asher covered his ears as the building was filled with noise.

The time-keepers from both lanes met behind the blocks. Two officials came over to the time-keepers. Their conversation was animated. Then they went to Miles and the other swimmer in the lane next to him. Miles and the other guy nodded. Miles held his hand out and shook the other guy's hand. They were both smiling. Was it a tie?

"Ladies and gentlemen, the race was so close that our timekeepers have the same time. Our officials need to go over the footage from the underwater cameras. We'll announce the new State Champion in the Boy's 200 Meter Freestyle as soon as we can. Let's give our competitors a hand." The building was filled with applause as Miles and the others got out of the pool.

When we finally stopped cheering, everyone sat back down and waited while the swimmers gathered into their teams. Miles spoke to a couple of the guys while everyone waited.

Eventually, the officials came out of the little room with medals. One of them moved to the side of the pool with the starting blocks and turned on the microphone.

"Ladies and gentlemen, after reviewing the footage, it's unanimous. The new State Champion for Boy's 200 Meter Freestyle is... Miles Huntington." All of us stood up and cheered.

Miles moved out from our school's team and met the officials. They put the medal around Miles' neck. His face and ears were flaming red when he bowed to the crowd. I could tell from here that he just wanted to melt into the background.

The crowd started to break up as the swimmers went into the locker rooms. The building was almost empty when I looked across the pool and saw the twins.

"We should find out if the twins are coming tonight," I thought out loud. Asher got to his feet, Zeke grumbled as he got to his. They both went over without another word. Guilt ate at me. I kept sending them over to get ignored.

Miles came back out in his track pants, shirt and sandals again, this time carrying a gym bag. When he reached us, Rory pulled him into a guy hug and whispered to him. Miles' face and ears turned pink before Rory let go.

"Thanks," Miles said quietly to him.

"Okay, now, I need to get back to work. Go rest up," Rory told us before he headed toward the others.

I looked over at Miles. "So, how close was it really?"

Miles let out a breath. "Extremely. A quarter of a second. Johanson really picked it up since last year."

"Well, win or lose, you'll always be our Miles and we're all proud of you," I told him honestly.

Miles' ears turned red. "Thanks," he muttered as he set down his bag.

"You're welcome, Nemo," I said with a grin. His eyes shot to mine.

"Did... did you just call me Nemo?" he asked, confused.

"Yep."

"You're calling me a fish?" he asked again.

"Nope." I smiled bigger. "I was thinking more like Captain Nemo, from 'Twenty Thousand Leagues Under the Sea.'" I shrugged, then looked down at Hades. "If you don't like it..."

"No," he said quietly, "I do." I glanced up only to meet his warm eyes. The moment stretched, my heart hammered.

"Those morons," Zeke growled, tearing my attention from Miles. Zeke was scowling as they came back over.

Asher didn't look any happier as he clapped Miles on the shoulder. "Congrats."

"Thanks." Miles looked back over his shoulder to the twins. "Give me a few minutes."

Miles headed over to the twins. Asher sat down in front of me next to Hades. It wasn't long before the twins left.

Asher got to his feet and turned to me. "Come on, Ally girl. We have snacks to make."

THREE HOURS later I was wrist deep in cookie dough. Asher was pulling potato chips out of the oven while I was making balls for thumbprint cookies.

Apparently, Miles' favorites were the ones with a dollop of chocolate in the middle. So, I was trying not to screw them up as Asher worked on the other snacks.

I looked at the ball I made in my hand and put it down on the wax paper. I made a thumbprint. Only the dough ball fell apart. I growled.

"What's wrong, Ally?" Asher asked as he changed the temp on the oven.

"This should be easy," I snapped. "Make a ball, make a thumbprint and move on." Asher came over to stand next to me. I sighed and looked up at him. "What am I doing wrong?"

Asher bit back a smile as he looked at my attempts. "Okay, grab some dough." I picked up a destroyed dough ball off the waxed paper.

He picked one up too. "I think you're not applying enough pressure to make it a solid ball of dough." He started rolling the dough in his hands. "If you don't get the air out it'll fall apart."

"So, push harder," I summed up as I started rolling.

"Yeah." He looked at the ball in his hands. "Now, we roll it to smooth it out. It makes a better circle if the surface is smoother." I mimicked what he was doing.

"Now put the dough on the baking sheet," he said. I put my dough ball down next to his perfect one. I grumbled wordlessly. Next to his, mine looked like a three-year old's work.

Asher took my hand and held onto my thumb. "Now, we lightly press down." His voice was soft in my ear as he lifted my thumb out of the dough. It wasn't perfect, but it was a thumb print cookie. I smiled.

"So," I said. "When do we put the chocolate in?"

"When they are almost done." He looked at the rest of my cookies and chuckled. "Why can't I teach you to bake?" He reached out and picked up another one of my destroyed cookies.

I shrugged. "I don't know." I looked up at him as he was re-rolling the dough. "It just doesn't stay in my head." I smiled. "Besides, my talents lie elsewhere."

He chuckled. "I hope so, because you certainly can't bake."

I looked up at him with a narrowed gaze while I reached into the bag of flour. "You brat." I tossed the flour at his face. It hit and flew everywhere. He threw the dough at me as I grabbed the flour bag.

He grabbed the sugar and nailed me in the shoulder. War ensued. At some point he stole the flour away from me and I went diving for the dough.

When we finally called it, we were both covered and the kitchen was a mess. Most of Miles' cookie dough was on the floor or covering us.

We were laughing as we cleaned up at the sink. Asher wet a towel and lifted my chin. He started cleaning flour and dough off my face gently. I met his eyes and grew still. His ocean eyes were warm, his hands slowly wiping the mess off my face. My body warmed for the first time in months. His gaze ran down my face then back to meet mine. He opened his mouth.

"Are you fucking kidding me?" A shrill shout had us jumping apart and turning around. Jessica was in the kitchen doorway. "You're really dating that skank?"

Asher sighed. "Jess, let's talk in the family room." He moved through the kitchen and closed the door behind him. I should probably go. If Jessica was going to have a shit fit, I wasn't interested in listening to it. I started washing my hands in the sink.

"This is my house too!" Jessica screamed. "And I don't want that slut in here! I don't care if you're fucking her!"

"Knock it off, Jess!" Asher shouted. I went still as I was drying my hands with a paper towel when Asher continued to raise his voice. "If you haven't noticed, you don't do shit around here. And I'm sick of it."

"What the hell are you talking about?" Jessica shouted. Wow, did the girl do anything but? I threw the towel away and put a leash on Hades.

"I pay the bills, I handle the house, and you go out and do whatever the hell you want!" Asher snapped. "Then you come in and expect to control who can come in this house? Not happening. In fact, forget having money. Until you help out around here, you're cut off."

"That's my money too, Asher!" she snapped. Yeah, I needed to go.

"No, it's not," Asher countered. "And until you stop acting like a brat, you're not getting a dime."

I was at the door when the sound of skin hitting skin echoed through the house.

My mind grew quiet. I opened the kitchen door in time to watch Asher turn back to his sister, cursing as a red hand print was already starting to show on his face.

Oh. Hell. No. I dropped Hades' leash and strode down the hallway to the foyer. Asher didn't see me until it was too late. Neither did Jessica.

I swung and clocked her with a right hook across the face. She stumbled, I grabbed her shirt and pulled her back to me.

"I fucking warned you," I growled. "You hit him. I hit you!" I

slammed my fist into her face again, the pain in my hand not register-
ing. She went down hard. Adrenaline had me going for her again.

Arms wrapped around my waist, I was lifted off my feet. I fought
to get free until a rich baritone cut through the blood rushing through
my ears.

"Ally! Calm down!" Asher shouted. "Ally, it's me, stop! You made
your point!"

"She can't do that shit!" I snapped as I tried to pry his arms off
my waist.

"Ally, stop!" Asher barked. I stopped fighting him. I hung in his
arms, trapped against his chest with my feet dangling inches off the
floor. I took deep breaths as a crying, bleeding Jessica scrambled to
her feet and turned to us. Her nose was bleeding and a bruise was
already forming along her cheekbone. Damn, I had been aiming for
her eye.

"I'm calling the cops," she snapped as she pulled out her phone.
Asher put my feet on the floor.

"Go ahead, bitch!" I snapped back.

"Jess, don't," Asher ordered, his voice hard. "If you do that, you'll
regret it."

Jessica wiped the blood off her face as she put her phone to her
ear. "Not when Dad hears about how you let her hit me," she
shot back.

"Oh, so you can hit him but no one can hit you?" I shouted, Asher's
arms tightened around me, keeping me in place. "You're a piece
of work!"

"I need the police, my brother's girlfriend just attacked me." Jessica
sounded pathetic on the phone.

"Jess. You don't want to do that," Asher warned. She shot him a
look and gave him their address. Jessica hung up with a smug look on
her face. Obviously I hadn't hit her hard enough.

"Can I hit her again?" I asked seriously. "If I'm going to be arrested
I should at least get a *really* good shot in."

"Don't even think about it," Asher warned. I grumbled wordlessly
as sirens came closer.

I couldn't stand the smug look on Jessica's face. So, I wiped it off. "Oh, I wouldn't be too thrilled, Jessica. I can still press charges against you for those pictures last October."

Jessica's smile dropped. I smirked. The siren stopped outside the house.

"I think you hitting me is going to speak louder," Jessica said, trying to sound confident.

I snorted. I let her think that. There was a knock on the door.

"Police. We got a call," a man's voice called through the door.

"Come in," Asher called. The door opened. The police officer walked in and surveyed us.

"Thank God, that bitch hit me!" Jessica immediately started crying. I rolled my eyes. I went to open my mouth.

"Ally, don't," Asher whispered. I hesitated. "Please. Trust me." SHIT. If I didn't call Jessica out on those photos I was going to go to the station. But Asher asked me not to... Fuck. I closed my mouth.

"We'll separate everyone and we'll figure this out," the officer announced. This wasn't going to be good for me.

IN THE END, two other officers arrived. Asher was in the kitchen, Jessica was in the family room and, being the less beat up of the two, I was in cuffs on the front porch.

The cop who put them on me recognized me from last January. He was nice enough to let my keep my hands in front of me. I thanked him.

We had attracted quite the crowd. Neighbors were out on their porches watching. Not the twins, or Maria. She was still helping her sister get her kids home.

Jessica was still crying crocodile tears when the first cop on the scene came out. He was the one who recognized me from January. Officer Daniels eyed me.

"You're Rory's niece, aren't you?" he asked bluntly.

I nodded. Guilt ate at my stomach as I looked away from him, only to see the hand cuffs and my scraped-up knuckles. Rory was going to kill me. Or send me away. My chest ached as my eyes burned. I bit my lower lip hard to push back the tears. Rory wouldn't do that. That's just your fear talking. I just wished it didn't have such a loud voice.

"Yeah," I muttered.

He nodded, then looked back through the front window into the family room. Jessica suddenly wasn't crying anymore. Shocker. Officer Daniels turned back to me.

"What's your story?" he asked.

"She hit Asher, I hit her... more," I stated simply. He nodded as if he expected it.

"Here's the deal," he said. "Jessica wants to press charges. However, Asher said if she did, he would press charges against his sister." I blinked up at him. Really? Asher would do that? I didn't know what to think, or how to feel about that. Except grateful he was willing to back me. "It's clear cut what happened, and quite frankly, it's a paperwork nightmare," the cop announced. "No charges will be filed by anyone." His gaze met mine. "Rory, however, is stuck at a traffic accident on the highway and wants you home now."

I blinked. "My Blazer is-"

"Rory said to leave it," he said as he uncuffed me. I picked up Hades' leash.

Officer Daniels grabbed my arm and walked me to his cop car. Every eye in the neighborhood watched as he put us in the back seat. He shut the door and walked around. I didn't even get to say good-bye to Asher.

The drive to Rory's was quiet. Officer Daniels didn't try to make conversation.

When he pulled up to the house, he had to let us out of the back. I could feel the neighbors watching as he walked me to the door.

"Thank you for the ride," I muttered before I closed the door. He just nodded and headed back to his car. I rearmed the alarm and let Hades off the leash.

When I turned Tara was sitting there, gaping.

Oh, come on.

"Did you just come home in a cop car?" Tara asked amazed. She smiled. "Dad is so going to kill you." I didn't answer. I simply turned and went upstairs to my room.

I closed the door behind Hades. I flopped down on my bed, different scenarios running through my head. Would Rory really send me away? My heart ached at the thought. No, no, he wouldn't do that. He knew I didn't have anywhere else to go. Mostly to stop myself from thinking those thoughts, I texted Miles.

Alexis: I don't think I'll make it to your game night tonight.

Miles: Why? What's wrong?

Guilt ate at me. It was Miles' big day and I'd just ruined it.

Alexis: Jessica hit Asher, I hit her, she called the cops. I came home in a cop car. Just the usual.

My phone rang instantly. It was Miles.

"What happened?" Miles demanded. I explained what happened and how I was waiting for Rory to get home to decide my fate. At the end, he was quiet.

"Are you mad that I ruined game night?" I asked cringing.

"No, not at all," he said softly. "I'm actually grateful. It's about time Jessica learned she can't just hit Asher."

"Well, she's got a bruise and a bloody nose from it," I assured him.

"How angry is Rory?" Miles asked.

I sighed. "I don't know, but he had the cop bring me home. The Blazer is still at Asher's."

"That's probably not a positive sign," Miles admitted.

A door slammed downstairs.

"Alexis Luanna Delaney, get your ass down here!" Rory shouted. My heart jumped into my throat.

"Shit, he's home. Gotta go," I said quickly before hanging up.

I got off my bed and headed downstairs with my pulse pounding in my ears.

By the time I came off the stairs Rory, still in his uniform, was pacing. Tara was still in the far armchair, grinning happily.

The furious look on his face made my lungs tight. I bit the corner of my bottom lip as I moved to stand next to the empty armchair.

"You had the cops called on you," Rory stated. I nodded. "You hit her. How many times?"

"Who did she hit?" Tara demanded. Rory turned to her.

"Tara, go to your room, now," he snapped. She huffed as she got up and headed upstairs.

The door upstairs slammed before he turned back to me. "Answer."

"Twice." I cringed.

"She hit Asher, so you hit her twice?" he asked, distinctly.

"Yeah, I was going for more when he pulled me off her. I kinda snapped," I admitted.

"That's assault, Lexie," he stated.

"I know," I muttered.

"She can press charges!" he barked.

"She's not," I assured him. "Asher threatened to press charges on her."

He sighed, ran his hand through his hair and met my eyes again. "I understand why you did it. But you came home in a cop car, Lexie." He met my gaze. "You're grounded for two weeks."

Okay….

"What does that mean, exactly?" I asked carefully. I had never been grounded before. Since Dad died, no one cared enough to know where I was.

Rory let out a breath, his shoulders sagging. "It means you're staying home," he said, his voice tired. "No leaving the house and no going out with the guys. Got it?"

"Uh, can I leave to go to the cemetery and come straight back? You know, soul crossing?" I asked, hesitant to even open my mouth. "Otherwise this place is going to get surrounded again."

He nodded. "Then straight back here. You understand?"

"Yes, sir."

He gestured toward the stairs. "Go to your room until dinner."

I hurried my ass upstairs and into my room. I sat down on the edge of my bed and let out a deep breath. He wasn't going to send me away. Something inside me finally let go. I didn't want to examine it too closely. I picked up my phone and used the group text.

Alexis: Well, I'm grounded for two weeks.

I didn't have to wait long for a reply.

Zeke: Asher told us what happened. How many swings did you get in?

I grinned as I typed.

Alexis: Not enough to make me happy.

Asher: Ally.

Alexis: I warned her before, I swear.

Miles: I assume Rory won't allow us to have game night at your house tonight?

I thought about it.

Alexis: If one of you ask, maybe?

Miles: Give me a moment.

Zeke: So, how are your hands?

I held my right hand out and moved my fingers. There was swelling, a few scrapes and some redness but that was it.

Alexis : Not bad. I'll get some ice after dinner.

Miles: Rory says not tonight but tomorrow can be a go.

Asher: Damn.

Alexis: Sorry guys.

I spent the rest of the afternoon texting with the boys.

I kept hoping Isaac or Ethan would chime in. But they stayed quiet. I went to bed that night worried about them.

CHAPTER 16

SATURDAY MORNING

*T*he next morning, I woke up late and drove to the cemetery. The large group of souls had grown overnight, again.

"About time," one of them shouted.

"Oh, forgive me for sleeping." I snapped. "I should be at your damn whim every moment of the day and night." The man went to say something but one of the women touched his shoulder. He shut up. "Alright, we're doing twenty again today. We'll try a few more after, so line up." I announced.

Everyone did as the others had. They all linked hands. I went to the first in line and felt my barriers shake. I reached out with my will and grabbed onto all of them. Then I dropped.

We landed in the Veil and I instantly let go of everyone. I stepped back and watched as they looked around. Balls of golden light began falling from the Way, doors opened. The dead crossed. It was nice, but I had seen it all before. A light rain fell through the Veil making me smile. It wasn't until the last soul had gone through the Way that I noticed there was still someone here.

It was a little boy. He had to be around eight years old. He had high waisted trousers with suspenders and a pin-striped long-sleeve shirt.

His hair was a bowl cut and his eyes made my heart sink. They looked older than they should have.

I walked through the grass towards him. As I moved closer he became more unsettling. I lowered my barriers just a little to figure out what it was about him. My throat burned and squeezed tight. He'd been strangled. Poor kid. I shut my barriers so I couldn't feel him anymore.

The rain was a light sprinkle now. He looked up at the sky and closed his eyes as the rain sprinkled onto his face. A small smile teased at his lips. I focused on him.

"I forgot that feeling," he said quietly as he stepped further away.

"Feels good, right?" I asked. He nodded slowly. Those unsettling eyes opened on the Way. He looked down at the muddy ground. "What's your name?" I asked gently.

"Dennis," he whispered as he crossed his arms over his chest. He wasn't talking, they always talked.

"My name is Lexie," I said in my soothing voice. "This is the Veil. It looks kind of scary right now, but that's because it's sick. I'm trying to make it better."

Dennis looked around, then met my eyes. My heart dropped. His eyes were so full of pain it was shocking. "What happened to you?" I asked before I could think.

"A lot," he said. It wasn't much, but from the look in his eyes it was more than enough.

He stepped away from me and strolled through the grass. Towards the ledge over the abyss. My heart slammed as I took a step towards him.

"Dennis, be careful," I told him, moving slowly through the grass. "You don't want to go that way."

He reached the ledge and looked down. "Why's that?"

I moved a little faster. Something was wrong. I could feel it. "It's where souls go to be unmade."

"That's an option?" he asked in his deadpan voice. I reached the ledge.

"It's only one way," I admitted. "But from what I've seen of those crossing, and those who go into the abyss, crossing over is much better."

He scoffed, "Sure, it is."

He was thinking about it. I had to reach him. I dropped my barriers further. His pain hit me like a freight train. I staggered under it; his memories, the abuse. The nightmare that his life had been. Tears fell instantly.

"Oh, God," I gasped as I fought to keep his memories his and not mine. My hands gripped the mud and grass, helping to ground me. He turned to me, those dark, empty eyes met mine. Because that's what they were. Empty. Empty of hope, love, empty of anything this boy had been in life. The horror and degradation he went through... it stripped it away. Stripped him away. I tried to breathe under the weight of it.

"Sometimes it's better to not exist," he told me.

I shook my head. "There's always a chance for a better tomorrow." I held his gaze. "The hope that tomorrow will be better. They can't hurt you anymore, not here. Tomorrow *will* be better."

He blinked at me, then looked back at the pit. "No, it won't." He stepped out onto the ledge.

Adrenaline had me on my feet and running the last steps between us. He jumped. I grabbed his hand and pulled back. He looked up at me with pity on his face as he dangled over the darkness.

"Zahur!" I screamed as I tried to pull him back up the side of the cliff. Dennis dangled limp against the cliff, the abyss just below him. "Zahur! I need you now!"

Hands grabbed my arms.

"What the hell are you doing?" Zahur shouted.

"He jumped," I growled through my teeth. Dennis' eyes were dead as he waited to drop.

"Then let him go!" Zahur snapped. I looked at her, her eyes blazing. "It's his decision."

I gaped at her as she broke my hold on Dennis. The boy dropped into the abyss. I watched as he disappeared into nothing, then dropped to the ground where I sat. Staring into the pit.

Zahur knelt beside me and forced me to look into her eyes. "You can *not* stop them from making this decision. You can try to talk them out of it, but you can not try to force them to cross. You bring them here, but from there, they have to choose and *you* have to respect it."

I nodded dully. I couldn't believe what just happened.

Zahur's eyes softened. "This isn't your fault, Alexis. Sometimes a soul goes through so much damage that they don't want to exist anymore." She let go of my chin and turned to look at the pit. "That's why there is another option." She turned back to me. "Go back, take it easy today." Still in a daze, I pulled myself out of the Veil.

THE SUN WAS STILL SHINING and birds were still chirping. The world went on like it always had, like it always would. In the world, it didn't matter that Dennis' soul was gone from existence. Not to the world at least.

The other souls frowned at me. "How many this time?" Mr. Davis demanded. I shook my head and walked away. "Hey! What about us?"

"No more today." I snapped over my shoulder before I climbed into the Blazer.

"That's not fair!" he shouted. I didn't care, I drove off.

I don't remember the drive home. I just remember walking in the door. I blinked as I looked around the empty living room, then let Hades off his leash. I didn't want to stay inside, not right now. I walked out back only to find Tara. She was in her two-piece slathering on the sunblock.

She looked up at me and scowled. "What do you want?"

"I'm going to sit on the dock," I muttered. Tara turned on her iPod and put her earbuds in.

"Yeah, well, leave me the hell alone," she snapped.

I ignored her as I headed out to the end of the dock and sat down. Hades followed and laid down next to me. I rubbed his ears as I watched the water and tried to deal with what I saw.

He just... jumped. Wiped himself from existence. I pulled out my phone needing to talk to someone, then hesitated.

I wanted to talk to Ethan. Tell him what I saw, but the way he looked at me... I closed my eyes and hung my head. It hurt. It hurt more than I ever thought it would. I put my phone back down on the dock.

Dennis' life ran through my mind. He'd been abused by his parents then given over to a boarding school in the 20's. Where he was tortured, raped, beaten, and treated worse than dirt. He had fought. Every day. After everything that he had been through, he still fought when the headmaster decided to kill him. Only to let him win in the end? I knew I couldn't really feel the hell he went through. I only felt a little and it dropped me. But I kept asking why?

I was so engrossed in my own thoughts I didn't notice Hades getting up, or someone coming down the dock.

"Red." Isaac's voice pulled me back. I got up and all but tackled him in a hug. He didn't seem to mind, in fact he squeezed me back just as hard.

"I was worried about you," I told him, my voice muffled against his shirt. He buried his face into my hair and held me tight. He took several deep breaths. I didn't want to let go, I just wanted to stay there breathing in limes until everything went away.

"Get a room you two!" Tara shouted from the shore. I flipped her off without letting go of him. Isaac took a deep breath then raised his head. I looked up at him and worried even more.

He had deep bags under his eyes. I reached up and held his undamaged cheek.

"Are you okay?" I asked lamely. Of course he wasn't okay, look at him!

He shook his head. "No, no I'm not." His voice was thick as he kept an arm around my waist. His amber eyes were shadowed as they met mine.

"I'm sorry-"

"No." He shook his head. "You don't need to be sorry. I get why you didn't tell us. I'm not even mad about it anymore." He let go and stepped around me to sit at the end of the dock. I joined him, my hip and shoulder touching his. He took my hand and watched the water. "What did Sophie tell you?"

I squeezed his hand. "She told me she calls you two Eth and Izzy." He kept his gaze on the water. "She's told me about the pranks she used to pull on you two." His jaw clenched. "And embarrassing things from your childhood. Did you really wear a Superman cape for a week straight when you were eight?"

He sighed. "Yeah... that's Sophie." His voice was thick. He turned to me the shadows in his eyes turning his usual amber to a deep chocolate. "Is that all she told you?" I nodded.

Relief filled his face. I only saw it for a second before he looked back at the water. What did he expect Sophie to tell me?

"Asher told us about the nightmares you had in December. That they were bad." He changed the subject, his voice still thick. I went with it.

Expecting a lecture, I answered, "Yeah."

"Miles and Zeke aren't too happy with you about that," he told me. I snorted hard.

"They can get in line," I grumbled. He looked down at me, his brow furrowed.

"Red, what's going on?"

"You and Ethan are mad at me. Now Zeke and Miles are too, and the dead..." I shook my head. He didn't need to hear this. He had enough to deal with already.

"Lexie, what's happening with the ghosts?" he asked seriously.

I looked into his eyes and finally gave in. "They're getting stronger, and pushier. The other day when I crossed that rotting ghost? It wasn't because I chose to. It was because they brought him to me and basically threw him at me."

"Shit," he said with feeling. I nodded. "Anything else happen this week?"

"This morning..." I shook my head and looked down at the water.

"What happened this morning?" he asked gently.

"A soul jumped into the pit." I tried not to see it again but I couldn't help it. "He unmade himself." A fresh wave of tears started to fill my eyes. "He was just a kid." Isaac wrapped his arm around me, I leaned against him and took deep breaths.

"I'm sorry, Lexie," he whispered as he held me. He let me cry on him until I was done.

When I lifted my head from his shoulder and wiped my face he broke the silence. "You need to tell the others."

I looked up at him confused. "Why?"

"Because, they need to know," he pointed out. "Hell, they want to know what you're dealing with. So do I."

"I just don't want the ghost shit to touch you guys," I said tiredly.

"So what if it does? It's our fucking choice." He reached over and lifted my chin, forcing me to meet his eyes. "You better start sharing. Or Zeke will put you on permanent probation."

I sighed. He gave me a small smirk then let go of my chin.

He looked out at the water. "Tell me something good that happened this week, Red, even if it's something ridiculous."

I smiled as I looked out at the water. "I told Tara that she was chasing Asher and Zeke like a bitch in heat," I offered. He snickered. I started smiling.

"Nice, Red," he said. "Anything else?"

"I hit Jessica," I admitted.

"I know, how'd that feel?" He wrapped his arm around me and gave me a side hug.

"Pretty good," I admitted. We broke into a fit of giggles.

We sat and talked about nothing important for half an hour. I was laughing when that chill ran down my neck like a blade. I slapped my hand to my neck and hissed.

"Red?"

"There's a ghost somewhere," I whispered. I got to my feet, Isaac followed. I started down the dock then paused. Where... where was the ghost? I looked up and down the shore ignoring Tara. "I don't see it."

Isaac looked down at me. "What are you talking about?"

I gestured with both hands towards the shore. "I don't see

anything. There's just Tara on the shore." My stomach knotted. This wasn't right.

"Let's get inside," he suggested.

I was mid-nod when something grabbed my pant leg and yanked. Cold water closed over my head as I was pulled under. Heart slamming, my barriers shook. I looked down. It was Mr. Davis from the cemetery. He kept dragging me down. SHIT! I reached for my will just as my barriers broke. The world disappeared as he poured in like stagnant green water. I couldn't patch my barrier, that was gone. He slipped in and tried to take control. Oh, hell no!

CHAPTER 17

Isaac

*L*exie went into the water hard. I stood there stunned for a second. When she didn't resurface I realized what was happening. No, no, no, no. Not again! I dove off the dock and into the cold water.

I opened my eyes and searched for her, my heart pounding against my ribs. I searched the water until my lungs were begging for air. I came up, took a lung full and dove back under.

I finally found the bubbles, and followed them. She was down near the bottom. Terror tore through me as I swam down towards her. She was unconscious, blood drifting off her face. By the time I reached her, the bubbles had stopped.

I grabbed her limp body and pushed off the bottom of the lake. I brought her to the surface as fast as I could, my own lungs burning for air. Come on, Red, don't die on me too. I broke the surface gasping. I brought her face above water. She took a big deep breath. Blood kept pouring from her nose. SHIT! I swam for the shore.

Tara was up and had her phone in her hand by the time I reached the shallows. I lifted Lexie into my arms and ran for the house.

"I'll call 911!" Tara shouted.

"No!" I shot back. As we got to the house, Tara opened the back door. "Call Rory!" I ran into the house and all but busted Rory's bedroom door open.

Then I had her in the bathroom. I sat on the toilet lid and started to strip her shirt off, tearing it in the rush.

"What the fuck are you doing?" Tara shouted, horrified.

"Call Rory!" I snapped. Tara was gaping at me with the phone in her hand. I reached over and started the shower with hot water. Then I lifted Lexie in my arms again and laid her down in the bottom of the tub under the spray. My hands went to her pants and peeled the denim off her legs. I threw them over my shoulder, then went to the cabinet under the sink and pulled out the large tub of salt that Rory had stored there since last time.

Tara was yelling names at me, calling me a pervert as I poured salt over Red's skin. I knelt down next to the tub and started frantically rubbing it into her arms, legs and shoulders. "Come on Lexie, don't do this to me. I can't lose you." My voice shook but I kept talking to her while I scrubbed. "Wake up Lexie, please..."

"Isaac! Lexie!" Rory shouted. I kept scrubbing.

"Bathroom!" I shouted back, my voice cracking. Come on, I can't lose you too. Come on, Red.

"Dad! He took off her clothes!" Tara screamed.

"It's fine! Move, Tara!" Rory growled as he shoved past her to get into the bathroom. "What happened?"

"Ghost pulled her into the lake and jumped her. She hasn't woken up yet," I answered quickly. Rory moved away then came back with a blue Lexie kit.

The kit! I forgot about the fucking kit! Rory pulled out the vial of salted holy water and poured it into her mouth then went back to working the salt into her arms. I kept scrubbing her legs.

"Come on Kid, wake up for us," Rory chanted as we worked. A few more heart pounding moments and finally, her lips moved. I couldn't hear her. But her lips were moving.

"She's awake," I announced with relief that left me limp against the side of the tub.

Rory held her face and pulled out a pen light. "Lexie, open your eyes!" Her eyes fluttered but they didn't open. Rory didn't wait. He forced her eyelid open and shined the light into each eye. She was crying by the time he was done. "No bleed." He leaned against the wall in relief.

Lexie curled up in a ball in the bottom of the tub, still crying. In only her bra and underwear, it killed me. I pulled a towel out from under the sink and covered her. It was soaked in seconds but it made me feel better now that she was covered.

Rory brought his hand down on my shoulder. "Go grab some of my sweats and a shirt to wear while we dry your clothes." I shook my head, my eyes still on Lexie.

"I'm not moving," I muttered, my voice thick. The bathroom was silent except for the shower.

"What the hell is going on?" Tara asked.

Rory hung his head and cursed. "Lexie almost died. So, let us take care of her, call the guys and then I'll tell you what's going on. Go to your room until then."

Tara leaned against the door jamb and crossed her arms over her chest. "I'm not asking, Tara." Rory snapped.

Tara stormed off. I ignored them, my entire focus on Lexie. She was completely limp, she must have passed out. It had been too close, way too close.

After a while, Rory got an ear thermometer out of the medicine cabinet. I moved the shower head so it wasn't hitting her in the face anymore.

Rory took her temp. "Okay, we can move her." I shut off the water, grabbed a fresh towel and switched it with the soaked one.

"Your room?" I asked as I lifted her out of the tub and cradled her against my chest. Shit, she always felt so small...

"Yeah, Hades is going ape shit out there. He'll be able to stay with her in my bed," Rory decided as he led me into his room. He pulled back the covers. I carefully put her in the bed, took the towel and covered her immediately with the blankets. I used the towel to start blotting the water from her hair.

Rory opened his bedroom door. Hades came charging in, jumped onto the bed and sniffed her body and face until he was satisfied. Then he nosed his way under the covers and disappeared. From the lumps under the blankets it looked like he had laid along her side like a living heater. It made the vice in my chest ease a little.

"Good boy. You take care of Red," I said. He thumped his tail once under the covers.

"Go change, and we'll call the guys," Rory said. I shook my head before sitting down on the bed.

"I'm not going anywhere," I told him, still watching her chest rise and fall. She's alive. I kept reminding myself as Rory moved around the room.

He held out some clothes. "I'll stay with her. Go change and I'll put your clothes in the dryer," Rory ordered. I hesitated. "She'll be okay, Isaac. I promise."

I nodded before forcing myself to take the clothes and go back into the bathroom. I wasn't going far from her side, not until she was awake. I changed quickly. Fear clenched my chest. I can't lose her. I can't. She's... I can't lose her. Eyes burning, I picked up my clothes and hers, then headed back into Rory's room.

She was still breathing. I handed Rory our clothes before moving to the other side of the bed and climbing on. I sat at the end of the bed and watched her chest rise and fall. She was breathing. She was alive.

Rory's hand came down on my shoulder and squeezed. "You saved her Isaac, she's going to be okay." I nodded absently but I refused to budge. He squeezed my shoulder again. "I'll call the guys," Rory said before heading out the door.

I moved closer and took her hand in mine, needing to feel her. Her hand was smooth, with calloused fingers from drawing so much. I memorized every detail of her hand as I thought about what happened.

I can't lose her. She's... she's Lexie. Losing her would be it. I couldn't take it. I decided to stop thinking and just watch her breathe.

Miles

MY CELL RANG. I looked away from my computer screen and checked the caller. It was Rory.

"Hi, Rory."

"Miles, it's about Lexie," he said, his voice troubled. My shoulders instantly grew tense at the sound of his voice.

"Is she alright?" I asked immediately. Please, let her be alright, please.

"She's okay," he assured me. I let out a deep breath, the tension in my shoulders easing as I relaxed. But Rory wasn't done. "I'm calling to tell you she was pulled into the lake and jumped about an hour ago. We were lucky Isaac was here at the time. He got her out of the water and in the shower. She's already woken up and passed back out." I took a deep breath and let it out. I had to be calm. I was the calm one.

"I'll head over. Is there anything she needs?" I asked as I braced my elbow on my desk and rested my forehead on my hand.

"No, she's out. Isaac won't leave her side," he said. I closed my eyes. That sounded like Isaac. He'd be sitting there watching her, looking for every twitch or eye flicker. Just like I was going to. I put that thought away and focused.

"Have you told the others?" I asked.

"I'm about to call them," he said. I nodded absently.

"I'll call them." I decided. "But Rory, could you watch Isaac? Make sure he doesn't leave?"

"I don't think that's going to happen, but yeah. I'll watch him." he agreed.

"Thanks. I'll be over after I tell the others."

"See ya then." Rory hung up. I set my phone down and leaned both elbows onto my desk.

This needed to end. She couldn't keep getting jumped. It had to be doing damage, right? I closed my eyes and struggled for control. Her face flashed in my mind, how she looked the last time she was jumped.

My poor Angel. We had to find a way to make it stop and not just when she's wearing her bracelets.

I took several deep calming breaths as I got to my feet. I picked up my phone and called Zeke. It went to voicemail. My blood boiled.

"Zeke. Lexie's been jumped. Rory says she's fine and that she already woke up. I know you're at your appointment but damn it, Zeke. Leave your phone on," I said in a cold voice. I hung up then swept my keyboard and books off my desk in a fit of anger.

Zeke was having a bad time, I understood how he felt. But he had the worst time when something happened to Lexie, and leaving a message wasn't going to help that. I took several more calming breaths. I needed to finish calling the others, then get over there and see her for myself. I picked up my phone.

Ethan

I WAS SITTING on the back porch of Ryan's house staring out at the lawn when my phone rang. It was Miles. I closed my eyes and took a breath. He probably wanted to talk about Sophie and I wasn't ready to. But... I never ignored Miles.

"What?" I answered.

"It's Lexie," Miles said instantly. I sat up straight as my pulse picked up. "She was jumped an hour ago." I grew still inside. She was jumped...

My lungs grew tight as I asked, "Is she okay?"

"She's alright, thanks to Isaac." His voice worried. "She was pulled into the lake when it happened. He got her out and took care of her." Isaac was there? He saved her? It took me a few heartbeats to take that in. Ever since Sophie died... "Ethan?"

"I'm here," I said, my voice tight.

"Are you going over?" he asked simply. I scoffed. It was Lexie. How could I not?

"Yeah, I'm headed over now," I told him, before hanging up. I rested my elbows on my knees and hid my face in my hands. She was okay. She was fine. It didn't help the tightness in my chest. I closed my eyes and fought back tears. We almost lost her. I hadn't talked to her in days and I almost lost her.

She had been right not to tell us about Sophie. It would only have made things worse. And Isaac didn't need worse. I dropped my hands and got to my feet. I needed to see her, see her awake and talking. Tell her that I'm an asshole.

I headed inside for my keys. I walked through Ryan's house, not really seeing it. I grabbed my keys off the table next to the front door.

"What's going on?" Ryan asked, coming from the kitchen with an orange in his hands.

I hesitated before telling him. "Lexie had a seizure, I'm headed over there to see how she's doing." Ryan's eyes snapped to me, his face stunned.

"Shit. I'll go with you," he said as he put the orange down.

"No, you're not." I decided.

He met my eyes. "I'm worried about her too, man."

"You need to back off from Lexie," I said before I could think.

He eyed me, then smirked. "You like her too." I shot him a look. Did it really take him this long to figure that out?

"No shit," I growled. Ryan's brows went up. I headed for the door. "I'll be back later."

Asher

I WAS LAYING in my room watching baseball when my phone rang.

"Hey, Miles."

"Lexie was jumped about an hour ago. A ghost pulled her into the lake," Miles stated, his voice weary. My world froze.

"Is she okay?" I asked instantly, sitting up with my heart in my throat.

"She's alright, Isaac was there. She's already woken up and she's passed out again." he said. I was already moving from my bed to my desk chair and began to pull on my shoes.

"You're sure?" I asked again.

"I haven't seen her yet, but Rory assured me," he admitted. That wasn't good enough. I needed to see her.

"I'm headed over now," I told him before hanging up. I grabbed my keys and hurried downstairs. I was in my truck a moment later. Ally... I fought for control as I drove. Miles said she was pulled into the lake. Did that mean she had water in her lungs when Isaac got her out?

When I get there I'll ask Miles to get the doctor to check her lungs. I'd heard about dry drowning before. I couldn't take that risk with her. I rubbed the back of my neck hard as I stopped at a stop light.

How bad was it this time? Would she have more nightmares? Was it the same ghost as the bowling alley? I needed answers, answers only she could give. It can't be that bad again. I don't think she could take it. Let Ally be okay.

"Please. God, I haven't asked for anything. Not since Mom. Please. Don't take her too." I whispered to no one.

I hadn't believed in God since Mom passed. But if it would help her, I'd believe, I'd beg.

<hr />

Zeke

I SLAMMED the office door behind me and strode down the hall. The fucking doc was being a huge pain in the ass. 'Talk to her about it.' Yeah, like it's that fucking easy. Like anything with Lexie was easy anymore. I stepped outside and headed for my Jeep. Nothing was easy with that girl except...

I growled at myself as I climbed in. That fucking kiss was still in my dreams, every fucking night. I slammed my door and took a deep calming breath. Now she couldn't even hug me. I would give anything to get my hands on Ordin, alone.

I took another deep breath. I remind her of him. That's the reality of it. I got it. I just hated it. I hated reminding her of him, I hated the sad look in her eyes when she looked at me.

My eyes burned and my throat tightened. I took another breath. I had planned to talk to the guys the next morning. Tell them I cared about her. Then… I got the call that she was in the hospital, and my world crashed around me.

For four hours, I thought we might have a chance. That we might work. Then life kicked me in the teeth. No, that would have been easier. Life kicked Lexie in the teeth, and then… I growled again in anger, then slammed my hand into the steering wheel over and over until my eyes stopped burning. I took several more deep breaths.

I wasn't there. I should have fucking been there! I fought for control while I sat there, not even starting the car. I ran through the exercises the doc told me to do. It is the past, I can't fix it. All I can do is work to make it better now. It's not my fault. It was Clay Ordin's. The last felt like a lie. It wasn't. I didn't do that to her. He did. I am not responsible for keeping everyone safe. That felt like a lie too. It wasn't, I know that.

Trying to distract myself, I picked up my cell from the console. I had a message.

"Zeke. Lexie's been jumped. Rory says she's fine and that she already woke up. I know you're at your appointment but damn it, Zeke. Leave your phone on." Miles' voice was cold before he hung up.

I barely noticed. She had been jumped again. I dropped the phone and gripped the steering wheel until my knuckles turned white. How much damage this time? Would she even fucking tell us if there was damage?

I took deep breaths as I fought for control. My Lexie was okay. She already woke up and was passed out again. She's alright. No one touched her, no one physically hurt her…

"God, Lexie…" I muttered as I fought the tightness in my chest to breathe. I needed to get over there. She was probably in bed, curled up with Hades. But I still needed to see her. Feel her pulse, see her breathe. I started the Jeep and focused on not running stop lights. I'm coming, Baby.

WHISPERS FROM THE DEAD

Lexie

I WOKE UP HURTING. My head was pounding and everything ached deeply. Even the bottom of my feet, again. Seriously, why did getting jumped do that? I ran through my memories.

For once in my life after getting jumped, I didn't have a ghost's memories. I had managed to protect myself that much at least. The fucker still surprised me.

I groaned as I opened my eyes slowly. Sunlight was barely coming through the closed curtains. It made the room bearable. I shifted, then gasped. Pain shot through me as my muscles protested.

"Lexie, I've got Rory's pain killers for you," Miles whispered gently. I smiled. Oh, I liked that voice. It soothed something in my brain.

I nodded, braced myself, then sat up quick and whimpered as I rested my back against the headboard. Miles pulled my blankets up to my chest. I held them as I started to be able to focus.

All the guys were sitting in Rory's room on dining chairs. I looked down and blinked. I was only wearing my bra on top. Miles handed me a couple pills, I took them and drank from the glass that he handed me.

"Well, it's official. The dead are getting pushy." I tried a joke. No one laughed.

Something moved against me. Hades peeked his head out from under the covers and climbed out to lay with his head in my lap. I looked over to Isaac. His face was pale. "Did I get dragged into the water?"

"Yeah," Isaac said quietly.

"We were real lucky you held your breath," Asher announced. I winced. I had hoped that I had remembered that wrong. I looked around.

"You guys didn't have to stay-"

"Shut up." Zeke snapped. I winced at the sound. His eyes were burning as they met mine. "While you were out Isaac filled us in on what's been going on with the dead. Why the hell didn't you tell us?" I whimpered and covered my ears as my head throbbed from the sound.

"Zeke, not now," Miles warned quietly.

"Just… give me a few minutes for the sensitivity to go." I mumbled.

Asher went to Rory's dresser and brought me a shirt. It was Zeke's huge blue thermal. I gave him a grateful smile before I pulled it on while keeping the blankets in place. The sleeves covered my hands and the neck hung off my shoulder, but it was exactly what I wanted right now. And pants, but pants could come when I could get out of bed.

"I'll go get your food," Asher said, his voice strained. He headed for the door.

"Thanks, Ash," I called.

He gave me a smile. "No problem, Ally girl." He headed out the door.

I looked at the others, they all looked tired.

"Guys, go, I'm fine now." I tried.

"Shut up," Zeke growled quietly. "We're not going anywhere. As soon as you're feeling better, you're answering some questions."

"I need some air…" Ethan got to his feet and headed out the door. Zeke growled and went after him.

Miles sighed. "Lexie-"

"Go, stop them from killing each other," I told him. Miles hurried around the bed and out the door, closing it behind him. Leaving me alone with Isaac.

He looked bad, and his eyes… he was barely holding it together. He was still, his gaze on the floor.

Needing to touch him I pushed the covers away and put my feet on the floor, repressing a groan at the pain.

"Isaac," I called softly. I needed to hug him, make him feel better but I couldn't reach him yet. Isaac raised his head and met my gaze. His eyes were scared as they filled with tears. He got to his feet then came to me. He dropped to his knees in front of me and wrapped his arms around me, his face pressing against my belly. I held his head and stroked his hair, ran my hands over his shoulders and arms, whispering that I was alright. That I was here. His breathing grew ragged as I held him.

At one point the door opened. I glanced over my shoulder to see Miles. He saw Isaac, then met my eyes and nodded. He closed the door quietly behind him.

"I can't lose you," he told me.

"You saved my ass today. I'm not going anywhere." I whispered back. At least, I hoped I wasn't. This one had shaken me. I hadn't even seen the asshole coming. I kept reminding him that I was alright until he could take a breath normally again. When he eventually let go, he sat back on his knees and wiped his face.

"Let's...let's get you dressed so you can eat," he said uncertainly. My stomach chose that moment to growl, loudly. His lips barely moved into a grin as he got to his feet.

He brought me Asher's Sylvester the Cat pajama bottoms. Asher must have brought my clothes down from my room. Who else would know to bring Zeke's shirt and his bottoms?

Isaac knelt and helped me get my feet into the bottoms. Then he steadied me as I stood. When I went to pull them up I groaned in pain.

He didn't hesitate, he helped pull the bottoms up. I tied the tie myself, awkwardly. I'd never had a guy help me get dressed like this before. Asher did my zipper on my dress for Winter Formal but this was different. It was... more.

He took my arm, we were about to head for the door when it opened and the guys filed through. Shouting came from the main room. Asher had a bowl of food in his hands and came straight to me.

"Change of plans, you're eating in here," Asher told me. I sat down carefully while Miles closed the door behind them.

"What's going on?" I asked as Asher handed me a bowl half full of pasta and the other half chicken. It was in some kind of pinkish sauce. It could have been poison and I still would have eaten it.

"Tara was here when you got jumped," Miles answered. I went still. "She saw everything."

"Shit." I speared some chicken and noodles then took a bite. It tasted familiar and great but I couldn't place it. After I swallowed I looked up at Asher. "This is great but what is it?"

"Cajun chicken fettuccine in a Louisiana sauce. It's what we had the ingredients for in the house." Asher explained. I nodded and kept eating.

I was almost done when I finally had the brainpower to ask. "What was she yelling about out there?" The guys exchanged looks. Oh, this wasn't good.

Miles turned to me. "Rory had managed to put off explaining for a while. They've been talking for half an hour now."

My heart dropped. "Did he tell her that she's not his?"

Asher shook his head while Miles answered. "He told her it skipped a generation once in a while."

I looked down at the comforter and muttered Rory's words. "Sometimes not telling someone something important is for that person's own good."

"Until it almost gets you killed," Zeke growled. I lifted my head and met his eyes. "You've been hiding a lot. It's time to start talking." I didn't even know what to say.

Miles leaned forward in his chair, bringing him to the side of the bed. "Lexie, we've noticed you've been keeping some things to yourself," he said gently. "For example, the dead becoming more aggressive. Or that you were having trouble walking into the house at night."

"Like, what the hell happened the other day at school?" Zeke snapped.

"Zeke," Miles warned. Zeke clenched his jaw. Miles turned back to me. "Is there anything else you haven't told us?"

Exhausted and tired of lying, I nodded. It took me a few heartbeats before I could answer. "I don't want you guys to have to deal with that stuff."

"Ally, we're going to have to deal with that stuff as long we're with you." Asher pointed out gently.

"And we're not going anywhere. So, start talking." Ethan stated.

Heart aching, I met Ethan's eyes as mine burned. "You're not?" I asked quietly.

His eyes ran over me before they met mine again. "I'm not. I know we didn't talk to anyone for a few days, but we just needed time." He looked at Isaac, who was sitting beside him. "We needed time to cool off before we talked to anybody so we wouldn't say shit that we didn't mean."

"It's better to say nothing than to tear into your friends. We don't always pull it off, but if we stay away, we do." Isaac explained. Hell, their silence made sense now.

"Which is why *we* took their lunch to them at the tournament," Asher explained.

"Yeah, they were being little shits," Zeke added. Ethan shot him a look before turning back to me.

"The point is, never doubt that we're all in," Ethan said. He gestured around the group.

"That's how this works. You're all in, or all out."

"We're not asking you to tell us anything you aren't ready to share," Miles explained. "We are asking you to tell us what you're dealing with. What's bothering you? With the dead, with the Veil. We want to know."

"Why do you want to know?" I asked, my eyes filling. My chest tight. "I don't even want to know this stuff."

Miles looked me straight in the eyes and said, "Because it's you. It has happened or is happening to you. And we all love you." He reached up and tucked my hair behind my ear. "So, we need you to tell us what's going on."

I closed my eyes and took a deep breath. My True Self's voice rang through my ears. 'Work on your fear of abandonment, it's annoying as fuck!' I took another deep breath before opening my eyes.

"What do you want to know?" I asked, not knowing where to start.

"Everything." Zeke stated, his voice quiet. Tears fell as I looked down at the comforter. I took several breaths before taking the leap.

"It started a couple of months ago." I began, my voice raspy. "Larger groups of the dead were coming into town more often. So often, I haven't been able to keep up." I reached out and took a drink of water, my trembling hand making it tricky. Miles was there in a heartbeat, steadying my hand so I could drink.

"How many dead would you say are in town?" Miles asked gently.

I shrugged as he set the glass down. "I'd say around five hundred," I estimated. The guys cursed, except for Miles. I continued. "The ghosts started complaining about how long it was taking for me to get them to cross. It wasn't bad at first, just muttering and bitching. Then this guy, Davis, showed up and it got worse."

"How bad, Lexie?" Zeke demanded.

I bit the corner of my lower lip before I could answer. "You know that rotting soul I crossed?" They all nodded or said yeah. "That wasn't by choice. He pretty much threw him at me." Zeke cursed a blue streak then got to his feet and began pacing.

"And you were at the cemetery alone?" Asher asked.

"Yeah. It sucked, but I figured it out, yelled at them and refused to cross anyone else that day," I told them.

Zeke stopped pacing and turned to me. "What happened at school?"

I took a deep breath and let it out before answering. "The ghosts found me in Math. They came right through the walls. I... I did something I'd never done before." I described how I shoved them all from the room and how it had made me sick. That I didn't know what it meant. If my abilities were growing or if I was just desperate. "It scared me," I admitted in a whisper.

"Maybe you should ask Serena," Asher suggested. I looked away from them and to Hades. I started scratching Hades' ears.

"Lexie," Zeke snapped, drawing my attention. "Why won't you go to Serena?"

"I can't trust her," I began. "She knows how to work with the dead, she just doesn't do it."

"That's not what she said before," Zeke growled.

I met his eyes. "She could have helped save Mary Summers and she didn't. But that's not the only reason. Apparently, there's a Witches Council somewhere that polices Magic users. And Necromancers are not their favorite."

"Keep talking, Beautiful," Ethan said with a frown on his face.

"They have rules and if you break them you'll, well, 'Be dealt with.'" Zeke stopped pacing. "And there's a specific rule for Necromancers."

"Which is?" Miles asked. I looked down at the comforter again.

"Raising the dead," I said. "Once that happens the Witches Council deals with them. I've interpreted it as killing them." Zeke cursed, the others were shocked. But I wasn't done. I met Ethan's eyes. "After we told you about Sophie, I went to her and asked some questions. Before I left she said something about... if my abilities are growing as fast as she believed, then it won't be long before I started raising the dead." The room grew silent.

"She threatened you?" Zeke growled.

I looked down at the comforter and nodded. "I took it that way," I said quietly, then muttered to myself. "Hell, maybe that's why no one's made it to thirty."

"No one's made it to thirty?" Asher asked sharply.

I sighed. I might as well tell them now. "No woman in my family has had a thirtieth birthday. The record is twenty-nine years, seven months and eight days."

"Damn it, Lexie," Zeke snapped. "You've been carrying this shit all this time?"

I nodded, waiting for the axe to fall. For them to say enough and walk out the door.

"You didn't need to take this on alone," Miles said softly. I met his warm eyes and could breathe again. "The fact the other women in your family didn't make it to thirty doesn't mean you won't." I gave him a look. "Lexie. They thought they were Seers. They were working with false information. You know what you are. And you have more people to support you than they did."

He had a good point. Why did he always have a good point? "If you're going to bring logic into it," I muttered.

"Well, someone fucking has to," Zeke snapped. "Anything else you're keeping a secret?"

I thought it over and winced. It didn't go unnoticed.

"Lexie?" Miles asked.

"When I found my center, I met someone who looked like me." I met Miles' eyes. "She wasn't my True Self, but she helped me. When I got to the Veil, she told me what I needed to do to fix the Way." I looked down at the comforter again. "And when I struggled with that, she helped again. Since then she's kind of... become my teacher, I guess."

"Does she still look like you?" Ethan asked. "Has she told you what she is, who she is?"

"She still looks like me and hasn't told me what she is," I admitted. "But she told me to call her Zahur."

The guys all shared looks. Some were worried like Asher's and Miles'. Others were angry like Zeke's.

"Anything else?" Ethan asked, his voice strained.

"Unless Isaac didn't tell you about this morning..." My eyes met his. He shook his head. I took a deep breath. "Okay. I lost a soul this morning."

"What do you mean lost?" Zeke asked.

I met Zeke's eyes. "He jumped into the pit. He chose to be unmade rather than cross over." His face softened, his eyes warming. I looked back down at the comforter and concentrated on petting Hades. "I grabbed him and tried to pull him back. When I couldn't, I called for Zahur. She made me let go." The silence grew heavy. "She said I couldn't stop them from making that choice. I could try to talk them out of it but I can't physically stop them." My eyes filled as I saw it all again.

"Lexie..." Miles breathed as he reached out and took my hand. "That's not your fault."

I nodded and wiped my face. "I know, but it still sucks." I took a breath and looked around the room at them. "That's everything except for a couple things I'm not ready to share. So... if you want to bail, don't leave me guessing. Do it now, because I'm done." I looked at each of them. "I'm done trying to keep you guys away. I'm done hiding everything. I'm tired of thinking someone is going to leave. I'm all in. If you guys are."

The air was thick with silence. Isaac moved first, he crawled onto the bed and hugged me tightly. Shaking, I hugged him back. Then Ethan climbed on the bed and joined the hug with his brother. "You're beautiful Lexie, but sometimes you can be so stupid," he announced. "Group hug time." I laughed softly.

The bed dipped, Asher appeared over Ethan's shoulder. He wrapped his arms around all of us. We lost our balance and tipped over. Hades yelped and squirmed out of the way. We started laughing.

A hand found my shoulder. Wintergreen mixed with cinnamon, limes and spice as I looked up. Miles had a small smile on his face as he squeezed my shoulder.

I kept giggling with the twins as I got squished. Over Miles' shoulder, Zeke stood by the bed. Instead of joining the dog pile, which was what it was at this point, he crossed his arms over his chest.

"Zeke," I groaned.

"Yeah?"

"I'm being squished," I complained.

He smirked. "Tough shit." His dry voice had everyone chuckling.

The tension left the room, leaving behind peace. I grinned up at them while the others squished me.

CHAPTER 18

SUNDAY MORNING

I put down the last ward rock, then stood up straight. The rocks were painted with symbols and a drop of my blood in the center. They now surrounded the house and I even put a few on the damn dock for good measure. I had started these in December but never found the time to finish them. I sure as hell found the time this morning. Now, hopefully, the dead couldn't come in at all.

I headed back into the house with Hades. I had slept until two this afternoon and I didn't care. I was taking the day off from crossing souls. They could just kiss my ass right now.

After my talk with the guys last night I felt better. Lighter. As if some of the weight I had been carrying was gone. Telling them everything had been difficult. Hell, I shook the whole time. But I was glad I did it. I let them in. I was all in, theirs, completely and utterly. It scared the shit out of me, but I'd deal with it.

I was opening the back door when my phone rang. It was Ethan.

"Hey."

"Hey, Beautiful." Ethan's quiet smoky voice rolled through my ear. "How are you feeling?"

"Better than I have in a long time," I admitted.

"Good," he said. "Lexie… do you feel up to trying to cross Sophie today?" I went still, my stomach knotted.

"Yeah," I said. "If you're ready to talk to her, of course."

"Miles and the others are going to keep Isaac company for a few hours," he said. "Meet me over at the house?"

"I'm on my way," I said before he hung up. Ethan was ready. Shit. Thankfully Rory lifted my grounding after yesterday. He figured almost dying was enough punishment.

I went inside and put Hades on his leash, then headed out to the Blazer.

The drive to the twins' house felt longer than it should have. The twins' car wasn't there when I arrived. Good, I needed to talk to Sophie before Ethan got here anyway.

I quickly headed inside and let Hades off the leash as that chill ran down my neck. I straightened to find Sophie sitting on the staircase just like the other day. Had she even moved? Probably not.

"Ethan's coming home now," I said. She gave me a sad smile. "Are you sure you don't want to talk to your mom too?"

Sophie shook her head. "Mom's doing alright. She's not holding on, but she hasn't forgotten." She gave me a watery smile. "This would just hurt her. She believes I'm okay, and that's what I want. And Isaac… talking to me won't help." I sighed.

We both walked into the family room. I paced while Sophie took the left chair and curled up in it. We didn't have to wait long.

Ethan came in with heavy bags under his eyes. I didn't think, I just hugged him.

He squeezed me tight for several minutes before letting go. He looked down at me.

"Okay, so what do we do?" he asked.

"We sit down, and you talk," I said. "At least, I think that's how this would work. We need to find what's keeping her here."

His eyes grew shadowed. "I think I know what's keeping her here." He moved away from me to sit on the couch. I sat on the coffee table in front of him. He leaned his elbows on his knees and was looking at the floor.

"When you're ready," I said gently. He took several deep breaths and let them out slowly before meeting my eyes.

"In order for you to understand, I need to tell you about the car accident that killed Sophie," he explained.

"Okay," I said.

Ethan stared off into the empty space over my shoulder. "We were coming home from our grandparents' place over in Baker, near North Dakota. Sophie was behind Mom. Isaac was in the back behind me. We got in the accident on I-94."

I reached out and took his hand. He squeezed mine before continuing. "A big rig driver had fallen asleep at the wheel. He crossed into the lane next to him and flipped his truck and trailer on its side, blocking off both lanes." Sophie got to her feet as he continued. "It was a holiday weekend, so the interstate was packed. We were the second car to hit the trailer." His voice grew thick.

"We hit head on, the front of the car crumpled, glass shattered. Mom was knocked out immediately, even with the airbags going off." He met my eyes. "A second didn't even go by and we got hit again, this time it smashed our side against the trailer. Then we were hit again on the driver's side." Oh, God.

Ethan looked down at our hands. "The crash kept going but we weren't getting hit every time. My legs were pinned under some metal from the car, my back was fucked up and I had a concussion from the second hit. So, I was struggling just to stay conscious." He looked over my shoulder again, his grip on my hand tightening. "The only thing that kept me awake was Sophie. She was hit hard in the third hit. She was crying, asking for Mom. She said her chest hurt. Isaac had a broken arm but he managed to pull her into his lap and hold her. We started telling her jokes to keep her calm."

"They were horrible ones," Sophie said with a teary smile. "They were a comfort, even with the sound of crashes still going on."

"I passed out while he was still telling her jokes." He met my gaze, tears running down his face. "What we didn't know was that the last hit broke her ribs and punctured her lung in several places. Isaac was alone when she died in his arms. He was alone with her for almost an hour after. Until the paramedics could get to us." My heart broke for both of them as tears fell down my face.

He looked down at the floor and took deep breaths. I reached out and pulled him into my arms. He clung to me as we cried.

Sophie moved to the couch next to Ethan, her face shining with tears. "Izzy kept telling me jokes after he passed out," she said, her eyes on her brother. "When he realized I was dying, he tried to get out of the car to get help. We were completely pinned and the pile up had just stopped. The ambulances weren't even close. He could only keep telling me jokes."

She wiped her face. "Then I had a lot of trouble breathing. He told me how much they loved me. How special I was to them. How I just needed to hold on." She wiped her face and met my eyes. "Izzy made me feel so loved at the end that I wasn't scared when I died. He made it okay for me."

I took a deep shaking breath and repeated what she said to Ethan. He pulled back, wiping his face, but the tears still fell. He shook his head.

"I thought I let her go," he admitted.

"He did." Sophie looked over to me with shining eyes. "He only pulled me back two years ago. Every night he lays in bed, his heart hurting. It's what drew me back."

I repeated what she said to Ethan. He looked down at the floor and cursed.

"That's when I realized how bad Isaac really was," he said quietly, his voice thick. "I was alone."

"You're not alone, Ethan," I told him softly. "You're surrounded by people who love you." He looked up and met my eyes. Those chocolate eyes of his were full of shadows.

"Isaac's changed. He won't talk about it, but he has," Ethan said. "Sophie was dead and Ma... Ma was finally doing better after losing Sophie." I reached out and held his jaw in my hand.

"You are not alone," I told him again. "Everyone is here, anytime you need us. I am here." I swallowed hard. "You'll never be alone. I promise. If you need me, I'm here." His eyes gazed into mine for several heartbeats. He nodded before looking away.

"I never got to say goodbye to her," he muttered. I wiped my face and looked at Sophie.

"Now you can," I said gently. When he didn't say anything, I had to ask, "Do you want me to go in the kitchen?" He shook his head, his gaze on my knees.

"Sophie, no perteneces aquí. Lo siento, te traje de vuelta aquí." he said, his voice cracking. "Te quiero, y te extraño cada día maldito, pero no puedo pedirte que te quedes, tienes que pasar a lo que viene y ser feliz. Adiós mi pequeña Sophie."

Sophie's tear streaked face turned to me. "Tell him I love him and I will," I repeated her words. He nodded and took deep trembling breaths. Sophie looked to me. "I can go now."

I turned to Ethan. "She says she's ready."

He swallowed hard. "Take care of her."

"Always," I answered. He gave me a sad half smile.

I turned to Sophie. She reached out her hand. It was barely a thought and that golden thread moved around her wrist. I closed my eyes and dropped down.

After the long fall we landed in the Veil. Sophie got to her feet and looked around, then froze. I looked to my side and blinked. Ethan stood there blinking and wobbling on his feet.

"W-w-what the hell?" I stammered. I looked down... holy shit! I had grabbed both of them with separate threads. Oh, God. What have I done? I'd never brought a living person to the Veil before. What if I killed him? Oh, God.

I took deep slow breaths as I let go of Sophie. I was too afraid to let Ethan go from the connection.

"Lexie, what..." Ethan trailed off as he saw Sophie. The little girl smiled the biggest smile. "Sophie?"

She ran to him, laughing as she jumped into his arms. He held her tight as they both cried.

"I've missed you, every damn day." He pulled back and kissed his sister on her cheeks, then her forehead. He smelled her hair. Then hugged her tight again.

"I'm sorry about your guitar," she told him as he hugged her. "I'm sorry about scaring you and Izzy. I was just mad at you!"

"I don't care! It got our attention!" He held her close again. "I wish Isaac was here."

She shook her head. "He doesn't need to say good-bye. He already did." She took a breath and squirmed to be put down. He reluctantly set her back on her feet.

"You need to help him," she said. "Tell him that he's wrong and that's coming from me."

A ball of golden light came down from the Way. A door shimmered into existence and opened. It was a kitchen. And there was a woman waiting there.

"Sophie," I said, getting her attention. She turned and smiled.

"Is that...? ¿Abuela?" Ethan asked, his voice full of disbelief.

"Yeah." Sophie turned back to us. "It's time to go." She hugged Ethan one more time.

"Good-bye, Sophie," he said. He had tears in his eyes but this time he also had a smile.

"Love you both," she said, before walking away towards the door.

I held his hand tightly as she crossed over and was immediately hugged by her grandmother. The door closed then turned into two balls of light that shot up into the Way like comets.

I looked around for Sophie's flower and smiled. A tree had shimmered into existence. An apple tree.

Ethan laughed. "She always loved apples." I smiled as the tree grew taller.

Then I turned back to Ethan. "Okay, bad news time," I said. He raised an eyebrow. "I've never brought a living person here before. I don't know if I can get you back. I might have just fucking killed you." His brow furrowed. "I mean, I haven't let go of your soul, so theoretically I should be able to just bring you back and you'll go back into your body. If taking a living soul from their body won't kill someone..." I was rambling.

He turned me to face him. "Beautiful. I just got to see my sister and say good-bye. That was a miracle. You can bring me home," he said with complete confidence.

I took a deep breath while he watched me. "You're insane," I told him. "The Veil has fucked with your mind already."

He chuckled as he looked around. "This place *is* weird as hell." He met my gaze again. "You got this, Beautiful."

When I was calm I said, "Okay, let's do this." I was about to pull us out when he stepped closer.

"But just in case..." he said softly, his hands cradled my face as he moved in. He kissed me hard, and fast. He pulled me into his body as his teeth bit my lower lip lightly. Desire rose in me as I kissed him back, my hands buried in his shirt as he took over my mouth. One of his hands moved down my spine to my butt where he pulled me against his hard body. Sparks shot through me.

When he lifted his head I was breathing hard, my entire body on fire. He smirked down at me. "I've wanted to do that for some time now."

"Ethan..." Stunned, I didn't know what to say.

He grinned at me. "Just take us home." I nodded. That was probably best. I focused on pulling us both out.

I opened my eyes and immediately examined Ethan. He was holding his head and wincing at the light, but he seemed okay. The ache in my chest eased.

"Ethan? You're okay, right?" I asked desperately, my body still aching from that kiss.

"Yeah," he groaned. "That place was strange as hell." He finally blinked his eyes open.

"What do you remember?" I asked carefully. He looked at me confused.

"I remember my sister, seeing my grandma, her crossing and an apple tree," he said, "why?" Shit. He didn't remember kissing the hell out of me? And why the hell was I disappointed? AGH!

I just shook my head not sure what to think or how to feel. "Nothing, I just wanted to make sure you remembered saying good-bye."

He eyed me as if I was acting strange before he got to his feet. "I need to call Isaac and tell him to come home."

"I'm going to head out then, unless you need me," I said. He gave me a small smile.

"I'll be okay. Isaac will be home soon and I just... need it to sink in," he said.

I nodded and put Hades back on his leash, then headed for the door.

I was on the porch when he called my name. I turned, not knowing what to expect.

"Lexie..." he said as he came out on the porch. "How do I not pull her back again?"

I stepped closer and rested my hand on the middle of his chest, just over his heart. "You heal. You talk. And you let us be there for you."

"Thank you," he said softly. "You've no idea what you've given me." He pulled me into a hug that sent my pulse sky high. I hugged him back then pulled away. I needed to figure out what the hell was wrong with me. He smiled at me. "What are you going to do now?"

I looked at the sun, it was going to set soon. "I'm going to go to the beach and watch the sunset," I decided out loud.

"Get some peace and quiet?" he asked. I nodded. I left him on the porch without a word.

My mind was racing as I drove to the beach on the north side of the lake. I walked out on the sand and sat, watching the waves lap at the shore with Hades playing in the shallows.

What the hell just happened? Okay, Ethan kissed me and I liked it. Really fucking liked it. I examined my feelings as I watched the small waves. Shit. I *liked* Ethan. Four, four guys now. Why was I crushing on four guys? Let alone my friends? I went around in circles as the sun sank further. Finally I said, fuck it.

Too much had happened this week, I was done thinking for the day. I looked down at my phone and only hesitated a second.

Alexis: Meet me at the north shore beach. We need to talk.

While I waited I focused on watching the water and the pretty sunset. I had accomplished everything I had set out to do this week except for two things, and one of those I could solve now.

Soon the jingle of keys came towards me. Zeke sat down next to me. We were quiet for several minutes.

"I came clean yesterday," I said quietly. "It's your turn."

"Lexie..."

"Don't 'Lexie' me." I turned and looked up at him. "The other night you left. You said you had to work but you didn't. Is this what you're going to do now? Avoid me?" He ran his hand down his whiskered face.

"You're right, it is my turn to come clean." He took a deep breath and let it out as he turned to look at the water. "Ever since you came home from the hospital and we learned you can't hug me..." I looked down at the sand, feeling guilty again. He took a breath and tried again. "With what happened to you and with you not being able to hug me... it raised some issues for me."

"What kind of issues?" I watched as he clenched and unclenched his jaw.

He turned back to me with those beautiful blue eyes. "I've been in therapy since we found out I could trigger you."

I sighed, feeling even worse. "It's not your fault-"

"I let you drive home alone that night. It's my fault you were taken in the first place. I should have been there." His gravelly voice was rougher than usual. He took a deep breath and let it out slowly. "That's the way it feels. My doc says it's bullshit. That it's not my fault. I guess he's right but still..."

I shook my head. "Zeke, it really isn't your fault," I said, narrowing my eyes at him. "You've been blaming yourself this whole time?"

He swallowed hard and looked out at the water. "Yeah. It's why Sylvie told me to get back into therapy." He clenched his jaw. "The fact I remind you of him-"

"But you don't, Zeke." I stopped him. "With you, I know I'm safe. That you'd tear into anyone who tried to hurt me."

"Then why can't you look at me without that sad look in your eyes?" He asked gruffly.

Tears fell down my face. "Because it's been killing me that I've done nothing but hurt you since I came home from the hospital." His gaze snapped to me. He reached into his pocket and handed me his handkerchief.

I took it and wiped my face. Then took a breath and continued. "My shrink wants me to try to hug you again. But I'm scared that I'll have a flashback and hurt you more."

"Lexie, don't worry about hurting me," he told me. I shot him a look. The corner of his lips twitched. "Maybe we can figure out what it is."

"How?" I grumbled.

"How did it feel when you hugged me last time?" he asked. I closed my eyes and remembered.

"Your frames are the same but different enough. It's…" I struggled to explain. "It's that you're so much taller than me. It's like you're looming over me the way he did when he was monologuing." I shrugged. "That's the only way I can describe it. I'm sorry."

Zeke gave me a small smile. "Lexie." His voice was gentle. He got to his feet then held his hands down to me. When I took them, he pulled me to my feet and let go.

"I don't want to hurt you, Zeke," I all but whispered.

"You won't," he assured me as he stepped closer.

My heart slammed in my chest as my lungs grew tight. But instead of hugging me, Zeke bent down and picked me up with his arm under my butt. I fell against him as an arm moved across my back. With my hands on his shoulders, I looked down at him surprised. He wasn't standing over me, and he wasn't triggering me!

I wrapped my arms around him and buried my face into his neck as tears poured out of me. I took a big, deep breath of leather and engine grease and it was the best smell in the world. His face moved into my neck, he took a deep breath.

"I missed you, Baby."

"I missed you, Tough Guy."

ETHAN

I looked up at the ceiling and watched shadows dance over the surface. Today had been a bitch. But I felt better. Like I'd been holding onto something so much that someone finally took the load away. With her, I didn't feel so alone anymore. I looked over to my dresser. Photos of Lexie and the guys were taped to the wall.

Lexie. Why did I lie? We give her a big speech about being honest and then I lied to her face. I remembered kissing her in the Veil. I remembered her lips, her taste, the feel of her... I remembered everything. I closed my eyes and cursed myself. You're falling for her, you ass. I ran my hand down my face. What the hell was I going to do? She didn't mention the kiss. Did that mean she didn't feel the same way? Or was she just playing it cool because I said I didn't remember? Fuck. I'd have to ask. That wasn't going to happen anytime soon. She wasn't even close to ready to ask her out. I let out a deep breath. I just had to forget about it.

Yeah, forget about the best kiss of my life? Not likely.

At least Isaac was home. I sat up, giving up on sleep. Isaac refused to talk about Sophie once he came home. When I told him that I told Lexie about the crash, he'd stopped talking again. He just went into his room without a word. He hadn't been out since.

ETHAN

I got to my feet and walked out into the hall. His door was shut still. Maybe I should talk to him? Or at least sit with him? I didn't want to be alone right now, I doubt he did either. I knocked on the door. No answer. I opened the door. Fuck! Isaac's bed was empty, the window open to the night. Isaac was gone. Damn it!

ISAAC

The loud music was barely enough to get me out of my head. I drank down a shot of tequila and poured another.

Josh had texted me about the party around ten, he'd been willing to pick me up down the block from the house. There was no point in asking Ethan. He got closure today, the ass was probably sleeping like a baby.

I drank straight from the bottle. It burned all the way down. I made my way through the crowd bumping into people here and there and not caring.

He told her. Ethan fucking told her. My chest burned as I moved into the living room. She knew. I took another drink, enjoying the burn. She knew about it all. I staggered into a group of guys. I straightened.

"Hey, take it easy man," one of them said.

"Fuck off," I snapped before taking another drink and moving away.

"Go fuck yourself," he shot back. I turned and sized him up. It was one of that prick Jason's friends. They looked like they could hold their own.

"Nah, I'll just go fuck your mom." I countered. It didn't matter. None of it fucking mattered.

"What did you say?" he snapped. He shoved me.

I stumbled back into the couch but I righted myself and raised my arms with a smile on my face. "I said I'll just go fuck your mom," I repeated only louder. Yeah, this was what I deserved. What I needed. They stepped towards me.

"Back the fuck off," a deep, gravelly voice growled. The dude stopped. Shit. I turned.

Yep, it was the Giant of the North. Scowling at me like I was a bug under his shoe. I snorted. Might as well be.

He grabbed the back of my shirt and started pulling me through the crowd. "Come on, shit head, you're going home." I took another swig from the bottle. I didn't care, as long as I got to keep-

Zeke knocked the bottle from my hand, it hit the floor as he kept pulling me. The air grew cooler as he dragged me outside.

"You killed my drink. Big party foul." I told him.

"Shut up." Zeke snapped. Oh, he must be mad. Who cares? The world was spinning as he dragged me through the parked cars. "You owe me, you were about to get your ass kicked."

"Nothing I don't deserve," I grumbled. I deserved so much worse. So, so much worse. I hung my head as I fell into that pit again. She knows...

"It wasn't your fault, you ass," Zeke snapped as he opened the door to the back of his Jeep and threw me in. I laid across the back seat. It was really comfy.

"She knows," I grumbled. The door closed. Another opened. The Jeep moved. It made my stomach churn.

"She knows what?" Zeke growled.

I closed my eyes as tears fell. "That I let her die. That I killed Sophie."

Zeke cursed and started talking, but I was too deep to listen. She knew. And now I'd never have a chance with her.

She knew... Darkness pulled me under.

EPILOGUE

"So, how are things?" Dr. Smith asked.

I bit the corner of my lip. How are things? I sighed. Isaac was pretending that Sophie had never been here and if you brought it up he'd walk away. We're all watching him carefully, but all we're seeing is the funny guy again. Ethan told me Isaac has been training harder than ever to get back into the octagon this summer. I'm not looking forward to it. But of course, I couldn't talk to her about that.

"I've managed to leave the house a couple times without Hades or the guys," I replied. It had been just down to the store but it counted in my book.

She smiled. "That's good, Lexie." She wrote down a note then looked back up to me. "What else?"

"My voice therapy with Ethan is still twice a week," I answered. I kept going because it was alone time with Ethan, and I seemed to be craving it lately. I didn't want to look too closely at that. He still doesn't remember our kiss. I don't know if I'm happy about that or not…

"Okay, anything else?" she asked. "Did you hug Zeke?"

I nodded. "Yeah, we figured out that it was his height that triggered me. So, he picks me up for a hug now."

She smiled. "Good, how is he doing?"

"We're still working on our issues. He's seeing his own shrink and he sometimes has homework that involves talking to me." I shrugged. "We'll get back to where we were, it'll just take time."

"How is school?" Dr. Smith asked.

I smiled. "Jessica, Asher's sister, spread rumors that I'm sleeping with her brother. So, every time we pass her in the hallway I make a point to hold his hand."

Her eyes narrowed at me. "And how does Asher feel about that?"

"He doesn't mind. He thinks she deserves it," I explained. She also still hasn't received a dime from the house accounts.

She tilted her head. "What about the job at the tattoo shop?"

I sighed. "I decided that I have too much on my plate right now. I'm rushing around already and to add something else to that would just be a disaster." Not to mention the ghosts are still being pushy, but after me not crossing them for a week, they showed up at the house. That's when I learned the guys and Rory had planted Betony around the house. The protective plant and the wards had held. When the ghosts realized they couldn't get in, it occurred to them that pissing me off was a bad move. They are starting to settle down... I think.

As for Mr. Davis, if I see that shit again I'm going to force his ass into the Veil so fast he'll be lucky if he doesn't get shoved into the abyss.

Dr. Smith smiled. "I'm glad you recognized that. You have a tendency to push yourself until you drop."

I nodded. "Right now, I'm just enjoying my time with my friends and trying to find my new normal. And I'm looking forward to summer." School breaks were supposed to be restful. I could do with a good, event free summer. That could happen, right?

SNEAK PEEK AT BOOK FIVE

JUNE

It was the end of the last day of school when I started pulling the old books from my locker.

Normally I wouldn't have any books left, but these were the books Serena had given me along with a few of my own. And since Tara found out about my ability to see the dead, she's been snooping around. I had even caught her in my bedroom a couple times.

I wiped the sweat off my face before tucking another book away. Summer had shown up with a heat wave that had me wearing denim Bermuda shorts and a gray V-neck. The shirt was stifling. I couldn't wait to get home to throw on a tank top.

I reached in and grabbed another book.

"Hey, Red, what's taking so long?" Isaac called. The guys came around the corner and I had to take a breath. There was no getting around it. My friends were hot. As in sexy as hell and not just sweating. Every one of them was muscled in their own way, not to mention definition… Stop drooling, Lexie. I focused on Isaac's question.

"I'm getting my books," I reminded him.

"Is Tara still snooping around your room?" Asher asked as he leaned against the locker next to mine. He was trying to beat the heat in cargo shorts, a tank top and an open button down.

"Yep, and now she's gone to rifling through my drawers," I grumbled.

"Can you put a lock on your door?" Miles asked. He still wore his usual jeans and a shirt in the heat. It didn't seem to bother him.

"I have one, but she keeps getting in," I answered.

"Then we need to get you a better one," Ethan said. Ethan still wore all black, only now it was cargo shorts and a tank top along with his black army boots.

I stuffed another book into my bag. "I was thinking about it, but I need to ask Rory."

"Ask him, and I'll bring one over," Zeke told me. Zeke's wardrobe never changed, he still wore black jeans, a black t-shirt and black boots with his wallet chain. Even if he was sweating just as much as the rest of us.

"Okay, I'll ask tonight," I muttered as I put another book in my bag.

"What is taking so long?" Zeke demanded as he stepped behind me to look into my locker.

"I was stashing a lot of books and research." I pointed out. My bag was taken off my arm. Before I could say anything, a big hand turned me around. Zeke bent down and I was suddenly over his shoulder hanging upside down with his thick forearm across the back of my thighs.

"You're going too slow. Isaac, get the rest," Zeke ordered.

I pushed myself up off his back to watch Isaac all but topple the books into my bag. "Be careful!"

Isaac ignored me as he zipped up the bag and shut the empty locker.

"If he tore any of them I'm coming after you," I warned Zeke. "Now, put me down."

"No way. It's the last day of school," Ethan stated. "You took too long emptying your locker. It's roasting and we're going swimming." I started to squirm, trying to get down.

"Okay, but I can walk you know," I pointed out laughing.

Zeke slapped his hand over my butt making me squeak. "Stop

wiggling. If I put you down you'll just find something else to stall going swimming."

My face red, I reached down and smacked him on the ass. My hand stung. Damn, glutes of steel. He chuckled at my attempt.

"Fine! But I'm just worried about your eyesight!" I countered, smiling.

"You're not that pale, Red," Isaac reassured me. "You've gotten some sun in the last month, you'll tan up."

I rolled my eyes. Isaac clearly had never known a red head before. "And since summer started I put sunblock on every four hours. That's why I'm not a lobster."

"Lexie, you can wear shorts and a shirt if you're that worried about it," Miles reminded me.

"Nope, she has to wear a swimsuit," Ethan declared.

Everyone walked out of the hall and into the parking lot. I started to sweat even more. I hoped it got all over Zeke.

"Okay! But when you go blind, don't say I didn't warn you," I warned, though it was undermined by my current position over Zeke's shoulder. The guys started laughing until they reached my Blazer. Zeke carefully put me down on my sandaled feet.

"I'll wear the damn swimsuit," I stated. "But if I turn into a crustacean, I expect you guys at my beck and call for aloe on my back."

The twins both raised eyebrows.

"Rub goo all over your body anytime you ask? Okay," Isaac agreed with a smirk.

The guys burst out laughing. I rolled my eyes. There were just some things you can't say to a group of guys.

FOR THE LATEST ON THE VEIL DIARIES

Visit the website
blbrunnemer.com
or
follow the author's Facebook page
www.facebook.com/BLBrunnemer-1575614369409677/
or
join the Veil Diaries Fan Page

www.facebook.com/groups/TheVeilDiaries/